Who knows? One day your luck changes. One day you take a look around and you see a thing you never thought you'd see, and there's no one you can go to with it and say, "Christ, here's the situation, show me what to do."

There are things like that, things you can't go to anybody with. So you go it alone. For better or worse. For better or worse, you reach with your heart and do what you do.

Crazy. The gentlest man in the world, with a gun. And his son, the one he feared, with nothing but a piece of string . . .

THE STONE BOY

JAMES GORDON

CHARTER BOOKS, NEW YORK

THE STONE BOY

A Charter Book/published by arrangement with
the author

PRINTING HISTORY
Charter Original/April 1984

ISBN: 0-441-78634-0

Charter Books are published by The Berkley Publishing Group,
200 Madison Avenue, New York, New York 10016.
PRINTED IN THE UNITED STATES OF AMERICA

For Carol Atkinson
and Luis Sanjurjo

One afternoon
in the middle of the night,
two dead boys
got up to fight;
back to back,
they faced each other,
sword in hand,
they shot each other;
a deaf policeman
heard the noise
and came and killed
the two dead boys.

—Children's folk rhyme

1.

I DO LAW. I do law the way some men do science or soldiering or race things. I mean, the law is more than just work for me, a way to fill the days until there aren't any left. What I'm talking about is a feeling you get from the thing you do, what's meant when they say you have a calling.

The law calls to me. Or, anyhow, it used to. I used to hear it as a major chord, three keys struck in matchless unison, a blend that bodies forth—majestic, glorious, thrilling.

I think that's how it was for my father and for his father before him. That's how long the Decks have been lawyers—and we've married lawyers. My wife, Emily, she's a lawyer. My wife, Emily . . .

We're not married anymore.

But that's not really a part of this story, of what I want to talk to you about. This story's not about me and Emily—or about how my feeling for the law's been changed. What this story's about is a friend of mine, a man and his two sons. I think it may even be a story about all fathers and all sons—and the terror that can sometimes overtake them.

They say the law has all the answers. They say that from the clattering machinery of its give-and-take there comes the artifacts of a durable morality, judgments that are reasonable unto the circumstances, solutions that are merciful, humane.

I used to think that. But now I'm not so sure anymore.
Ever since the world fell in on Ben Garrison, I'm not so
sure of anything. I feel shaky, vulnerable. I see where a
man's luck can go bad and where there's nothing there to
catch him—not the rule of law or any other rule, not
even the arms of those who love him.

I love Ben Garrison.

Everyone loved the man. I think even Willa, his first
wife, did. What Willa did to Ben Garrison had nothing to
do with not loving the man. And Peter? Did Peter Garrison love his father?

Despite everything, I think so. But sometimes love is
not enough.

That's what Ben Garrison found out when his luck
went bad. No one could help him—not me or his second
wife, Joan, not even Andy, the son Ben Garrison so
adored.

Who knows? One day your luck changes. One day
you take a look around and you see a thing you never
thought you'd see, and there's no one you can go to with
it and say, "Christ, here's the situation, show me what
to do."

There are things like that, things you can't go to anybody with. So you go it alone. For better or worse. For
better or worse, you reach with your heart and do what
you do.

Ben reached. He reached for his sons.

He had his hands all the way out and his heart opened
wide. And that's how it ended, with Ben Garrison
trying.

But before that, he tried reaching for everything in
sight. He was a man frantic to grab the right thing. Even
a gun, a Colt Buntline, a long-barreled weapon that fired
a small-caliber load.

Crazy. The gentlest man in the world, with a gun. And
his son, the one he feared, with nothing but a piece of
string.

2.

SOMETIMES I THINK it was ordained right from the start.
But that's ridiculous. Besides, where was the start?

I'll tell you something. When I was in the Navy, I saw
them cut loose an anchor once. It's quite a sight—those
giant links racing into water. But where is it they start
falling? Up where you can see them? Or down there on
the bottom? Maybe the answer is the whole chain goes at
once. Maybe the chain starts falling the day they weld
the links together. Maybe it was like that with Ben and
Peter and Andy. Maybe it all started down the day Ben
was born.

But I don't know much about his beginnings—except
that it was in Ames, Iowa, and that he was the only child
of a man who got forced out of farming and went on to
try his hand at a small machine shop until a rotary belt
took his arm off.

It was a grim life from start to finish. Ben left it when
he was fifteen, making his way East, doing this and that
until he landed in New York. It wasn't that he didn't love
his folks. Far from it. It was just that he couldn't bear
seeing them suffer because they couldn't give him much.
It was easier to go off and send them what he could, a
letter every day and once a week all the cash he could get
along without. Besides, he wanted a life, a different life,
a farm boy's dream of big-city success.

He got it, too, more than he ever bargained for, the
works—money, a certain fame, prestige. But his folks
never lived to see it. The father died while Ben was still

doing bits and taking classes in New Haven. The mother
went a few months later.

That's how I met Ben. It was when his dad passed
away, some foul-up on the insurance, the burial policy
the Garrisons had. Ben's mother wasn't getting any
action on it, and Ben was desperate to find someone
to help. Somebody in the Drama School had given him
my name.

It was a common practice at Yale in those days, those
days being the mid-sixties. The brighter, more experienced law students got a little unlicensed practice and
some perfectly good beer money, whereas their clients,
other Yalies, sometimes got some worthwhile advice.

Ben wasn't a Yalie, though—and the unwritten rule
was that you did this sort of thing only for fellow students. But he made no effort to hide it.

I still have the note. My God, I've got so many things
that once belonged to Ben. But, no, I don't have the
notebooks and I don't have the gun. The Buntline went
back to Colorado—evidence. A fishing guide found it
the next summer, and it went from Maine to Colorado,
rusted and useless from a season in the snow, but still of
interest to the police in Cortez.

I don't have the little black pouch, either. But I know
what was in it.

I know the whole story—from one source or another.
Let's say it starts nowhere exactly, because it starts with
Ben Garrison being the good and loving man he was. But
I came into it years ago in New Haven, the morning I
found that note in my box.

> *Dear Steven Deck—I need your help with some-
> thing legal. Could you please meet me at Naples
> Pizza at 5 sharp this afternoon? I have very light
> hair and I will be by the door. Yours truly, B. W.
> Garrison. P.S., I am not a student at Yale but I
> have some classes here in the Drama School, and I*

*hope it will be OK anyway. I'd be very thankful if
you could come.*

He didn't need to describe himself. You stepped into
that place crowded with college kids, and you knew
instantly which one was *Yours truly, B. W. Garrison*.

It was the clothes partly, and not just because they
were the wrong ones but also because it was February
and freezing. Yet the young man I found standing just
inside the door at five sharp was wearing no more than a
thin pair of wash pants and a short-sleeved shirt.

His teeth were actually chattering. But even this and
the clothes weren't what first seized my attention. It was
instead that Ben Garrison was easily the most striking
man I'd ever laid eyes on.

I suppose I must have been gaping at him, the big-
framed body, the regal way he held himself. He turned
out to be six years my junior, and certainly he'd had
none of the privileges I'd grown up with. But when Ben
Garrison smiled in greeting, I felt favored by a king.

"Mr. Deck?" he said, and I could hear his teeth clicking.

"Steve'll do," I said, and shook his hand.

"I'm real obliged. B.W.'s what they call me," he
said, still pumping my hand and looking nervously toward the counter and the tables, as if uncertain as to what
would be the next graceful move. "But I'm trying to get
them to call me Ben." He laughed, and I could see it was
chiefly to fill up an empty space, an embarrassment. He
just didn't know what to do next.

"Then I shall call you Ben," I said, instantly disgusted with myself for the fancy language and the note of
condescension.

"We could get us a pizza," he said. "Would you like
that?"

"I'd like it fine," I said. "So long as it's strictly
dutch."

He started to protest, to say the whole thing was his

idea, his treat. But I didn't let him. Pride struck out all over the man. But so did real poverty.

What I remember best about that first meeting is how it broke my heart that I never offered him my coat or one of the sweaters I had on underneath it, how I didn't even mention my amazement that he could bear such intolerable cold, how I didn't do either of these things because I knew I was about to form the one great friendship of my life. Little as I knew in those days, I knew enough not to risk blowing the best thing that was going to happen to me just because I valued my own charity over another man's pride.

But I got away with never charging him the standard amateur rate for the advice he was looking for. It didn't come to much anyway—a letter or two to an old Yale lawyer in Ames, to ask him to check the Iowa statutes, to get on the insurance company's ass, and to let Ben's mother know there was somebody looking after her interests. In the end it didn't matter—Mrs. Garrison died less than four months later—and what burial costs were required the Ames lawyer and I sort of took care of, doing it in a way that left Ben thinking it was the insurer paying off, after all.

No, you couldn't *give* anything to Ben Garrison. He could only give to you—the shirt off his back if that was what was needed, and if it wasn't, then more loyalty and affection than you'd ever need to have.

All through February and March we saw each other regularly, if only for a beer and a recap of the day. My life was law school, my last year—and Ben's was doing bit parts at the Long Wharf Theatre, a professional group in town, that and some special setup that let him sit in on directorial classes at the Yale Drama School.

Anyway, we saw each other constantly until Ben met Willa. I was there for it. I was there when he met her. I was there because I'd brought her. So, in a way, I did give Ben Garrison something.

I gave him Willa Stafford.

* * *

It was opening night at the Long Wharf—*Tea and Sympathy*, that was the play, with Ben in a small role, and even at that, one that was all wrong for him. But so what? Ben wasn't much of an actor. It embarrassed him, acting—and I suspect this was because he was so handsome and felt disgusted by having to capitalize on his looks. For him it was just a trade because he couldn't get any other. No education, no training. But in New York he'd finally gotten a couple of very minor things way the hell off-Broadway, and from there he'd gone on to Boston, for a season or two of cabaret theater. It was when he was on his way back to New York that he stopped off to take a look around New Haven. Luck, timing, whatever it was, he'd scored himself a spear-carrying walk-on at the Long Wharf, and the chance to audit directing classes at the Drama School.

He was twenty. I suppose he was doing okay, considering.

Willa was my age. But whereas I was still a student and Ben was worse off still, Willa Stafford was already a pretty big deal, even a minor celebrity—at least in certain circles.

The reason was a book. It was called *The Dream System of the Havasupai*, and whatever it was, it was way beyond me. What I know is that it was her doctoral thesis, and that it was a highly regarded piece of anthropological research, earning her not only a one-year appointment to the Yale faculty but also the esteem of her senior colleagues. But what really set Willa off from the rest, what accounted for the reputation she had, was the nervy way she'd gone about her work, living for two years with the Havasupai Indians, a small tribe that scratched together a meager existence at the base of the Grand Canyon.

Not bad for a graduate student, a young woman all alone, going into a situation like that and sticking it out for two whole years until she had what she wanted.

She wasn't bad to look at, either. Sultry, on the exotic

side—and very sensual, at least to the eye. I'd dated her once or twice, gotten her story, *not* gotten her into bed. But I was still hanging around, hoping. Besides, there was something very compelling about Willa, a sort of wild, unshakable resolve.

Why she got interested in Ben I'll never know. To begin with, I think she was more interested in women, so far as sex and friendship went. Men bored her. God knows, I did. What Ben had to offer was great looks, yes, but the rest of his virtues were scarcely the kind to excite a woman like Willa. Ben was just a simple, straightforward guy. Ideas didn't interest him. Feelings did. I think his chief enthusiasm in life was people. Whereas people ranked on Willa Stafford's list just about as low as you could get.

Anyway, he took after her like a shot. And she let him.

It's strange. She didn't even seem to notice him in the course of the play. Even though he was hard to miss. But afterwards, at the cast party, all she wanted to know was who was the one standing off by himself, and of course it was Ben, not aloof by any means, but just too scared and embarrassed to really join in. It was how Ben always behaved at those backstage things—trying not to be impolite, but afraid to place himself where people could get at him. He didn't like those sessions that came after performances. He didn't like having to stand around with the actors and crew, everybody hugging and kissing and making a great show of being theater people, while meanwhile the people who weren't theater people milled around trying to catch your eye and be introduced, tell you how wonderful you were, and how they just adored the play. But mostly what Ben didn't like was when they'd say, "Uh, now I hope this won't make you un-*com*fortable, but I've been just dying to tell you how much you resemble—" And then they'd name some movie star, and Ben was supposed to say, "Aw shucks, no, not me, not really," and blush.

They were always telling Ben how much he looked like James Dean or Alan Ladd, depending on how old the speaker was, when the truth was he didn't look a thing like either one—or like any other movie star, except maybe Paul Newman. Yes, he looked a little bit like that, especially the eyes.

But before Ben died, he didn't look like anyone you'd want to look like. What he looked like was a man with too many miles on his heart.

Years after Willa left him, we got good and drunk one night. He was in awful shape. Talking about Peter started it. Some men would get silent with a thing like that. Ben, too—most of the time. But when it came out, it all came out, and his eyes would fill up with tears—and then he couldn't speak even if he wanted to. So we drank right on through it until Ben could talk again. And then the talk shifted to Willa.

"You remember how she looked that night? You remember, Steve?"

"You mean that night backstage at the Long Wharf?"

He nodded. He almost fell onto the table doing it. We were both in a pretty bad way.

"It was this funny thing about her. The way she slouched, sort of. So tall and that straight smoky hair, and that funny slouch she had. You know something? I even remember what she was wearing that night. Flat black pumps. Shiny. Patent leather, I guess they were. And that black dress, loose-fitting, with an Indian belt hung low on her hips."

"A concho belt," I said.

"Yeah," he said, "a concho belt. But it was this way she had of sort of folding herself up, shoulders crooked up high and just a little forward, so that her breasts were kind of shielded, and the rest of her spilling down and coming at you, thrust out. It make her look—*exposed*, like she needed to be protected because she was all uncovered. But at the same time it was bold, almost brazen, offering you her pelvis, inviting you with her—"

He stopped himself and took up his drink.

"The hell with it. You know what I mean."

I knew what he meant. I remembered. The look of the woman was strangely sexual, maidenly, yet wanton. I listened to Ben, and I remembered—the way it was raining that night when the three of us came out of the Long Wharf—a thin mean drizzle that kept trying to turn into ice. The plan was for coffee and sandwiches and more talk about the play. But the two of them got very silent, and it didn't take much to see why. It was something sudden and furious. So I more or less got myself out of their way and went home.

You could tell. You could tell they were going to go at each other as soon as they had the chance—and that's just what they did, sleeping together that first night in Willa's room on campus. Which was where they worked over each other's bodies for the next two weeks—until there was a second note in my mailbox.

Steve—hey good buddy, what say you stand up for me marriage-wise! If yes, meet me at Naples tomorrow at 3. Your pal, B. W. Garrison.

He was there when I got there—at his usual station, standing at near-attention close to the doorway, same outfit as always, the threadbare wash-pants, that short-sleeved shirt, his hair damp and his face glowing as if he'd just come out of the shower.

"You're shitting me," I said when I'd gotten him to a table with a pitcher of beer in front of us.

He raised his glass to clink it against mine.

"Here's mud in your eye," he said, grinning like an idiot.

"Jesus, Ben—she'll eat you alive."

But there was no talking him out of it. He was dazzled. She was a scientist, a scholar, an intellectual, and pretty dishy to look at. Best of all, she was brave, a hell of a woman who'd gone out on her own and done something that really mattered.

"Done *what?*" I asked.

That grin. "She wrote a book."

"About what?"

"About Indians," he said.

"Ben, you haven't even read her book."

"Well, neither have you," he said. "And don't worry, I'll get around to it."

I tried arguing with him. But it was pointless. She was the one I should have been arguing with. At least I might have made an effort to find out what her motives were. To hear it from Ben, it was love, pure and simple. But based on what?

"You don't even know the woman. You couldn't possibly know her."

"You ever see that tooth of hers?"

I didn't know what he was talking about.

He pointed. "Over here. Up here. Little tooth that didn't come all the way out?"

I shook my head.

"No," I said. "What about it?"

Ben grinned. "Nothing," he said. But he had the look of a man who thinks he's proved something.

"I don't get it," I said.

But he just smiled and nodded as if he knew something no one else could possibly comprehend.

What was I supposed to say?

I quit raising objections, or pointing out the obvious. It was useless. And for all I knew, maybe this was the way it worked, real love. Maybe it was all a matter of crazy things like a tooth.

A year later they were living in New York, the routine young New York couple on the way up—husband beginning to make his way in theater circles, wife lecturing at Princeton and NYU and working on a new book, but doing it on West Eighty-sixth Street and not at the bottom of the Grand Canyon. And just to complete the picture, there was a baby now.

There was Peter.

Myself, I was a long way from marriage at the time, a long way from meeting Emily. I was just getting down to New York and setting up in my father's office. So I suppose I didn't know much of anything about what matrimony and paternity can make a man feel. But, based on guesswork, I'd say Ben Garrison was about as happy as a man could get.

Until Willa disappeared that spring.

Just like that. No message, no letter, no little note or warning.

Just gone. For good.

With the boy. With Ben Garrison's son.

3.

HE THOUGHT IT WAS a game. That's what he thought at
first. That morning when he woke up and neither of them
was there.

The apartment on West Eighty-sixth was small by
West Side standards. It didn't take him long to search
everywhere. And then he went back and did it all over
again. He must have looked a dozen times in some of the
same places, as if his looking one more time could make
them reappear. He looked in places where they couldn't
possibly be. And all this time he kept listening for
them—for whispers, for stifled laughter, for a sudden
shout—*Guess who's here!*

The one thing he didn't want to do was go to the
telephone and call the police. Because that would make
it real. And what would he say? *I got up this morning
and my wife and son were gone.*

He kept on looking, going from room to room, calling
their names. All that morning he kept it up because
he didn't know what else to do. Until he was shouting
the words of the game. *Come out, come out, wherever
you are!*

When he didn't know what to do anymore, he tele-
phoned me. But I couldn't make out much of anything
over the phone. It's an awful thing to hear a grown man
cry like that. I tell you, it's an awful sound.

I got over to his place as fast as I could, did my best to
get him calmed down. But it was hopeless. The best I

could do was to get him to go around the apartment with me to see if things were gone.

They were. A few items of clothing—Willa's and the baby's—and certain essential things you'd need for an infant. And then we saw that she'd taken her books, too. Six or seven books Ben said she referred to all the time, and one copy of her own book, the one she'd gotten Margaret Mead to sign.

He put his hand out toward a shelf and then snatched it back.

"What?" I said. "What is it?"

"She means it," he said.

"Why?" I said. "What?"

"All those pages she typed up. The book she's been working on. It's gone."

I got Ben into the kitchen and I got some coffee and whiskey into him. He kept getting up and going back into Peter's room. I'd follow him after a while. He'd just be standing there staring at the crib. I'd come up behind him and lead him back into the kitchen.

"It'll be okay, Ben. I swear, man, I swear."

I said something pretty much like that for the next five years, years when we tried every clue and guess we had.

It'll be okay.

But it wasn't.

It must have been when the nights came that Willa knew what she was going to do. Lying there sleepless, her vision must have flamed. She must have seen canyons, deserts, the fierce wastelands of the American West.

Sometimes I get a picture of how it must have happened, Willa lying there, trying to sleep, her heart thundering beneath the bulb of a furious sun, until she could bear it no more and threw off the covers and got to her feet, gasping. I see her standing there for a long time, her face twisted with the passion that must have gripped her blood. Perhaps she stood there praying for Ben to stran-

gle on his saliva or to swallow his tongue, some kind of
spontaneous thing that would wipe out her one mistake.
In time she must have turned from the bed, her body
convulsed, a fist. Maybe she went to the kitchen first or
maybe she went straight to Peter's crib, reaching her
hand down, spreading her fingers, shaping the soft globe
of the boy's head. I hear her saying, ''Yes, yes,'' as if
acknowledging something or surrendering at last.

The police tracked her to Chicago. We know she flew
TWA, the first flight out that morning. From there, Willa
left no trace. But it wasn't hard to guess where she was
headed. Not that knowing it would do any good.

It didn't. Because we never ran her down. Even when
her second book came out, it was hopeless. She was too
clever, too careful. She'd handled everything through
intermediaries. And as for royalties, they were paid into
a Delaware trust in Peter's name. Court orders got us
nowhere. If the people she did business with really knew
her whereabouts, we couldn't, as a practical matter,
force them to tell. One dead end led to the next, and after
five years of it I advised Ben to give it up. It was killing
him, the search.

''Write it off. Make a new life.''

''Are you crazy? He's my son.''

''He's not your son. Not anymore, he's not. It's
useless.''

But it was just as useless to say that to him. Ben
Garrison couldn't write anything off—not if it had people in it.

Two years ago she sat here in this office and told me
the whole thing. She could have come for Ben's funeral.
It would have meant coming one week sooner than she'd
planned. Because she'd been scheduled to film an inter-
view in New York, a segment that would go into a Time-
Life special devoted to her work.

She looked the same—only weathered, skin seamed

from the sun, and she wore her hair in a short, mannish bob now. It was still that same smoky color.

I wanted to know how she had managed to vanish so effectively, and she was more than willing to tell me. I think she was proud of it—the way she was proud of pulling off those two years alone with the Havasupai.

You can't blame her. It was quite a stunt for a woman with a year-old child.

"You didn't go back to the Canyon, did you?"

"No. That would have been foolish. I'd already been a fool once. I wasn't about to be one again."

"You mean by marrying Ben?"

She didn't trouble herself to answer. But I was stupid to ask the question, and stupid enough to ask a worse one.

"How come you married him in the first place?"

She shrugged. "I don't honestly know. Do you know the motive for everything you've done?"

"For the important things, yes."

"That's nonsense—and I dispute it. On the contrary, it is the basis for our most binding actions that we probably understand least well."

"Forget it," I said. "It doesn't matter. The thing is, if you didn't go to the Grand Canyon, then where? Cortez?"

She shook her head and smiled. I saw that tooth, her first gift to Peter.

"There is a town called Kayenta, just south of Monument Valley. Actually, I stayed there for a week—in a Holiday Inn, of all places. I saw to it that the word got out—to the Navajo, the Zuñi, the Ute, the Hopi, the Mescalero. All one has to do is spend a bit of time in the Kayenta washateria. They all come there—the women —and the men wait outside in their pickups. I had diapers to do. I hung around. I told the men. The word got around. So it was easy after that. I always had a place to go. For three years I kept moving. I went from one tribe to the next. I was all over the Four Corners area."

"That's just where we looked."

"Well," she said, "that's just where I was."

"We had the state police checking. The Indian police, too."

Again that smile. "It did a lot of good, didn't it? You know how far you get, asking an Indian a question he doesn't want to answer?"

I lit a cigar, and watched her frown with annoyance. "And then what? After the three years?"

"Nothing really. I returned to a normal existence." She gave a little laugh. "Normal for me, that is."

"You moved to Cortez."

"I moved to Cortez, yes. I hired a Hopi crew out of Tuba City, and I had them build the bunker. I designed it myself, you know. A rather remarkable dwelling, actually. But I imagine Ben must have told you about it before he died."

She moved in her chair and crossed her legs.

"You understand," she said, "I didn't come here to justify myself. But I know how you felt about Ben, and I thought I might explain a few things—from my point of view. From my point of view, I had no choice. I married Ben. It was a dreadful mistake. I had to undo that mistake—surgically. Had Peter never turned up Ben's whereabouts, who knows? Perhaps it would have worked out. Hadn't Ben adjusted, gotten used to a life without Peter? After all, the child was only a year old when I took him away. There's no end of studies that prove the weak connection between a father and a child when the child is still an infant."

I wanted to interrupt her. I wanted to say, "Sure, sure, maybe that's true, but it's all crap when it comes to a man like Ben Garrison." But I just sat there and let her talk.

"A clean break," she said. "In my judgment, that was best for all concerned. And for a while it all went perfectly. I had my work on the nearby reservations, and the townspeople kept out of my way. I took him with me whenever I went into the field—sometimes months, just the two of us. But then, when school came, other kids came with it—and questions. After a while, the usual answer didn't work anymore. He'd gotten too smart for that. But it was more than mere intelligence. Sometimes I felt he could reach into my mind with his fingers.

"Yes. Yes, of course. I admit it. Until Peter was six, I'd told him his father was dead. But then one day he said, 'If he's dead, then where is he buried? Take me there. I want to look at his grave.' I told him that was absurd, that it was too far to go. But he insisted that I name a place, that he wanted to think about it, that he had to have the name. That's how it started, the questions, the answers. Eventually I told him his father was *not* dead, that in fact he had abandoned us. That I'd told him the other thing only to protect him. He said, 'Protect me from what?' I said, 'From hating your father.' So of course I planted the idea. It was what I had intended to do. But I believed it was better that he hate his father than that he long for him. I beg you to understand this, Steven—I had no idea that it would get out of hand. I would have thought Peter too controlled for that, too intelligent. I was wrong. I suppose I should have been more mindful of his secretiveness. After all, that's how I am, too. I make no secret of my secretiveness," she said, and she gave a little laugh.

"You make it sound so harmless, Willa."

"It *was* harmless. Don't you see? What I did would never have gone beyond Peter and me if it hadn't been for Ben getting those notebooks, that and—"

"Ben's running out of time."

"Yes."

She studied me as if to say, "Don't you see? I am not the guilty party." And when I said nothing, she lit a cigarette and moved the ashtray closer to her hand.

I took her to dinner that night. I wanted to hear more. But it wasn't for Ben anymore. I think it was mostly for

me. I wanted to grieve—for Ben and for Andy and for
Peter. But as I sat there talking to Willa, it was Emily I
was thinking about—Emily and Joan and Willa, three
woman, so different. But were they? Were they really?
Maybe it will always be fathers and sons and the physical
drama between them, a game for who gets the woman,
even if the getting is only in the mind. Maybe that's what
families are, not people in groups, but arms and legs and
animals in heat, the moral law and the social law no
more than the desperate work of males without females
hoping to get closer to the fire.

Creatures in caves . . . what it must have been like for
Ben in that cave, Peter cross-legged, eyes rolled back
into his head, lips parted, dwarfed tooth showing, that
strange word.

Anasazi.

How much can God take from a man? The answer's
simple. How much does he have?

I ordered brandy, and we sat for a long time, the
waiter returning again and again with fresh coffee. I
didn't want the night to be over. I wanted to keep asking
her questions, trifling things just to keep her there.

I started to light a cigar. But then I remembered, and
put it away.

"Another brandy?"

She nodded, and I raised my hand.

"You were going by your maiden name. That was the
only name Peter knew. Didn't you realize what you'd be
doing if you told him the name Ben? The name Garrison? Was it because of school? Because you had to produce a birth certificate?"

"No, I don't think so." She sipped from her glass and
put it down. "I imagine I could have found a way around
that. No, it was because it legitimized my story, gave
Peter something actual and specific. That's why I told
him his father was an actor, a director, whatever."

"Then why not show the boy a picture of Ben? He

was famous, you could have found a photograph. That would have done the job even better. A face.''

She had her glass halfway to her mouth again, and she lowered it to the table. "Oh no," she said, almost smiling. "Ben was far too handsome to risk it. How much better to let Peter conjure up his own vision. What could compete with his imagination?"

She lifted her glass again, and this time she finished what was in it.

"I'll tell you something interesting, Steven. It's just an observation of mine, and scarcely more than a parochial one. But you know how it is often remarked that no man can actually disappear in the United States—that he's tied to the apparatus by a hundred strands. Numbers, all sorts of numbers.''

"That's what they say," I said.

She smiled. "Yes. Well, I suspect the principle doesn't hold for a woman.''

She took up the brandy the waiter had placed in front of her, raising her glass to me in a sort of toast. "So you see, Steven? There's something to be said for the inequalities.''

She stayed on in New York for three days. But I didn't see her again. There were a few things I still wanted to ask her, bits and pieces to fill out the picture, a lawyer's habitual curiosity. I still couldn't fathom how she'd brought the whole thing off, stayed attached to two or three universities without our ever finding her.

But there was only one thing I really wanted to ask about, and of course I couldn't. Not just about regret and whether she felt any—for Ben or for Peter or for Andy, or, most of all, for Joan. But for *herself*. How does someone get that way, freed from doubt, liberated from all those uncertainties that hold the rest of us in check? Didn't she realize she'd already destroyed Peter, long before Ben bought the Buntline?

No, she realized nothing, and regretted less. She drank her brandy and sipped her coffee and eyed me—

and in three days Willa Stafford vanished again, as absolutely as she had that morning, so many years ago.

But I see her sometimes. I see her the way I see the rest of them, even Jack and Eric and the girl, the whole story and everyone in it.

All my life I will see it—Peter sitting half-ringed by the arc of *luminarios*. The cave in Mesa Verde, its blank face forever gazing at the blank, cracked earth, its great mouth ceaselessly grinning, ceaselessly screaming, the toothless gums forever agape. And my friend—in my mind I will see him forever on sandstone, climbing, falling forever on ice, while the child Andy—or is it Peter?—forever calls out to his father, howls forever in terror or in delight.

But whenever I think of Willa, everything blazes. I see her striding and striding forever, under the flame of a stupendous light. I see her cross and recross that ancient desolation, pelvis offered, dark hair streaming, and above her, held overhead, the infant Peter, silent, triumphant, aloft.

I see it. *All of it*.

I see it as if what happened to Ben Garrison had happened instead to me.

4.

It started in July—a little pain, a little chill. Later in the month, it was pain all the time, an agony so constant that he could almost forget about it until it boiled over into a sudden torrential scalding of tissue and bone. By mid-August he had undergone tests, complicated tests that emptied him of everything except the taste of sheet metal on the roof of his mouth. But these he kept to himself, just as he had the pain. Besides, he had a show to get out, things to get done, people counting on him, big money riding on his name. All right, he had pain, chills, and certain tests were being done. Was there anything conclusive yet? Was the verdict in?

He checked his watch. An hour to go.

The appointment was scheduled for eleven-thirty. So the answer was no. Meanwhile, he was thirty-four years old and healthy as a horse, with about an hour to go before he might know otherwise.

He reached for the aspirin bottle in the pocket of his heavy tweed sportcoat, shook out four tablets, and swallowed them with the cold black coffee from the Styrofoam cup. Four rows in front of him, up there on the stage, an actor was going through a similar sequence of motions.

"Hey, Roger!" Ben Garrison shouted from where he sat in the darkened theater. "Hey, pal—give me a break, okay? You *pick* up the brandy snifter! You *hear* the music! You *drop* the powder into the brandy! In just that order, with no funny business in between. Got it?"

22

The actor came downstage and shrugged, squinting out beyond the footlights to where he guessed Garrison was sitting.

"Sure, Ben, I know—but I thought the guy might—"

"You're thinking again, Roger! Honest to God, pal, quit it. The point is, it's by the numbers. Like a drill team, okay? Beat, beat, beat—snifter, music, powder. A chain reaction. Okay, Roger? Okay, everybody? Everybody all set?"

It was a funny play, this thing that Billy Dillon had written and that Curt McIver was producing. It would be Ben's fourth comedy hit in a row, and it would put Billy Dillon on the map and make McIver even richer than he already was. As for Ben, he loved bringing in the winners. Not because of the money or the glory so much as because a hit made everybody so damn happy. And after this one, he'd knock off for a year and get some rest. He'd promised Joan. And he owed it to Andy. After all, the boy needed a father to see him through the years. It'd been five seasons since Ben had had any real time off. That's what these pains and chills were all about—just too much work, is all.

He lowered the big yellow pad to his lap again. "Miss Farrar! Cynthia, love!"

The actress turned to face the row of seats.

He checked his watch again as he took her through it. Flood's office in less than forty-five minutes. A clean bill of health. That was what he wanted now, a clean bill of health and the peace of mind to deal effectively with what was in his briefcase in a big manila envelope.

"Love, be a good cupcake and throw your head back *after* Roger turns on the machine!"

"Sorry, Mr. G."

"No problem, Miz F."

"You're doing just great, baby!" It was Billy Dillon yelling to the stage from somewhere in the back of the theater.

He wanted to turn around and tell Dillon to shut up, to

carry on his seductions somewhere else. But instead he raised the pad to jot down a note about a blocking change he wanted to try in the second act, and when he moved his right arm, the pain took him and lifted him halfway out of his seat. He grabbed for the back of the seat in front of him and sank to his knees, gasping, trying to catch his breath and hold himself off the floor.

He could hear Cynthia Farrar calling from the stage. "Mr. G? Shall I take it from the entrance?" But he couldn't speak at first, and when at last he could, his voice was thinned out, breathy, as if he'd just swallowed a feather.

"No, love, just from the last line. That'll be fine, thanks."

He didn't hear much after that, and he didn't see much, either. Maybe it was because he was sitting in darkness and looking into stage light, but he was finding it harder and harder to focus his eyes. Tiny clouds drifted across his vision, and when he tried to blink them away, they spread out like drops of ink soaking into blotting paper. Minutes before eleven he called it quits and convened the afternoon rehearsal for two o'clock. When he stood to leave, he had to steady himself before he could make it into the aisle.

"Dynamite!"

It was Billy Dillon. He'd caught up with Ben in the lobby, and he had an arm around his waist, and he was grinning like a fool and trying to slow Garrison down.

"Jesus, Benjy, all I can say is Jesus. Honest to God, man, it's on the fucking money, you know? We'll run fucking *forever*."

Garrison was checking his watch and edging toward the doors and the street.

"You hear me, man? It's fucking dynamite! You're a goddamn *genius*, and I owe you my fucking *life*."

Garrison kept moving.

"You gave me a good script, Billy. Just relax, okay?"

"Oh man." The man was hugging Garrison and trying to step in front of him. "Relax, he says. Jesus fucking Christ! You hear him? Relax!" He pulled at Garrison's waist again, and then he let him go. "Me? What about *you,* you son of a bitch! You're fucking *wasted,* man. Skin and fucking *bones.* Eat something, for Christ's sake. Eat pussy, man. Or, hey, hey—let me take you to lunch, let me buy you some fucking *food.*"

Garrison smiled and kept trying for the doors.

"Thanks, pal, but there's somewhere I've got to be by eleven-thirty sharp. I'll catch you later, okay?"

"Hey, hey," Dillon said, still trying to block Garrison's escape. "I understand, man—believe me, I *understand.* You probably got to cut home for a nooner with that gorgeous old lady of yours. Only there's this one thing, you know? Which is *where* is *McIver?* On account of there's this thing I've got to ask him about. So what's *doing* with the son of a bitch?"

"This afternoon. He said he'd fall by this afternoon."

"Right, right. Well, that's *good,* Benjy, thanks. Because he made a little promise to me about sweet Miss Cynthia, you see. So he'll be *in,* you think?"

"You bet," Garrison said. "Call his office and check."

"No, no, that's good," Dillon was saying as Garrison kept trying to push past him. "It's just that the son of a bitch swore he'd set it up, you know? And, hey, Benjy, I don't mind telling you, that's all right, you know? I mean, you can't blame me, cunt like that—can you?"

"See you at two, pal," Garrison said, cuffing Dillon on the shoulder and shoving through the doors onto Forty-fifth Street.

In the cab, heading through midday traffic, he reached into his briefcase and drew out a large manila envelope, the heavy paper so worn from handling that it was furry in spots and almost torn through with the thickness of its contents. He held it in his hands for a while, hefting the

package and turning it over to read the address and the
return address for what seemed to him the hundredth
time. Then he leaned forward and rolled both windows
all the way up. He stayed hunched forward, huddled into
himself.

It was hot for mid-October. But even with his heavy
wool sportcoat and the thick turtleneck he wore under it,
Garrison was very cold. The icy wind that had been
blazing up in him since late July shot through his body
with full fury now, and it seemed to have brought with it
a curious yellowing of his skin, as if the frost he felt
widening inside him were scorching the surface of his
body darker. All through August and September he had
kept himself under extra layers of clothing and two or
three blankets at night. Probably overwork, overwork
and a bad diet, meals eaten at a dead run. A good rest,
that was what he needed—a good rest, some sunshine,
and regular, well-balanced meals. A holiday. It would be
good for all of them. The three of them would go somewhere, maybe the Bahamas, maybe Acapulco.

But right from the start he'd known he was kidding
himself. He'd known it was more than fatigue and a
lousy diet. He'd known that whatever it was, it had to be
serious. But he just hadn't wanted to know more than
that—not until he'd done his best for Dillon and McIver
and gotten the damn thing opened and running smooth.
But then Joan noticed the weight loss. How could she
help but notice the piled-on clothing and blankets at
night in the midst of the summer heat? And his skin, the
way it looked shaded, as if he'd been blast-frozen, she
couldn't miss seeing that.

She'd pestered. She'd begged him to see someone. At
least to talk to Paul, Paul Fiore, the internist who'd
served as the Garrison family doctor since Andy was
born. And so, finally, if only so she'd stop worrying,
Ben promised. "I'll give Paul a ring. I'll make an appointment. I promise, honey."

But he didn't do it. Instead, he waited for whatever it

was to go away and just leave him alone so he could work. All he did was promise—until halfway into August, when she caught him shivering on a broiling day.

She made the appointment herself.

It was Paul who had seen him and who had, that very same day, referred him to Flood. Only Garrison hadn't told Joan about that part of it. He hadn't said anything about going directly from Paul's office to Flood's, about walking from East Sixty-second Street to East Sixty-eighth and stopping along the way to go into a coffee shop and check the Yellow Pages. He knew there was a section in the directory for physicians, where certain ones were listed according to the specialty they practiced. He found Flood's name among them.

He wished he'd never looked.

It was listed under something called *oncology*.

He didn't need to know what the word meant, exactly. He just had to see it to get the general idea.

Oncology. An *oncologist*.

It made something turn over inside him. For a time he stood there gazing at the page of names and numbers, and then he moved into the phone booth and called Paul Fiore.

"Not a word to Joan. No matter how she rags you for an answer. You just tell her I'm fine—that I'm a little overworked, is all. You swear?"

Paul Fiore had given his word. And later that day, Flood had ordered an elaborate series of tests.

The taxi was stalled in traffic on Madison. The driver was cursing and trying to catch Garrison's eye in the rearview window. But Garrison didn't want to talk. He didn't need to hear anyone tell him how lousy the whole stinking world was, and how the worst of it was this totally screwed-up city.

He moved out of the driver's line of vision and gingerly eased himself all the way back against the seat. He glanced at his watch. It wouldn't be long before he'd have his answer, an answer to tests which sometimes left him so weak that two nurses would have to help him to his feet again. They'd stay with him, vigilant, watching for fainting or vomiting as he sat in some cold white cubicle, waiting to regain his strength before he tried to get back into his clothes.

He studied the return address: *J. S. Breaker, c/o Graduate Division in Social Sciences, University of Colorado, Boulder Campus, Boulder, Colorado*. And he looked once more at the mailing address: *Mr. Benjamin Garrison, c/o The Plymouth Theater, 326 West 45th Street, New York, New York*.

A man who ignored zip codes. Did that suggest anything about him? Hastiness, arrogance, ignorance, impulsiveness, what? All of the above or none of the above?

There was a third address, and no zip code followed that one either. It was in the typewritten letter clipped to the speckled cover of the grammar-school composition book, the one that came first in the group of four that Breaker had put inside the envelope. It was an address for which Ben Garrison had searched for almost thirteen years—at first with a singleminded ferocity that almost drove him mad, and then later, as the effort proved useless, with the patient, abiding determination of a man who would never give up. And now here it was: *Dr. W. Stafford, Box 91, Rural Route 1, Cortez, Colorado*.

But now that he had the information he wanted, he didn't know what to do about it. The postmark on the envelope went back to June. It was the middle of October now, and Garrison had done nothing about it.

He murmured the boy's name—*Peter*—as if the utterance of the name might conjure up a vision, a face, some idea of the face of the child who could write the murderous sentences the four booklets contained. But all Garrison could see was her face, Willa's face, long and narrow and wondrously serene as it gazed upon an infant in a crib.

Who belonged to the name Peter? What kind of boy?

The taxi cut a sharp angle through the intersection at 57th, and then it jumped free of traffic and sped ahead toward 68th. A sudden chill flashed through Garrison as the cab turned at the corner and pulled up before a small building midway down the block. He hugged his arms to his chest, and then he realized he had to get out his wallet. "Jesus," he said, grinning as if he'd just done something funny. "Jesus," he said again as he reached for his wallet, and then he actually laughed as he paid the driver and fished in his pockets for more change for the tip.

Why not laugh? It was all ridiculous. He was in the pink, goddammit!

Inside the double doors, he said, "Garrison. To see Dr. Flood."

The receptionist did not smile. She touched her hair, nervously pushing at little wisps.

She said, "Yes, of course. Mr. Garrison. I have you down for eleven-thirty." And still she did not smile when she lifted the intercom receiver and buzzed for a nurse to come get him.

5.

HE WAS MORE than an hour late getting back to the theater. He was more than an hour late because he had walked, and he had walked because he wanted some time to think.

But he could not think. Nor could he see or hear. All he could do was walk and walk, taking no particular route, just going where his blind motion led him.

He passed Forty-fifth Street unawares, and was almost to Thirty-eighth Street before he understood that he had gone too far. It was then that he took a firm grip on his briefcase and was able to grope beyond the blunt language that had just sentenced him to death. Perhaps there was something he was missing, some loophole, a way out.

Of course! He could get a second opinion. A third, a fourth.

But two hard truths caught him squarely and stopped him where he stood.

Was there time for a second opinion? If so little time remained, wouldn't it be crazy to waste it on a round-robin of doctors?

And then there was the second truth—that Paul had said when you went to Charles Flood, you went to *the man,* that there was no one who could top him in his field.

Two months. Approximately. Approximately sixty days. The pancreas. Inoperable, untreatable. Too god-damn late.

He was still trying to decide which seemed longer—
two months or sixty days—when he found himself back
at his post in the fourth row of the Plymouth. He could
see the cast and crew waiting respectfully onstage, but he
scarcely heard himself when he called out an apology
and told them to run the second act all the way through.

He sat down, dazed, and pulled out the big yellow
pad. But he made no notes. Nor did he hear what was
going on up there. If Garrison heard anything, it was the
voice of Dr. Charles Flood going off in his head.

He thanked everyone at four-thirty and sent them
home. When the lights came up, he went quickly to the
back of the theater to cut McIver loose from Dillon.

McIver seemed glad to be rescued, and within minutes
Garrison had him out of the place and in a booth at the
rear of a joint on Eighth Avenue, a double shooter of
bourbon and a Campari and soda standing like two sol-
diers on the damp table between them.

"There may be a problem," Garrison began.

"*What* problem?" McIver almost sneered with delight. "You got a hit, you got a problem? What? You
can't find a big enough bucket to carry your money to the
bank? Don't talk problems, Ben. I don't want to hear."

McIver was a big man, thick gray hair theatrically
styled, money from a third wife who spent her days
learning to sit up straight on the back of a horse somewhere on the North Shore of Long Island.

He leaned forward, his voice confidential.

"You looking for a larger cut?"

Garrison took up his glass of bourbon and downed half
of it. He could feel it grab in his stomach, warming him.

"Nothing like that." He put the glass down. "It's
something personal, Curt. A private matter."

He did not want to explain. He did not want to talk
about it. If he talked about it, then it would get back to
Joanie.

"So? So talk to me, Ben boy. I'm right here with you.

I'm your friend and associate. Right? You want me to go for a prize and guess?''

Garrison was searching for a way into this. He started again. "You've been fair with me, Curt. We've always been straight with each other."

But McIver wasn't helping. "Yeah, yeah, enough shit, okay? *What,* for Christ's sake! What's eating you, Garrison? Trouble at home? There's nookie in the picture?''

McIver smiled broadly and leaned in closer.

"It's the Farrar bitch. Am I right? Dillon's after her, but you want your action first. No problem, lad. That faggot gripes my ass anyway. So you want me to set it up? You can trust me, Ben. Talk to me. I'll fix it. I got that particular little cock-teaser thoroughly wired, Ben boy. Just say the word.''

Garrison sat back. He lit a cigarette. He looked at McIver, but what he saw was Flood's face, and he heard the words *pancreas* and *fastest of the cancers.*

"All right," he said. "It's this in a nutshell. I have to step aside from the show.''

Again McIver smiled grandly. He pushed his glass to one side, as if clearing a space for battle.

"Forget it. Can't be done.''

"It has to be done," Garrison said.

"Ben boy," McIver began, rolling his heavy shoulders, "let's not fuck around, okay? I'm tired, you're tired, we're deep into rehearsals. Meanwhile, the story is like a kid's story—it's that simple. We have paper, right? There is a piece of paper. You signed it, I signed it. Black and white. So forget it, sweetheart. Deck's got a copy? Do me a favor and call Deck and ask him to read it to you. You want a dime? I'll give you a dime.''

Garrison heard his brain scream. He pinched the bridge of his nose, rubbed his eyes. His vision was fogging again, tiny clouds that only spread out worse when he rubbed his eyes to get rid of them.

"Look, Curt," he began again. "I don't want to hassle with you. There's no room in this thing, no leeway at all. I'm out. I'm sorry as all hell, but there's not a—"

McIver didn't let him finish. He held up his hand like a cop stopping traffic. "I've heard enough, buddy boy. You fuck me over, and I'll sue your ass all the way into the twenty-first century. They'll have to come get you from Iowa and take you home in a shovel, mister. You hear me? Now this conversation is over!"

McIver stood up, tossed a twenty-dollar bill onto the table, and walked out.

For a time Garrison just sat there, slowly swallowing bourbon. And then he unbuckled his briefcase and got out the envelope. He slid the four notebooks and the letter onto the table and fanned them out in front of him. In the middle of each speckled cover there was a square of white, the word COMPOSITION printed at the top, two thick black lines below, the name PETER STAFFORD written across the first of these lines, four different dates across the second: *1972, 1974, 1977, 1979.*

Garrison downed the last of his bourbon and signaled the waiter for a refill. He lit another cigarette, picked up the composition book headed *1972,* and opened it to the first page. Andy was seven now, the age Peter had been when he filled these lines from margin to margin, the words formed in very small, very precise script. Andy was seven and yet he still printed, and the result was a logjam of lumpish sprawling letters that only a parent or a teacher would have the patience to decipher.

There was a title entered at the top of the page, centered perfectly on the first ruled line: *How the Monster Got Killed.*

Garrison read the first three sentences. But he didn't need to. He knew them by heart.

Everybody was running because the monster was after them, a big green thing with lots of eyes and claws and gick dripping out of its mouth which had long black fangs in it and a tongue like a lizard. The monster's

*name was Daddy and it made everybody scared to see it
because it ate people and tore them to tiny shreds, even if
they screamed help me help me. But there was a boy in
the town and he wasn't scared because he had a magic
trick which was to hold his breath and he also had a big
enchanted dagger too and it could kill anything even
Daddy.*

What was it? A cry for help? Or a wish to murder? Or
was it both of these things—or neither of them, just a
small boy's imagination running riot? No, it was more
than that—infinitely, dreadfully more than that. For
every page of the booklet was covered over with the
evidence, and there were three more booklets to go—a
total of four selected from the cache of eight that Breaker
said he had discovered in the cave. But what of the four
that Breaker did *not* send? Did they refute the evidence
here? Or did they simply confirm it all the more power-
fully?

The waiter came with Garrison's drink, and he
promptly drank from it, stubbed out his cigarette, and lit
a fresh one.

He picked up the letter to study it yet again, his eyes
straying from phrase to phrase, groups of words that he
had circled with red pencil the day the envelope came.

". . . *this urgent matter, because you must handle it
in strictest confidence . . .*"

"*I'm no psychiatrist, but these notebooks . . .*"

"*She must never know that I . . .*"

". . . *my humanitarian duty to inform you that . . .*"

". . . *gravely disturbed, in my inexpert judgment.*"

". . . *fixated on eventually securing the death
of . . .*"

". . . *a normal fourteen-year-old boy to all outward
appearance . . .*"

". . . *if not you, then who?*"

". . . *hideaway in a nearby national park, a cave,
which he has turned into a kind of . . .*"

"But whatever you do, she's my thesis director—so leave me out of it because . . ."

A flame of frigid air ignited under Garrison's heart and fanned out, waves of frost pulsing through his chest. His hand gripped the glass of whiskey as the seizure whipped through him, and then it left him as abruptly as it had come. Sweat stood out all over his body, and he was breathing as if he'd just been chased.

He folded his arms and rested them on the table and let his head down on top of them. He stayed this way for a long time, hating himself for giving in to the pain, and yet amazed at how much he had already withstood without crying out in despair. Perhaps it was like that, dying. Perhaps you did so much of it each day that, by the time it got around to the big one, you just slid right into it, a man with plenty of practice. Hours ago he'd been given the word that in a couple of months he was finished, done with, as dead as this table, this glass, the floor beneath his feet. With everything to live for, life was over—except the hardest part, the dying still to be done. Then why was it that he wasn't devastated, shrieking at the top of his lungs? Was it possible that in mere hours a man could put a thing like that under his belt and then hitch up his trousers and take two steps forward and wait for his guts to explode? Had he already had the worst of it? Perhaps half of him had died the morning Peter wasn't there—and the other half the day this envelope came. Perhaps it was a ghost that Flood had sentenced to death.

He drank off the rest of his bourbon and shoved everything back into the briefcase. When he stood up to go, he staggered slightly, but quickly recovered his balance and made his way past the bar to the door.

The letter was dated June 12. It was October now, October 17. In all this time he'd done nothing, because everything he'd thought of seemed the wrong thing to do. But there wasn't time for doing nothing anymore. A serpent was unwinding inside him, and in two months it would swallow him whole.

Two months—give or take a little margin for error. Two months to save Peter, to invent an antidote for the poison that had been fed him. Two months for Garrison to protect from harm the people that he loved.

Peter, first Peter—and then Andy and Joan.

6.

THE HOUSE ON West Eleventh Street stood just as he had left it that morning—and yet it seemed to him different now, exposed, vulnerable, worn down in places he hadn't noticed. The roof—he had better see to the roof. Maybe a paint job—inside and out. And a burglar-alarm system, that was an absolute necessity. Insurance. The mortgage. Countless things that needed attention, and how would he ever think of them all? A list—start making a list—and put Peter right at the top of it.

He climbed the steps to the front door, taking his time, stopping to look again at the exterior of the house, the shutters on the second and third floors. Insulation. That was essential, too. With fuel costs rising like crazy, he'd better take care of it first thing. The car! The station wagon. It was a gas-eater. Get rid of it. Get something less expensive to run, something smaller. Something easier for Joan to manage. But what? Weren't those compacts sometimes death traps? All right, he'd have to think about it. A little car would be less hassle in the city, but couldn't they be dangerous? On the other hand, maybe the city itself was too dangerous. Maybe he ought to see about selling the house, moving Joanie and Andy somewhere else. Back to Ames, maybe. He still had some aunts and uncles in those parts. Wouldn't that be a better idea? What were they here for? For him, and his work. So why not somewhere clean and safe?

He'd have to think about that, too. After all, it was up to Joanie and Andy, wasn't it? They couldn't just give up everything, could they? Maybe with him gone, the best place to be was right where they'd always been. Maybe it was crazy to think about changing things. Maybe the best thing was to leave everything just the way it was. He'd have to think about it. It was too much to decide all at once. A list. That's the thing. Do it in an orderly, careful fashion. Give it some time, some thought. But how? In two months? All right, all right. He had to slow down. One thing at a time—and the first thing was Peter. Do something about Peter. Save him. Hold him and hold him and make him well. *Please, God, give me time to make my son well.*

He touched his key to the lock and the door fell open, and he almost fell forward with it. He stood in the middle of the foyer, dizzy with fear, appalled. They could be up there, throats cut, bullets in their heads. New York! It was crazy to live here.

He cried out for them and lunged for the bottom of the stairs.

"For God's sake, Ben honey, what is it? Something wrong?"

It was Joan at the top of the stairs, face flushed from the Indian-summer heat, her graceful hands tucking at the long syrupy hair she wore drawn gently back and folded in on itself at the nape of her slender neck.

Garrison stood there at the bottom of the stairs, looking up at her in relief, his heart still racing.

He had to swallow before he could speak.

"It's nothing," he said, but his legs still trembled, and he had to hold tight to the railing. "It's okay," he said.

She smiled and started down the stairs, coming toward him, barefooted, her long sleek legs shimmering from beneath the flowery cotton skirt. Garrison gazed at her coming at him—the legs, the strong bone where they joined.

Two months. Sixty days. And the nights were numbered too.

"But you were hollering so. Somebody bite you today?"

"The door," he said. He felt paralyzed. He wanted to smile back at her, but he couldn't. "Unlocked. Don't do it anymore."

She stopped midway, leaned a little, put her hands to her lovely knees. "Um, yes—somebody bit him today. Is it rabies, then?" With her hands still on her knees, she took a little jump to the next stair down. "If I come any closer, will I catch it?"

"You bet," he said, and held out his arms to her.

She reached him and slipped her golden arms around his waist, and his arms closed around her and he lowered his head and put his lips in her hair.

"Joanie," he said. Just that, and all at once he wanted to weep.

"Where'd they bite you, darling? Show me," she whispered. "Come upstairs and show me."

"Just the door," he said. "That's all. Promise me you'll watch out for things like that."

He held her close so that she would not see his face.

"Hey, honey, cut it out. It's just that Andy and I came home loaded down with groceries and all, and then I had to get him right into his tub. All this over an unlocked door?"

She swung away from him, her fingers knitted behind his back, her breasts jogging under the loose T-shirt she wore.

He kissed her throat and pulled her close to him again, and it felt to him that the warmth of her body was like an armful of sunshine and that his own body was already dead.

"You *do* want to go upstairs, don't you?" She pushed away from him. "Well, I'm sorry, but you can't. There's a seven-year-old person in this household, if you don't mind my reminding you—and your bedtime comes after his.''

"Promise?" Garrison said.

There was nothing playful in his question, and she knew it now.

"Oh, darling, I promise."

He let her go and moved to the stairs.

"Andy's in the tub?"

"Andy and, let's see, Henry the octopus and Henry the sea monster."

He started up the stairs. When he heard her close and latch the door, he stopped and turned.

"I'm sorry, baby. Okay?"

"You see some grisly headline today?"

"Hey, it's not that," he called down to her. "It's just that it's a good policy, you know? You can't be too careful, right?"

She stared at him, worried at this sudden change, the tension. "Like hell you can't," she said. "If you ask me, that's what most New Yorkers die of—the willies, the jitters, the good old heebie-jeebies. Now *relax*, sweetie—everybody's *safe*. You go scrub the Andy and the Henrys while I get dinner."

Again Garrison tried to smile. He turned away from her and started shouldering up the stairs, trying to clear his mind of everything save the pleasure of the moment, the happiness it was possible for him to give.

When he made it to the first landing, he started calling ahead to the third floor. "What's this I hear? There's a boy in my house? By God, is there a real live boy up there?"

He kept it up until he heard the laughter and the splashing that were meant to answer his teasing.

"A boy! A boy!" Garrison shouted as he mounted the last of the stairs and quickened his pace to the door at the end of the third-floor hall.

He did his best with the food. But he couldn't get

much of it down. And he did even less well with the talk, the routine reports of the day. All through dinner he wanted to get up and go find a sheet of paper and start his list. Or just get up and hug Joan, hug Andy, draw them both to him and never let them go. But instead he gazed blankly at his food, the tablecloth, their faces, and even when a jolt of pain came, he did not stir.

"Hello, hello."

"You bet. Sorry. Rehearsals, is all."

That seemed to satisfy it, but he knew they were watching him, and he tried to come out of it, to say something, say anything.

"Hey, Garrison family, for the record, I'm not unhappy or anything like that. And I don't have anything but the highest opinion of this here meal Mama cooked up. It's just that, number one, I had a tremendous lunch today and, number two, I'm still sitting in the Plymouth Theater."

"Fourth row, center section?"

It was Andy, pleased with himself for remembering.

"Are my habits that famous?" Garrison said.

"You bet," the boy answered, hoping his father would notice.

He did. He turned to Joan. "You hear this boy say, 'You bet'? Is this what happens when I turn my back? The words get stolen right out of my mouth?"

It got them smiling, and it seemed to quiet Joan's anxiety. At least she didn't nag him for the rest of the meal—eat more, try this, try that, you've got to get something in your stomach.

Later he took Andy into the living room, and for a while they talked about school and about football, and then Garrison read to his son for an hour or so, the boy in his lap, his spill of golden hair, still damp from the bath, like an angel's wing caught beneath Garrison's chin. He read to the boy from *Treasure Island,* doing the voices of Long John Silver and Squire Trelawney. It was a thing Garrison loved to do, and it delighted Andy. The boy would never have guessed how far his father's thoughts were from the people he made leap off the page. The boy was lost in a dream of curving swords and lusty men and young Jim Hawkins, bravest of all. But then, just when Long John Silver was saying, *Six they were, and six are we; and bones is what they are now,* the boy felt something snap inside his father's chest.

Garrison dropped the book. He lifted his son from his lap and sagged a little to the side, breathing fast.

"You okay, Daddy?" the boy wanted to know, standing there watching as his father struggled for air.

"Oh yeah, oh sure," Garrison was able to say, grinning to prove it. "Just a little stitch, is all."

But the boy could sense something more, something hinted in the bunched muscles in his father's jaws, a secret, a grown-up mystery whose content might be hidden but whose shape you only had to look to see. He reached his fingertips to Garrison's cheeks and lightly touched his face.

"Sweet Papa," the boy said, his wide light eyes searching his father's face for more signs, the answer he knew was somewhere there. And then, as if he could think of nothing else in all the world, the boy put his lips against his father's, murmured, "I love you, Papa. I love you so much."

She found him under two blankets and a quilt when she came naked from the bathroom, her body fragrant from the plain soap she favored, her hair undone, a honeyed cataract that swept to just below her shoulders, a slow liquid, undulant. She lifted the covers, and on hands and knees she crept close to his trembling body, her cool slim fingers reaching for the knotted muscles that ran like ribs across his belly.

"So thin, so tense. What is it, Ben? What's wrong?"

He turned to her in the darkness of the room, his hand moving to take her between the buttocks and urge her down so that she lay athwart him, a warm weight to keep him anchored to the earth.

"Ben, Ben." Her lips were pressed to his ear, whispering. "Honest, honey, I can't help it. You've got me scared to death."

He knew what she meant, but he acted as if he didn't. "That rumpus about the front door? Forget it. I just get jumpy sometimes, you and Andy all alone in this big house." He kept his hand where it was, his fingertips inching down and around to work the delicate tissue that moistened under his touch, her hips moving slightly now, little jumps as if fired by sparks.

"You know what I mean—you're still losing weight and you're freezing, I can tell. Please, honey, let's call Paul tonight—let's both talk to him."

He whispered when he spoke, talking into her throat, his lips pulling at her skin.

"I talked to him, remember? He checked me eight ways from Sunday. Says it's nothing but nerves and too much work. Now come on, let's skip it, okay?"

"I can't," she said. "Without you, Andy and I would go right down the drain."

He eased away from her and sat up and switched on the reading light on his side of the bed, a polished steel globe that angled from the wall. It was matched by an identical fixture that sprang from the wall on the other side of the bed, and between the two of them rose a broad length of tapestry—knights jousting while courtiers and ladies looked on. The bedroom was high-ceilinged and large, and the objects in it gave off the impression of dark waxed wood and plush velvet in deep green.

He reached to the night table for his cigarettes and a book of matches, and when he opened it, he saw the words *See Steve: mortgage, insurance, estate taxes* penciled the long way across the inside cover. He lit up and carefully closed the book of matches and put it back on the table with his cigarettes, turning his hand over so that the pack would rest on top.

"I say something that bad?"

"Yeah," he said, leaning his back against the wall. "Yeah, you said something pretty bad."

She pulled away from him and sat back on her haunches. "Like what?"

"Like going down the drain without me around. I don't like to hear you talk like that."

"Aren't you going to be around?"

He looked at her, those wide light eyes, the effect of half-surprise. Andy's eyes were like that, enchanted eyes, so expressive, so open, so trusting.

"Oh, baby, you bet I'm going to be around. Forever and forever. It's just that I like to think you can handle things without me. I mean, if you had to. You know, Andy and all."

She leaned forward, her back straight, sweeping her hair to one side. "Is that what you're thinking about? That I might have to manage alone?"

He forced a small laugh. "No, honey—for God's sake, no. But even so—" He didn't know how to finish it. "Forget it. Skip it. It's the Dillon thing. It's got me all tight inside."

It was then that he thought of the lie, and he began to move it into place.

"Honest to God, I'm thinking of chucking the thing. It's gone sour. Sappy material, uninspired cast, and life with McIver and Dillon is no treat. So what do you think? You think I should get out from under?"

He could see how the prospect pleased her. She crept closer on her knees, and then let herself down against him, her head resting on his belly. When she spoke, he could feel her voice inside him.

"Best thing I've heard all day. And it's just what Paul would recommend. We don't need the money and you don't need the credits—so, sure, honey, do it, get out of it."

"McIver will litigate. It's serious. I'd be in serious default."

She turned her head and nibbled at his skin. "Who cares? So what? Steve'll handle it. And besides, if you want to know the truth, those two beauties you've got give me the creeps—Roger and whatsername."

"Cynthia Farrar? *Miss* Farrar? 'Cynthia love'?" Garrison laughed. "Roger Wiseman, bless his soul, turns out to be McIver's wife's college roommate's boyfriend, and Dillon tells me that 'Cynthia love' and old Curt have been eating a lot of breakfasts together since she did a bit in a show of his four years ago. Oh hell, I don't know— maybe I'll do it."

"Quit?"

"Quit," Garrison said, and stubbed out his cigarette.

"Hoorray," she said, mouthing the word into his belly and hugging his hips.

"That way," he began, "I can take a crack at this movie thing."

It was the first of the lies he had to tell her.

"What movie thing?"

"They called Steve this morning."

"A directing assignment?"

He nodded. "Nothing definite. But at least they want to talk."

"Terrific," Joan said, and kissed his belly.

"It means going out to the Coast for a week or so— meetings, looking things over, this and that."

"But you'll get some rest first. We'll take Andy out of school, and we'll go somewhere gloriously sunny, and you'll get a good long rest. Is that a promise, B.W.?"

"It's a promise," he said. "Right after I run out to the Coast and see what's what—whether they like me and I like them. Fair enough?"

"Um." She made the sound in the back of her throat, and this time, when she kissed his belly, her tongue was between her lips.

He reached his hands to her shoulders and turned her

onto her back, bending to her and kissing her lips upside down. It was a long kiss, slow and musing, and she could sense that something had come over him, something that had nothing to do with their bodies. They stayed this way for a long time, her back resting on his outstretched legs, his head bent to hers, and when she felt how hard he was beneath her, she turned herself over and pushed against his shoulders and drew her knees up to either side of him so that he could enter her and feel how, for him, she could make her body into water.

"Slowly," he said, and Joan Garrison understood.

7.

HE WAITED UNTIL they left the house. He waited until Joan had trundled Andy into the station wagon to drive him off to school. And then Garrison packed a small overnight bag and left the house.

He did not want a good-bye—not one where he had to face them with his lie. It would be easier to do it later, to do it by telephone—to explain why he was going now and not the next day or the day after that.

He had stood by the garage door to give them hugs and kisses—and if he had held them a little longer than usual, perhaps they did not notice, and then, when they were gone, he sat down at the kitchen table and drew up a list—*mortgage, insurance, estate taxes,* and the rest of the things he could think of.

I still have the list, of course—his handwritten version and the typed copy I made from it. It's a thing to see, what a man in a hurry to get ready for death thinks to worry about for the people he's leaving behind. I have the list. And Joan has the letter he wrote later that morning.

She has it now, all the things he tried to say to her in there, all that frantic summation, so many things to get said in such a hurry. About Willa and Peter and the secret of all those years. About why he had never told her because how do you tell about a thing like that? And now he had to go away when there was so little time left. About that too, about Peter, and about why there was so little time. About the extra blankets at night and the

47

sudden loss of weight and what these things really meant.

Emily and I had taken the girls on a long weekend to Boston, so I was late getting in. Adele told him to wait, that I'd be along presently. But Ben asked to use an empty office.

He called Flood.

He asked Flood if there was any chance of error, even the slightest—and Flood said there was none. He asked Flood how bad the pain would be, and Flood said bad, but asked him to come in and discuss it because the telephone was no way to handle such questions.

Ben hung up. It wasn't rudeness, discourtesy, or anger. It wasn't in Ben to be that way—nor was it in him to take out whatever he was feeling on someone else. It was just that he was in a hurry, that for the first time he was beginning to understand how much of a hurry he had to be in.

I knocked, and when there wasn't any answer, I opened the door and went in. He was on the phone, talking to Joan this time. I started to back out and close the door, but he motioned for me to stay, to sit down, and then he said, "Hold it, honey, Steve just got in," and to me he called, "I won't be long."

I sat down and got out a cigar, not listening until I heard him say he'd call her from Los Angeles and please not to worry. Los Angeles? How could he be going to L.A. when he was in the middle of rehearsals? And then he said, 'A week or two, maybe a little more. You check with Steve. He'll keep you posted in case there's any trouble reaching me, because who the hell knows where I'll be half the time. They may want me to check out locations, things like that—but Steve's office'll be keeping tabs. Not to worry, honey, promise? I love you like crazy, and tell old Andy how come I had to hurry off and how he's my best buddy, okay?''

His voice was cheery, that remarkable voice of his, so full of life and warmth, but I could see from his face that it was an act, and when he kissed the receiver and whispered "I love you, yes, yes," his eyes closed and his jaws clenched.

I didn't want to say anything for a while. He stood there over the phone, his hand still on the receiver, looking at me and then out the window.

"Okay," I said, "just let it go easy, man. I'm right here. No hurry."

He jammed his hands in his pockets and started pacing the room. I think he was struggling to get on top of his feelings.

"As long as you're going to walk," I said, "let's move it to my office."

I followed him in and shut the door. He sat on the couch and lit up, and I pulled a chair over close.

"Trouble?"

He nodded.

"You're quitting the Dillon."

"I'm quitting the Dillon."

"McIver letting you out?"

He gave me a sort of lopsided grin, and then he straightened it out.

"Sorry," he said. "Sorry, old buddy."

I saw him blink hard, as if there were something sticky in his eyes. He rubbed at them and ran his fingers back through his hair, and for the first time I noticed how the silvery blond had begun to turn white. He was thinner too, much thinner.

"No," he said, still smiling, "McIver's not letting me out. Not by a long shot. He'll go to law, but it doesn't matter. You do your best with it, hear? If it'll cool him out, negotiate a pay-back instead of fighting against damages. Give him everything I got since signing."

"Like hell I will," I said. "You tell me why you're out, and I'll decide what our legal posture should be."

He waved his hand as if to dismiss all this.

"Forget all that shit. On moral grounds, the man's got the right. Let him have his money back, and just try to hold it to that if you can."

I shouldn't have pushed him. But I did.

"You tell me what your reason is, and I'll decide whether McIver's got moral grounds."

Ben sighed and got to his feet and started pacing again. "Look, good buddy, will you just do what the goddamn hell I ask you to do and skip the rest of this hassling?" He was shouting, and I realized I'd never heard Ben shout before.

I tried to get him to sit down. But he wouldn't.

"Then tell me what's all this about L.A. and locations."

"Forget it. I lied. And you're going to have to cover for me."

I said sure I would, no problem, but why?

He came back to the couch and sat down.

"Steve, I know where Peter is. I've known for months."

I wanted to shout, jump up, do something to show my happiness for him. But I could see that wasn't what he wanted.

"Where?" I said.

"It doesn't matter. Out West. Right around where we were looking all those years."

"He's with Willa? I mean, how'd you find out? He's all right, isn't he?"

"Yes," Ben said softly, nodding very slowly, his eyes fixed on a point somewhere to one side of my head. "Now just listen," he said, "just listen and remember what I tell you."

I got up and came back with a notepad. He waited until I was ready, and then he started to talk.

"Call my family doctor. Paul Fiore. Adele's got his number somewhere. You tell Paul he's bound by the privacy of the patient-physician relationship, and that you're holding him to that bond, and that goes for everyone, even Joan—especially Joan. Do the same thing with this other guy, Charles Flood. He's on Sixty-eighth—or you can get him through Sloan-Kettering.''

I did my best to keep it the way he wanted it—to be the attorney and not the friend. But when I heard him mention Sloan-Kettering, I began to guess the score.

He took out a sheet of paper and put it in my hand.

''You'll see a lot of things there that I've written down. What I want you to do is check them all out for me, and add in anything else that should be taken care of. You'll see what I've marked down there at the bottom, and that's the biggest thing. I won't be around to work with you on it, so what I'll do before I leave is sign over a power of attorney, and then you can just go ahead and take care of the rest without me.''

He paused while I glanced at the list. The word *Will* was scribbled at the bottom.

''You just take care of it the right way. I know I can count on you to do that. Only thing is, whatever arrangement you make for Andy, do the same for Peter, hear?''

I nodded.

''Half and half.''

''Right,'' I said. ''I'll take care of it.''

''Now the other thing is this. I'm going to write out a letter for Joanie, and I'm going to leave it with you. It's the eighteenth of October today—so if in one month I'm not back here or you haven't heard from me, you give it to her. Now you go take care of that power of attorney and let me be by myself in here for a little bit.''

I stayed where I was. I said, ''Ben, you listen to me for a while. I heard you. Now you hear me. Let's talk awhile. Let me help.''

''Talk's no good,'' he said. ''You're helping me fine if you just go take care of that thing.'' And again he blinked as if he couldn't see clearly enough and was trying to get something out of his eyes.

''I can help with Peter.''

''No,'' he said. He shook his head, that same dazed

motion, looking out into the middle distance. "Only I can. Only me." He blinked again, and then he looked at me. "I'll tell you this, Steve, just this. I'm going to give it a month. And then I'm coming back. One month for Pete, and one month here. That's the fairest way I know. You understand?"

I nodded my head, said, "Sure—I understand."

"You bet," he said, and stood up.

I didn't see him after that. Sure, I saw him again after it happened. But it wasn't the same Ben. How could it have been? He was gone by then, destroyed, even though he wasn't yet dead.

There were things I left out that morning in my office. All sorts of things I should have said, questions I should have asked. Even if he wouldn't have answered them. But instead I tried to be the way he wanted me to be. A lawyer doing his work. So there was a lot I didn't say or do.

But Ben was right. Nothing would have helped. Whatever it was, it was between him and Peter. And the clock was running fast.

8.

The cab got him out to LaGuardia just before noon.
But there was no space on anything into Los Angeles
until eight that night. And the story was even worse on
flights from Kennedy.

He knew he couldn't sit it out that long, wait hours
when his life had been reduced to days. Sitting around
LaGuardia for eight hours was out of the question, impossible, whereas an immediate flight into Denver was
no problem. Plenty of space was available. But he didn't
want to go to Denver first. He wanted to fly first to Los
Angeles. Once there, he'd check in at the Beverly
Wilshire and then leave word at the desk that all callers
were to be told he was out. He'd keep the room, and as
soon as he could, he'd catch a plane back to Denver.

But there was nothing, not one seat into Los Angeles
until eight. It couldn't be helped; he'd have to abandon
the idea and fly instead directly into Denver. He understood that it was going to be impossible to put Joan off
for a whole month. But at least he could hold her off for
a while by having a good enough story for two weeks.
And then it occurred to him—he'd tell her he was in
Colorado to check out locations. He'd wait a couple of
days, and when he called, that's what he'd tell her. At
least it made a little sense.

Garrison booked a seat on United, and by Indiana he'd
long since finished off the pint of J. W. Dant he'd picked
up at the airport, and now he was working his way

through his third plastic glass from the galley. But the whiskey wasn't getting anywhere close to the pain.

He closed the notebook marked *1977*, moved it to the bottom of the stack, and opened the one dated *1979*.

The fourth entry was titled *Justifiable Homicide*. There followed a paragraph in Peter's small, precise hand, the lines perfectly even, the words so evenly sized that a machine might have made them, the letters condensed and scored deeply into the paper.

There are a variety of conditions providing the context for murder without guilt. Through history, man has recognized certain grounds where the taking of human life is entirely acceptable and, if not exactly condoned by law, nevertheless countenanced by the culture. In other words, both in complex societies and in tribal communities, it is understood that murder might be, in spirit, moral, though not necessarily legal. A higher law takes over, the unwritten code that has, over thousands and thousands of years, evolved out of the practical experience of human relations. This code is understood the world over, even in those places where the written law precisely contradicts what is implicitly understood. Everyone is aware of the more commonly experienced cases of what I shall call "justifiable homicide," such cases as warfare, self-defense, the protection of property, etc. But who dares to speak of the more subtle cases, even though we all know what they are? I, Peter William Stafford, so dare! And I make so bold as to list them below!

Garrison took a swallow of bourbon and reread the passage, marveling at the intelligence that had produced these sentences—*his son!* Incredible that a fourteen-year-old was capable of writing such a thing.

He lit a cigarette and let his eyes stray to the window. For a while he gazed down at the clouds, shallow furrows of white, like cream in a bowl beginning to curdle. He was trying to put off reading the list that followed the opening paragraph. He'd read it before. He'd read it

dozens of times since June. It was item six that he'd
read the most often, until the words were so etched
into him that it was as if he were the paper they had been
written on.

6. *When a person hates another person, whether for
good reason or not, and when that hatred is so intense as
to be disabling, then such a person is justified in destroying the object of his hatred. Such an act is merely a form
of self-defense—insofar as the hatred is destroying the
person in whom it exists. Q.E.D.*

Had the boy copied this from somewhere? Was the
idea his own, the language his own? Garrison marveled
at the display of logic, and was sickened by the question
on which it turned. But all right. He could deal with it.
His son wanted him dead. When you thought about it, it
really wasn't so awful as all that. Lots of children probably wished their parents dead. It was just the fantasy life
of a lonely, frightened boy. And besides, Peter couldn't
help himself. His mother had done this to him. Somehow, some way, Willa had poisoned the boy's heart. The
thing to do was to show him how wrong it all was, how
far from the truth. It would be easy. Wouldn't it be easy?
Just go there and tell him, tell him how his mother had
taken him away, tell him how all those years his father
had never stopped looking for him, how he'd kept it up
until it almost drove him crazy.

Garrison leaned against the window, staring down at
the clouds, but his eyes were turned inward. They
searched the gray landscape of his thoughts, sighting
questions that he refused to consider, wincing as he be-
held possibilities too terrible to confront head-on.

How do you undo in one month the work of thirteen
years? And what if you couldn't? What then? Then all
his life Peter would be crippled with hatred. But was that
the worst of it, or was there something Garrison was
missing? Perhaps there was something subtle here, a
consequence much more devastating than anything he'd

thought about so far. When Peter found out he was dead, for example. That would be the end of it, wouldn't it?

Or would it?

It was then that it first came to Garrison. It was then that he thought of it for the first time.

He squeezed shut his eyes and tried to empty his mind. He reached for the glass and drank down what was left. He opened his eyes and looked at the man sitting next to him.

Anything, do anything! Just don't think!

He took the glass and the composition books off the service tray, and shoved the tray back into its place on the back of the seat in front of him. He stuffed the glass into the pouch and put the books on his seat. He pulled himself up and pushed through to the aisle.

Do something, do anything!

Just . . . don't . . . think!

He used the bathroom at the rear of the aircraft, and when he was through, he checked the magazine racks. But there was nothing that would hold his interest, and for a while Garrison stood there, fingering through the titles passed over by everyone else: four copies of the same trade magazine for industrial products, two farming magazines, and a handful of inspirational journals with such titles as *Beacon, Modern Faith, Christian Leader*. He walked forward to the galley area, where two stewardesses were cleaning up the mess from lunch, and he stood there for a time, making absurd small talk— "What time do we get into Denver?" "Do you fly this route often?" "What's your favorite city for a layover?" "All these DC-10 crashes, are passengers edgier than they used to be?"—until the stewardesses started eyeing him and stopped answering. Until Garrison just stood there with his mouth open and his heart screaming.

When Peter came looking for him to act out the thing he wanted, when the boy came looking and found him dead, what then? Cheated by cancer out of the thing he had to have, where would Peter turn? Who would be his target instead?

"Can I get you something, sir?"

"What?"

"Are you all right? You don't look well."

It was a stewardess, a different one from the two in the galley. She stood close to him, looking worried, peering up into Garrison's shocked face.

"Perhaps you've had too much to drink. Are you air-sick? I could give you something for it. You don't feel faint, do you?"

"Yes—I mean, no, no. I'm fine," Garrison said. "It's all right. Sorry."

"Perhaps you had better return to your seat, sir. Would you like me to help you back?"

"No. No, I'm all right. It's nothing," he muttered.

He turned away from her and made his way back to his seat, his heart drumming with the name that now beat inside him, its rhythm no longer soft and familiar, but crisp, fragile, morbid.

Andy, Andy, Andy . . .

He was cold sober when he stepped off the plane in Denver. Less than twenty minutes later he was heading west along Interstate 70 in a big blue rented Ford, his eyes narrowed against the enormous clarity of light. The sudden change in distances and scale confronted him on all sides, the hugeness forbidding, threatening, every-thing rock and brusque and glittering with geometric power. Even the names of the tiny towns that sped past him seemed hostile, not the names of places where peo-ple lived so much as statements of force—Dawson, Ed-wards, Ott, Eagle. The names seemed to dart up out of nowhere and chase the car, a streak of snarling pursuers collecting behind him, snapping at the tires as the Ford fled along the brilliant curving highway.

Dawson, Edwards, Ott, Eagle.

He turned up the collar of his sportcoat and gripped

the wheel hard, and then he let go with first his left hand and then his right hand to try to tighten the windows. But the air still rushed in from somewhere, a high, thin, piercing note like the cry of an unseen passenger. He turned on the radio to drown out the noise, but the radio seemed only to heighten it, as if the noise knew it must cry all the louder to be heard. A seizure of pain took him and threw him against the wheel. It felt like lengths of tissue were being torn out of place, long strips yanked loose to get at the cord of virgin nerve beneath. He screamed, howled, eyes wide open, brain grabbing to hold on to the shining rush of road.

When it was over, when the snake lay quiet again, its bright coils flexing with new food, Garrison flicked off the radio and lit up a cigarette, drawing the smoke in and holding it as if to fill the hollow the snake had opened up.

Dawson, Edwards, Ott, Eagle.

It was eerie, hypnotic, alien—more foreign than Paris, Tokyo, Rome. Not long ago he had been a man sitting across from another man in a small white conference room on East Sixty-eighth Street. Not long ago he had been a man walking aimlessly along streets whose names were numbers. Only yesterday he had sat among empty rows of seats while brightly lighted figures stood waiting for him to signal them into motion. Only this morning he'd been a father and a husband, his wife and son beside him at the start of a new day. And now he was a lone traveler on a planet whose vast landscape spread its colossal distances before him, a raging desolation, bleak, brutal, frozen.

He saw a sign for Cortez, so many miles to go, and his heart jerked to one side, a fierce ramming in his chest, and then, when the big car crested for a long slow rise, Garrison could see what he was heading for, an even greater vastness, staggering space, a colossus of high cracked plain, pink, vacant, crushed flat under the fabulous burden of light. It was the great gaping emptiness that geographers call the Four Corners area, a quadrant of blank earth made from land nobody wanted, the void where four states—Arizona, Utah, New Mexico, Colorado—come together to form a limitless vista of packed sand and powdery rock. And somewhere in it, there was a place called Cortez. And a child. *Peter! Oh, Peter!*

He pulled the big Ford off to the side of the road. He left the motor running while he got out to urinate, left it running to hear the sound of something familiar, something man-made in the midst of the wide, roaring silence crashing all around him.

He zipped up and started back for the car. He saw the door flung out toward him like the tongue of an exhausted animal. But a sudden bolt of pain knocked him down and made him cry out again as he knelt there at the side of the road, freezing in the flaming desert.

By three-thirty, he was slowing for a speed zone through a place called Glenwood Springs. Its broad, windblown streets tilted freakishly into his vision, jerking out at him like pop-ups in a children's book. Everywhere he looked, the word CAFE punched dark slots in the fiery light—GREEN'S CAFE, BIG SPRUCE CAFE, TOWN CAFE, HOLIDAY CAFE—signs like flat birds perched at crazy, skidding angles, and then it was all suddenly behind him, ripped away, an obscene photograph snatched out of sight. Just as suddenly the car picked up a running partner, a band of flaring water that raced with the Ford along a straightaway and as abruptly vanished when the road bent under another settlement, a swift distortion of service stations, storefronts, and squat, faded motels. He guessed it was the Colorado, and that somewhere farther on, it did its work on canyons and turbines, a river whose violence matched the mean earth it ran on.

The car hurtled past New Castle, past Silt, past Rifle, and just before six o'clock it stabbed a blue line through the town of Grand Junction and cut straight south for Elk. At Elk, he shut down at a Union station, and while the Ford was being gassed and checked, Garrison went next door to Moon's Cafe, ate eggs and toast and coffee, amazed that he wanted food.

He got a pile of change at the cash register, and gave the operator the number in New York. "I'm here," he said when Joan answered. "Just calling to let you know I arrived."

"You're *where?*" he heard her say, her voice so clear it startled him. "Where exactly? What hotel?"

"Nowhere yet," he shouted, looking around the room to see who might be listening. But no one paid him any attention, the half-dozen men in dusty work clothes and hardhats at the counter, the sullen waitress who stood glaring at them, her dyed hair piled high on her head in a complicated system of tiers. "I'm still at the airport. Just wanted to catch you before Andy went to sleep. Is he there? Can you put him on?" Garrison spoke quickly, trying to head off further questions.

"Hey, old chap!" he shouted when he heard the bell-like voice. "You okay? You taking good care of Mama? Mama tell you I had to hurry out to California to see about a movie? How was school today, pretty terrific? You give Mrs. Flynn any trouble?"

He saw the waitress peering over the heads of the man at the counter, and he lowered his voice.

"Hey, old scout." He turned to face the wall. "You tell Mama there's a limo waiting and I had to hang up. Here's a giant hug for you. Got it?"

When he heard the boy say yes, Garrison hung up.

He took two containers of coffee with him, and before he got back into the car, he drank from one of them to swallow four aspirin, and then he opened the small valise and got out a second sweater.

At Durango he picked up U.S. 160, turned due south again, and by midnight he was making his way into the outskirts of Cortez.

It seemed right to him, this place; even in darkness, it seemed to him the kind of place where Willa would live—arid, brooding, remote, gutted of everything human save the grit it took to choose such a place. Even the buildings seemed to shrink from one another, as if they couldn't get far enough away. As if they were afraid.

He took a room at the Oasis Inn, the first motel he saw, surprising himself when the registration card was placed before him and he wrote the name *Roger Farrar* and made up an address in Boston. If he hadn't planned it, then why had he done it? In the instant when it happened, he didn't know, and even later, in his room, he was still unwilling to accept the thing that had taken his hand and shown it what to write.

What was he doing here—really—in this room that looked like a cell? Wasn't he here to resurrect his child, to cover the boy with love, to shout, "Peter, my God, my precious, precious son!" Then what was he hiding from?

The room smelled like rot and disinfectant, and in the corners of the bathroom there were clusters of specks that looked organic. He watched them as he showered. But nothing moved.

It was nearly one o'clock when he got out and stood there drying himself, avoiding the mirror now because he did not want to see the man who'd written *Farrar* where the name *Garrison* should go. He got back into his clothes and, shivering, moved across the filthy carpet to the telephone.

He dialed the desk, asked if there was a coffee shop. The answer was yes, but it was closed until six. Was there someplace else? Yes, the Buckdancer Cafe stayed open till four—up the road at the south end of town.

At the Buckdancer, he ordered a hot beef sandwich and a glass of milk, but he couldn't get much of it down. He sat there trying to finish the milk as locals came and went, men mostly, workers whose clothes suggested hard, dangerous jobs. After a while he gave up on the milk and just sat there at the counter, smoking and drinking coffee. He did not want to go back to the motel. He did not want to sleep, think, or wait for morning. He wanted to die—right now—be dead before he had to face the thing that had made him write *Farrar*.

He watched the door in the mirror behind the counter. The place was filling up now—six young Indian men in high-heeled boots, sheepskin jackets, Stetsons, one of them with a T-shirt pulled down over his jacket, the words I'M UTE, WHAT'RE UTE? printed across the front. They piled into a booth, laughing, pushing at each other, pounding the table for service. Two highway patrolmen followed them in and took stools at the counter. Garrison could see them examining the Indians in the mirror, and then one of the officers smiled into the mirror as if acknowledging a greeting from somewhere behind him. Or was it the Indians he was smiling at?

It was then that Garrison realized it was for him the highway patrolman intended his smile. But he acted as if he hadn't noticed, and instead looked down at his coffee and trimmed the ash of his cigarette along the rim of the saucer. He was suddenly aware that he was being watched, that he must be an object of considerable attention—his clothes, his obvious difference from everyone around him. Surely, in a town this size, everyone was known and strangers aroused immediate suspicion. These policemen, wouldn't they know Willa? What if they asked him to identify himself? Suppose they asked him what he was doing here, demanded that he accompany them to the Oasis to see if he really had a room there? What if they checked the register?

How would he explain? Say that he is a father who hasn't seen his son in thirteen years and now he's come to claim him and is signed into a local motel under a false name? What would he do? Show them the composition books? Say that a man he doesn't know found them hidden in a cave and that they prove his son wants to kill him?

He signaled for his check, and while the girl stood

before him writing it out, Garrison looked past her and into the mirror. They had their heads down. It looked as if they were studying something on the counter between them—a magazine, a menu?

He paid and started for the door. Two Indian boys and a girl were coming in, holding white motorcycle helmets the way you'd hold a football. He stepped away from the door to let them by. The Indian girl said, "Now ain't that nice." Garrison gave them a half-nod and started past them, and when he heard someone behind him call, "Mister!" he just kept going. But this time the call was louder, more insistent. He turned, his hand still holding the door, and he saw one of the highway patrolmen, the one who'd smiled, striding toward him, his sidearm, a huge revolver, jogging low on his hip.

"That your vehicle yonder—the blue one?"

Garrison nodded. "Something wrong?"

The patrolman smiled. He wore eyeglasses, thin silver frames. It seemed strange, a policeman with eyeglasses of that type—the lenses so thick, the eyes behind them watery and large.

"Not anything that can't be fixed if you get the pressure up in your front left tire. See to it," the man said, and turned away before Garrison could answer.

When he got to the car, he knelt for a moment as if inspecting things, as if to show his willingness to be concerned, hoping that he was being observed through the glass door. And then he straightened up and gazed at the night sky. He had nothing to hurry away from. He breathed deeply. The air was cold and it felt laden with something, a sort of charged density, something vaguely chemical.

He drove slowly, cruising back through town, looking at the little there was to see. Despite himself, he watched in the rearview mirror for approaching lights.

There was a car pulled into the slot in front of his room—even though there were more than enough free spaces. He parked, locked the Ford, and left the door to his room open until he'd snapped on the overhead light.

He didn't bother to get out of his clothes. He slept, but within the hour, pain woke him, a single blade of agony that lifted him off the mattress with a shriek. Or had he only dreamed the shriek?

It was pain that had awakened him, but it was what lay ahead of him that kept Garrison staring until dawn at the plywood dresser that stood opposite the foot of the bed, its ill-fitted drawers looking back at him like grins that were slipping off a face with three mouths.

When at last the light came up, Garrison closed his eyes. But even then he could not sleep. He lay there in the milky light, thinking about another morning a lifetime ago, and he heard himself softly calling, *Petey? Willa? Hey, you guys, you're scaring Daddy*. He lay there remembering—*Come out, come out, wherever you are!*—until the tears came, and he cried.

And then, with his eyes wide open, Ben Garrison prayed.

9.

HE BOUGHT A LOCAL MAP at the desk. It was a sketchy affair that quickly dispensed with the town of Cortez and then spread out to concentrate on the outlying area, the nearby national parks that made up a small portion of the immense wasteland that sprawled over the Four Corners region. At the post office—a Plexiglass cubicle in the town's hardware store—Garrison showed the map, and the clerk reached through the hole and marked the spot where Box 91 would be situated along Rural Route 1.

Garrison sat studying the map while the car was being fueled and the attendant checked the front left tire, and then he drove south, taking his time, trying to make up his mind what he'd do when he got there. He didn't know—but he guessed it would come to him. It had to. Because the clock was running—sixty days. No, no, *fifty-eight.*

He found the mailbox a half hour later. But it took him all morning to find the house—because it wasn't a house. All morning he drove up and down the same length of highway, tracking from the mailbox to every dirt road that cut off the pavement and looked like it might go to somewhere people could live. He tried them all, sometimes driving miles into the desert only to turn around when the road faded to a path and then washed away into open land or ended in the front yard of an abandoned shack. Just before noon he followed a particular path as far as seemed safe to go. He was about to turn around when he caught a glimpse of what looked like something hopeful farther on. He left the car and walked the rest of the way, chewing aspirin and shivering in spite of the startling force of the sun.

But it was a cluster of trailers, six in all, one in the middle and the rest arranged like an asterisk. From the one in the middle there rose a kind of flagpole. At the top, wildly colored streamers were whipping in the steady wind.

Garrison moved in closer, and then he called out, "Anybody home?" He tried again, louder this time, and then he tried once more before he finally gave up and started back.

He could see them when he was still yards from the car, two girls sitting in the front seat, one behind the wheel, the other with her arm up through the opened window on the passenger side, the hand gripping the roof in the manner of ownership, a deep intimacy with the object touched. They looked like sisters, hard, flat faces, and the eyes, small and slitted, so that no whites showed until he was very close and had his hand on the door.

"Trying it on for size?" he said, and leaned down a little, enough to keep the girl on the passenger side also in view.

"Hooo-*eee*, damned if he ain't the funniest one. How's that for quick, Sister Sunshine?"

"Oh, Lord," the girl on the passenger side said, rapping her knuckles on the roof, "you got to go some to outquick a dude like that. You reckon these here his wheels?"

"This automobile any kin to you, Brother Sunshine?"

"That's right," Garrison said to the girl behind the wheel.

"Man blooded to a *machine*," the other girl said, and made a face as if to show disgust. "You think he been to see if Eric can cut him loose? Hey, Brother Sunshine, you been to see *Eric*?"

"No," Garrison said, easing the door open. "I'm

looking for some people named Stafford, is all. Can you help me?''

''Well, *shit,*'' the girl near him said, ''let's first see if *you* can help *us.*''

''That's right, Sister Sunshine,'' the other girl said, ''you enter into *negotiation* with the man. Tit for tat, Sister Sunshine, tit for tat. He won't do much for finding him no Stafford. See what you can get off the man for feeling up on your tits. Foxy dude like that been getting away too long with copping feels for free. You go *deal* with him now, Sister Sunshine.''

He'd had enough. Garrison yanked the door all the way open. ''Out! Do it *now!*''

The girls seemed alarmed. Something in his face that suggested a man at the end of his rope. But still they kept to their places. ''Okay, man, okay,'' the one behind the wheel said. ''Be cool, okay? Just funning. Get so goddamn sick of no one to shoot the shit with, you know how it is. We're Eric's girls, man. You know how it is.''

''Out!'' Garrison said.

''How about a ride? Just up to where you got to cut off for the Stafford place. Deal?''

''You know where it is?''

The girl nodded.

''Yeah, sure,'' Garrison said. ''Move over.''

He got in and fired up the engine, backing up until he'd made it to a place wide enough to risk turning the car around. The girls kept asking him how come he was looking for the professor woman, was he a reporter or something, was he with the TV? He didn't answer until it occurred to him they might know Peter, might even go to the same school.

They laughed at that, at the idea of their being in school.

''Hey, no, man,'' the one next to the window said. ''We're from Barstow, man. California? You know Barstow? Like in California? We're Eric's girls,'' she said, and rapped her knuckles on the roof again. "We don't go to no fucking *school*."

Back on the highway, they told him to turn left, toward Cortez. Garrison made the turn, guessing they were just leading him on to get a ride into town. But about fifty yards past the mailbox he'd been using as his reference point, the girl next to him told him to stop the car across from the clump of mesquite trees that stood off to the left.

"Down there," she said, pointing.

"Where? I don't see a road."

"There!" the girl said, still pointing, flexing her finger.

Garrison blinked and tried to see through the small clouds that were moving across his eyes in little puffs of motion. He kept looking. But he could not see what the girl was pointing at.

"You bet," he said. "Thanks."

"No problem," the girl said, and elbowed her friend to open the far door. "Everybody around here knows where the professor lives." The girl laughed. "In a fucking hole in the ground."

"All right," Garrison said again. "Thanks. Many thanks."

"Sure," the girl said, not moving yet, not following her friend out the door. "Hey, tell the truth, Brother Sunshine—you're with the TV, right? Like it's okay, man—we won't tell. She's some fucking kind of celebrity, people around here say. Lives in a fucking hole in the ground."

"No," Garrison said. "Just an old friend."

"Sure, sure," the girl said.

She slid toward the door, her tight jeans squeaking on the plastic seat.

"I'd take you into town if I weren't in such a hurry," he said. "Next time."

"Anytime," the girl said, her hand still on the inside

handle of the door. She leaned a little way back into him, her voice low now, conspiratorial. "Anytime you want your rig lifted, you just drive into old Eric's. Me and Lynn'll smooth out that joint of yours like you wouldn't *believe,* man. One bill for the two of us, you understand?" The girl winked and stood away from the door. "Take the starch right *out* of it!" she said, and pushed the door closed. "Like for a *month,* man. Guaranteed!"

He waited until they had moved off up the highway toward town. When they'd gone far enough and it seemed they'd lost interest in him, Garrison nosed the big Ford across the asphalt and headed straight into the mesquite trees, the hidden entrance to the unpaved road not revealing itself until he was almost on it.

He drove slowly, checking the rearview mirror to see how much dust he was raising. For a while the road dipped and curved, and then it straightened out for about a half-mile, gradually lifting toward a shallow hill. When he got to the top of the hill, he could see a length of paved road ahead. He stopped the car, stared down at the sloping land that bellied up on either side of the road. He saw nothing, no sign of life, no structure. He started up again, and again he stopped, raising himself in his seat and peering over the wheel.

It was then that he saw it. About a hundred yards ahead, just before the section of pavement ended and the road continued in dirt again and then wound around a sharp bend. It was a cattle guard, the iron grid painted dayglo orange. Garrison saw the cattle guard, and then he saw the double line of ruts leading off from it to the right. He saw where they ended at an abrupt hump of land, as if the desert there had gotten down on its hands and knees and lifted up its back.

To one side of the hump there were six piñon trees standing in a row. As he drove closer to the cattle guard, he could begin to make out a vehicle of some kind drawn up under the piñons on the other side, its finish worn so

dull and so laden with dust that the shape of the thing
virtually vanished against the backdrop of the mesa
beyond.

Garrison stared. The hump itself was clearer now. He
could see two round windows, like portholes, one to
either side of what must have been the entrance. But it
was impossible to see the entrance itself because the land
immediately in front of the hump was scooped out into a
kind of basin.

He remembered what the girl had said—*in a fucking
hole in the ground*. But it wasn't that. It was more like a
bunker, a kind of outpost built into the bleached earth.

He let the Ford roll forward to just beyond the cattle
guard, shut off the engine, and turned in his seat to see
better. Could his car be seen from there? Probably. It
was an awesome sight, a blunt lump squatting on the
desert flats, its concrete shoulders the color of sand,
those two portholes that gaped like eyes, stark and un-
yielding, the stolid way the thing occupied the ground it
rose from, as if it dared you to approach.

He moved to the middle of the seat and sat very still,
his heart pounding and his body trembling with the
waves of cold that washed through him. Even with the
engine off and the air-conditioning shut down, even with
the interior of the car like an oven, Garrison shivered and
hugged himself against the cold.

It was Wednesday. Peter would be in school. Did he
come home for lunch? Doubtful. Not at these distances,
not when he lived so far from town.

Was Willa inside?

What was it like in there? Did Peter actually grow up
in a thing like that, a home so strange and forbidding?

The vehicle—he could see it was a Land Rover
now—was it Willa's? Or did it belong to the man
Breaker? Were they in there right now? Working, making love? She could be inside, seated at her typewriter,
setting down the secrets of America's Indians. Perhaps

she sensed his presence, was ready and waiting for him to dare to come closer.

What should he do? Go up to the door and say, "Look, Willa, let's be reasonable—I've found you and I'm here to see Peter. I'm here because I love him with all my heart, and I want him to know that. I want him to know it so he'll stop hating me, so he'll stop making himself sick with hatred—because, you see, Willa, I'm dying—and I can't go to my grave knowing this is how things are."

Should he say, "Willa, look, you've got to tell me, please—will Peter hurt my son when I'm gone? Do you think he'd do a thing like that? Willa, is Peter dangerous? Could he really kill? Or are these things he's writing down just talk, just wild kid-talk he's going to outgrow? Don't you see, Willa? *I've got to know*. Help me, Willa. The past is the past, and I don't bear you any hard feelings, I swear it. But I'm dying and I must *know*. Do you think Peter could commit murder? I'm begging you, Willa. *Tell me*. Tell me if you think he could!"

It was absurd.

She would tell him nothing.

She would be very civilized—appalled at what he was suggesting, but restrained, courteous, aloof. She would express regret over his dying, that it was a terrible misfortune, of course. But in the great chain of being, his death was a small matter—for, sooner or later, doesn't death come to us all? But to question the possibility that Peter might be insane with hatred, obsessed with the idea of one day killing his father? No, no, she would never admit to that. How could she admit to the child's having a disease that she, his own mother, had infected him with? And besides, who could really say what Peter would do except Peter himself?

Garrison lit a cigarette. His hands were shaking, and

he felt sick to his stomach. Had he eaten anything? This morning, did he have coffee? He couldn't remember.

He had to collect himself, slow down. He had to try to think very hard. Get all the possibilities clearly in mind, try to see it all clearly and reasonably and then act in some way. But what? *Do what?* What exactly should he do? How long could he just sit out here staring while everything got crazy in his head?

What if he went up to the door and showed her the last entry in the composition book dated *1979?* If she saw that, would she believe? And if she believed, would she help?

No, not Willa. She would never concede the chance that Peter might try to kill someone, take the life of another boy. That his rage might shift from Garrison to Andy. That one day Peter might be a threat to a boy who would never even know such a threat existed.

"My God," Garrison whispered, the thing very real to him now. "What if it's *true?*"

It was madness, a nightmare, a monstrous scenario that he alone could imagine—his two sons grown into men on the wide arc of the earth, the one hunting the other.

He shut his eyes against the vision, and when he opened them, his heart clenched. She was there! As if from nowhere, Willa was suddenly there, her tall figure outlined between two trees.

He stubbed out the cigarette and looked again, blinking to clear his eyes of the drifting puffs of clouds.

She was standing in front of the Land Rover, a length of garden hose coiled under her arm. From where he sat, she seemed unchanged, the same dusky hair, the same long body, the shoulders and hips canted oddly forward. She wore blue jeans, their bottoms tucked into high rubber boots, and a plaid shirt whose tail stuck out on one side as if she'd dressed hurriedly or just didn't give a damn. He could see that she was folding back her sleeves, and he could tell she was doing it very carefully, the same methodical motions he remembered from years ago.

He saw the spray of the hose, the stream of water iridescent in the hard light, one strong brown arm moving back and forth like a wand as she held the nozzle high and rained water down over the roof of the Land Rover. Her back was to him, but what if she turned and saw the car? Was it unusual for a car to be parked out here? Did the light hide him, so she could not see that the car was occupied? The brown mesa landscape between them was fisted here and there with low scrubby growth. But Garrison could see her plainly enough. If she turned, would she see him?

He saw her drop the hose. She moved out of sight. He saw her go, the slouch, the deliberate tread. She disappeared back behind the bunker. To do what? Turn off the water? Call the police to report a suspicious automobile on the road in front of her home? And then he saw her again, stepping slowly toward the Land Rover. She was gathering the hose into precise coils, winding its length into a loop. He saw her glance in his direction, and then she went quickly toward the back of the bunker and disappeared.

He waited for her to show herself again. He half expected her to come flying out of the place, suddenly emerging from the basin between the portholes, hair wild, face contorted with rage, running at him and screaming with contempt as a squad of emergency vehicles from the sheriff's department converged on him from behind.

Garrison waited five minutes, ten minutes, staring at the bunker, watching for movement, the two portholes gawking mutely back, a face that gave no answer, and then, feeling as if he'd done something unspeakable, he started the engine, wheeled the car around, and went back the way he had come.

10.

HE STOPPED FOR COFFEE at the Buckdancer, and got directions to the high school, all the way north past the Oasis, on the other side of town.

It was larger than he would have expected, a one-level glass and steel structure that looked as if it had been erected yesterday. He passed the building and parked a safe distance away.

The heat beat at him when he stepped from the car to the road. But he liked it. He liked the way it parched his lips and tongue and lungs, drying up tissues as if cleansing them, leaving them cauterized, the decay of cancer scorched off.

There was a stadium behind the school, goalposts at either end, a cinder track ringing the field, two small grandstands on either side. He made his way to one of them, and when no one challenged him, Garrison climbed to the topmost row and sat watching the football scrimmage taking place below, two sets of boys in vivid jerseys stretched over shoulder pads twice the size they needed. How old were these boys? In helmets, it was impossible to tell. But they could be freshmen. It could be the freshman team. Isn't that what Peter would be now, a freshman? Would he be athletic? Did he like football? Peter could be among these boys, this close at last.

But then Garrison remembered the notebooks, a passage written when Peter was twelve: *I refuse to participate in sports of any kind, for sports were invented to*

*channel aggression into socially acceptable forms, to
drain off the natural homicidal impulse and to provide
suitable entertainment for those who are moral and intellectual spectators. It is a corruption, the worthless play
of fools and cowards. Try to imagine Einstein playing
dodge ball!*

Garrison checked his watch—almost two o'clock.
School would probably let out soon. How did Peter get
home? A school bus? Did Willa come pick him up? How
would he know who Peter was, unless someone pointed
him out? Was it possible to go up to the principal's office
and identify yourself, say you were here to see your son?
No, they'd call Willa to check on him. And what if they
didn't? If they didn't, then they'd go tell Peter, and from
that moment on, the boy would be vigilant, on guard—
and once he was on guard, that would finish it and you'd
never know the truth. You would die never knowing.

For an hour he sat there following the spectacle of his
thoughts and the bright jerseys on the playing field, and
then he started back for the car, quickening his pace
when he heard someone calling. But what was he afraid
of? He'd done nothing wrong.

He forced himself to turn around.

He saw a short boy or a short man coming. At this
distance Garrison couldn't tell. He shielded his eyes
from the sun, waiting for the figure to cry out again. But
whoever it was, man or boy, he bustled silently along the
cinder track, a short burly figure coming at Garrison with
a curious rolling gait, as if one leg were impaired, the
knee fused.

"Yo! Fella!" It was a man's voice, and Garrison
could tell from the tone that it was an order to halt. With
the sun's blazing eye behind the man, it was impossible
to see his face. But as the figure heaved from side to
side, Garrison could make out something glinting on his
chest—and then he saw it clearly, a silver whistle swinging from a chord that went around the man's thick neck.

A coach, then—a school official of some kind.

Even though he was only yards off, the man called out his command again—"Yo! Fella!"—loudly, as if he were still a great distance away. Garrison could see the barrel chest, the close-cropped hair, football cleats, the tight T-shirt that said CORTEZ COUGARS.

"Sorry to holler at you," the man was saying as he stepped in close. "There something we can do for you around here?"

Garrison smiled. "No," he said evenly. "I don't think so."

The man shifted his weight and toed the sandy turf. He was shorter than Garrison by about a head, but he must have outweighed him by at least fifty pounds—and though his manner seemed friendly enough, he appeared to be having trouble containing himself. As he talked, his powerful arms moved in the air uncertainly, and when Garrison dipped his head to notice this, the man took a quick step back and moved his hands to his hips.

"Don't be shy now," the man said. "We get all kinds around here—so if there's something on your mind, you go right ahead and speak up."

"Really," Garrison said, "there's nothing."

"Nothing?" the man said, his tone mocking now. He was settling in, bending his knees slightly and looking Garrison over, as if an accusation had been lodged and it was now up to Garrison to clear himself.

"That's right," Garrison said, and started to turn away. But the man spun him back around, and when Garrison faced the man again, he could see there was no pretense of friendliness any more.

"Hey, come on," Garrison said, for an instant considering the truth and as quickly discarding the idea. "Let's just take it easy, okay? I'm a salesman, and I thought I'd kill some time and watch the kids work out."

"Prove it!" the man snapped back incredibly, his expression all business now, fingertips at his hips, as if he were readying himself for some sort of calisthenics.

"What?" Garrison said, stunned.

"You heard me, buster—I said prove it!"

"Prove what?" Garrison said. "Are you crazy?"

"Prove you are who you say you are!" the man snarled, his face reddening now, his stance suggesting there was no backing him off.

Garrison stared, dumbfounded.

"You going to prove it or am I going to have to get tough with you? Because we get a lot of goddamn creeps around here, and a lot of wiseacres too, guys who think they can just sashay in here and scout my boys and get the hell away with it. Now, I saw you up there with your eye on my boys, and I'm asking you for the last time, what's your story?"

Perhaps it was his explanation that seemed to betray the man's bluff—or perhaps it was just that Garrison was tired of standing in the sun.

"Stick it," Garrison said very quietly, and then he turned on his heel and strode away, expecting to hear the rush of feet behind him. But there was nothing.

All the way back to the car, he held to his slow, even stride, not turning, fists balled at his sides in anger with himself.

He'd made a crucial mistake. It was a small town, and he was a stranger in it. And now he'd made himself all the more conspicuous.

For a while he drove randomly, trying to shake the feeling of being pursued, keeping his speed leisurely, checking in the rearview mirror when he came to corners and turned. Was he being followed? Perhaps a note had been made of his license number. But why? He'd done nothing wrong. Yet he felt guilty, drenched with shame. He struggled against the impulse to floor the accelerator, cut north again to the highway, and drive straight back to Denver. From there, he would give it all up and go home. But he understood that would be to abandon Andy to an uncertain future, a future that might have an assassin in it.

When Garrison saw the sign for the Buckdancer, he parked, got out, and walked the rest of the way, breathing the baked air, noticing again the trace of something sharp in it, like gunpowder or woodsmoke. He took a seat at the counter, lit a cigarette, ordered coffee. The air-conditioning chilled him, and he turned up the collar of his sportcoat. But then he had a sense of looking furtive. He flipped his collar back down and reached into his pocket for the aspirin bottle.

"Mr. Farrar! Hey, Mr. Farrar!"

The man down the counter must have called it out three times before Garrison understood and turned.

It was the night clerk at the Oasis, the man who'd been on duty when Garrison had registered, a young man, mid-twenties, a full red beard and freckles where the beard didn't cover. He was gesturing with his eyes at the empty seat next to Garrison, and when Garrison nodded, the man picked up his dishes and moved over.

"They did you last night," the man said as he slid up onto the stool. He smoothed his beard and took up his utensils again.

"What?" Garrison said.

"Last night," the man said. "They did you here. Like they hooked you in down here. The Buckdancer."

Garrison understood. He wanted another cup of coffee. But he also wanted to be away from this man. He nodded and studied his empty cup. "You're the one that told me. I remember."

"Right," the man said, forking up a mouthful of fried egg. "Jack's my name. You're from back East, right?"

"Back East?"

Garrison felt trapped. He looked to see if anyone was listening, such as the patrolman who'd warned him about his tire last night.

"Yeah, sure," the man was saying. "Boston. Like I could tell. I didn't even have to read your card."

"Yes, Boston," Garrison said,

"Sure," the man said, his lips wet, the red bristles ringing them flecked with bits of egg and toast. "I could tell, all right. You know, the clothes. The way you carry yourself. Anybody could see you're not from around here. Me neither. I'm from Barstow. Hey, more civilized back there, you know? You going to be around here long?"

"Long?" Garrison muttered as he tried to remember where he'd heard *Barstow* before. He buttoned his jacket and picked up his check from the counter. The four aspirin were still there. He wiped them off the Formica onto his hand and put them back into his pocket.

"Just thought I'd give you the word," the man said, grinning as if Garrison had just confided something secret. The young man stopped to chew, and then he licked his lips and continued, "Keep off that coffee shop in the Oasis. Poison. Take my word for it, poison. I'd say it's the Buck or starve, you know what I mean? Unless you got people around here. You got people around here, Mr. Farrar?"

Garrison didn't answer. He got down from his stool.

"Just a tourist," he said, and turned away, moving along the counter to the cash register.

"Well, that's good," the man Jack was calling, spinning on his stool to keep Garrison in range. "Lot of touring to do around here. Mesa Verde, Painted Desert, all kinds of shit. People from back East, it takes them apart."

Garrison took his change from the girl at the cash register and edged toward the door.

"Yeah, right," the young man called, swiveling to keep Garrison in view. "You got a problem, you check with old Jack!"

"You bet," Garrison called from the door. "Thanks."

"Good!" the young man said, grinning wildly.

Garrison was touching the door handle when he heard him again. "Yes sir, day or night, big or small, you check with old Jack and his man Eric."

He stood on the sidewalk and glanced at his watch. Three-thirty. He figured the time differential. Yes, Andy would be home from school. But he didn't want to call from the room. He went up the block to a gas station, feeling in his pocket for the change he'd need.

He found a phone booth back near the washroom, dialed direct, and when the operator came on to give the amount, he had the coins ready, hesitating before he deposited the last one, in order to give himself time to make sure he had his story straight.

But he was in luck. It was Andy.

"Hello. Garrison residence."

"Uh, excuse me, is Mr. Garrison home?"

"No, my daddy's in California."

"California, is he? Where's that?"

"It's next to the Pacific Ocean. Do you want me to get my mama?"

"Now just hold on a blessed minute there, mister— because I do believe you misunderstand me, sir. It's actually Mr. *Andrew* Garrison I'm calling for. Is he home or is he next to the Pacific Ocean too?"

"I'm Andy Garrison."

"Well now, that's okay, but it's *Andrew* Garrison I want to talk to."

"That's *me*. It's the *same*."

"By thunder, Andy boy, don't you *recognize* me, lad? It's your old friend Henry calling!"

"Henry who?"

"Henry Henry! *That's* who!"

"Papa!"

"Hey, old thing, how the heck are you?" Garrison roared in his normal voice, grinning with true pleasure for the first time in days.

"I'm fine, Papa. How are you? How's Hollywood?"

"Hollywood's find, son—just fine. Oh, it was feeling right poorly a couple of hours ago, but just this minute it's feeling fine. Mama okay?"

"She's great, Papa, you bet. You want me to get her? She's in the shower."

"No, no—just let her soak in there, okay? Tell her I called and that I had a good old chat with you, and that you and I decided it was best if we talked a few things over man to man, as it were. So, speaking strictly man to man, old chap, how the heck *are* you, anyway?"

"I'm fine."

"Well, that's good. I'd say that's just about the best news I've had since I heard they found a way to grow stringbeans in the can."

"Oh, *Daddy*."

"Don't you oh-Daddy me, old thing. You doubt my word?"

"Oh, Daddy, come on."

"There you go again, oh-Daddying me. How would you like it if I oh-Andied you every whipstitch? Wouldn't be so hot, would it?"

"*Dad*-dy."

"Ah God, I sure do love you, old scout. You just hunky-dory?"

"Hunky-dory, Papa."

"Swell. Kiss Mama for me and don't forget to tell her I called and how we thought it was better not to bother her in the shower—and here's a gigantic, a tremendous, a huge old humdinger of a kiss for you! Got it?"

"Got it."

"Good. So long, son. I love you."

He didn't want to move away from the phone. He wanted to stay close to it, to keep touching it, as if to touch it were to touch Andy, to touch Joan. His body rang with what he felt, this feeling that Andy could produce in him. Yes, he'd been right never to tell Joan,

never to drag all that was past and confused into what
was new and so very, very clear. It was an infection, that
old life, and it could do nothing but spread to the new.
So he'd kept his mouth shut and lived with his secret,
glad that it could hurt no one but him. The important
thing was to protect them, to shelter Andy and Joan.
What good would it have done for her to know? Or for
Andy to be told about Peter?

But now that he reconsidered the question, he was
willing to understand that the old answer wasn't the right
one anymore. Because to know about Peter was to be
warned about Peter, was to be ready for him to come
at you.

He tried to think of Andy, tried to recapture the good
feeling that just moments ago had been in him. What was
it? A kind of ringing. But it gave way to a clicking at the
base of his spine, a tinny, metered ticking that he could
have sworn he heard, the clack of a metronome picking
up the pace, until his chest clanged with it, a terrible
noise that swelled to a catastrophe of sound. He staggered from the phone booth and then sagged against it,
frantically whipping at the air and trying to draw breath,
trying to stay on his feet, but going down, his knees
buckling under him, whole orchestras of noise crashing
in his brain.

It was minutes before he was able to stand again, and
even then he wasn't sure he could make it to the car. He
moved back inside the phone booth and leaned himself
against the telephone, his hands raised to cushion his
forehead. When he thought he could walk again, he lit a
cigarette, sucked the smoke deep into his lungs, and
pulled himself upright. But he stayed in the booth. He
lifted the telephone and dropped in a dime and dialed
Manhattan information. But when the operator asked for
the name he wanted, Garrison did not say *Charles
Flood*. Instead he said, "Sorry. I changed my mind."

He passed a drugstore on the way to the car, really

more a five-and-ten with a prescription counter in the
back. He went in and was immediately cold. He moved
aimlessly up and down the aisles, and then, not to attract
attention, he picked up a few items—a candy bar, two
packs of cigarettes, a large bottle of aspirin. These he
carried to the cash register at the back, and stacked them
on the counter. He waited for the pharmacist to appear.
When a clerk came instead, Garrison moved to a nearby
display and took a pair of sunglasses off the rack.

"These too, thanks."

"Will that be all?"

"Is the pharmacist back there?"

"He's off duty until after supper. If it's something
important, you can call him at home."

"That's okay," Garrison said, picking the sticker off
the eyeglasses and fitting them on. "Just these. That'll
do swell. No, wait a minute. You don't sell liquor, do
you?"

"Next door."

He checked his cash when he paid.

"You take a credit card?"

"Sorry, sir—not for small items like these."

He went next door, bought a quart of Dant 100—and
then took his purchases back to his room at the motel. He
started on the candy bar, and then he started on the
bottle.

He never got back to the candy.

At first he thought it was a horse screaming. And then
he understood that the sound was coming from inside
him. Yet how could that be? It was not possible. Because
he could *see* the horse—blocky teeth ajar, dripping
nostrils flaring—and the horse was deep inside him. But
then he understood that he was wrong, that his eyes had
tricked him. He saw that it was not a horse, but a winged
thing of some kind, a thing with talons and feathers, a
bird with the face of a horse. He saw it wheeling through
the widening space inside him, beak open, head shriek-

ing, his body a cavern in which the bird flew. It soared,
turning circles above him, which was miraculous, because it was also inside him, wings stretching until the
bony tips pricked the walls of stone and bits of flesh fell
from them, fell into the horse mouth that was a snake
mouth when it closed on the falling gore. Garrison
looked up. He threw back his head and looked straight
up. He saw the scabby neck, the eyes, the teeth, the
snake face grinning over the hunch of shaggy shoulders,
wings collapsing back into the body, the neck reaching,
the mouth opening, the scarlet throat, and then he heard
it shriek again—horse, bird, snake—plunging toward
him, teeth grinning, tongue stabbing the red wind that
rose to catch the claws . . .

"Yes!" he shouted into the receiver when he had it off
the hook.

"Mr. Farrar?"

"Yes," Garrison said, not shouting now, rolling toward the night table so that he could move the phone to
the bed. It was twilight, and even darker in the room, but
he could see the half-empty quart of bourbon lying on its
side on the other bed.

"Sorry," Garrison said. "Sorry I shouted. I was
asleep. Dreaming."

"Hey, listen, I know about dreams," the voice said.
"It's Jack. Don't you remember? You left a message for
me to call you when I came on."

"Right," Garrison said, trying to remember. He
wiped at his face as if bits of gauze were stuck to it.
"Yeah, sure, you bet," he said, remembering. "It's
this. I want to talk to you about something."

"That's good," he heard the man say. "Hey, that's
real good. Check with Jack. You name it, just say the
word."

Garrison pushed himself up against the headboard.

"How about I see you on my way out?" He looked at
his watch. He had to blink to see the numerals. Six-

something. He could make that much out. "About seven-thirty, okay?"

"Seven-thirty. No problem."

Garrison imagined the vivid red lips, naked and wet within the frowsy verge of beard. He was sure of it—he'd tried the right man.

He snapped on the table lamp, wincing from the sudden blast of light. For a time he sat on the edge of the bed, eyeing the half-killed bottle, amazed that he'd somehow capped it before tossing it onto the other bed. His head hurt. His chest hurt. His back hurt. So much for whiskey as painkiller. Somewhere in the thicket of his drunk he must have realized this, called the desk, left word for the night man to get in touch. But he didn't remember doing it. What he remembered doing was sitting with the bottle in one hand and the *1979* composition book in the other, staring and drinking, trying to find some harmless interpretation of the very last entry.

It was a page long, but not a handwritten page. Instead, Peter must have typed the single paragraph on his mother's manuscript paper, trimmed away all the blank space, and then pasted the square of typewritten sentences onto the last page of the book. He must have used a ruler to mark the heavy inked border that went around the square of typing.

Garrison got to his feet. His head throbbed with the exertion. He leaned over, took up the whiskey bottle, and on his way to the bathroom he dropped it into the empty trashcan. It made an ugly sound. Hammers went to work deep inside his head.

He flipped on the bathroom light and started getting out of his clothes. He piled everything on the sink, first trying to shut off the leak in the faucet and then giving up on it. It was hopeless—there was nowhere else clean to put his things, and he was too cold to leave them in the other room. He kicked the door shut and turned the shower on, just the hot water, running it full blast until the room filled with steam.

It was a good feeling. Talking with Andy—that was a good feeling too. He tried to remember what Andy had said, the sweet chirp of his voice. But it was useless; as soon as he sought to recall phrases, snatches of the language in Peter's last entry drove everything else out.

He adjusted the water and got in. The steam thinned enough to reveal the patches of specks in the corners where the tiles joined the fiberglass of the tub. The growth—if that was what it was—seemed denser, as if it had flourished overnight. He took the sliver of soap in his hand, but he did not use it. He was sure he didn't have the strength to wash. It took all his effort just to stand there and let the water run over him.

He tried to focus his mind on what was next. A plan of some kind. But his mind recoiled from thought. That was the trouble—he'd been thinking too much. If he had not thought, if he had instead just acted, then he would be somewhere with Peter right now, holding him and kissing him and reassuring him, making up for all that lost time, all those insane lies, making his peace with Peter before going home to give the last of his life to Andy and Joan. But he had let himself think. All the way back to the time when the envelope had come from Breaker, all the way back to June, he'd been trying to think the thing out. And now thinking had brought him to this, like a lone climber arriving at some desperate height and in panic discovering there was no way down.

But there was a way. He could stop Peter. He could stop him now. Stop him before the thing went any further. He could stop him before cancer finished its work and there was no one left on earth to stop him.

He shut off the water and got out, so dazed with what was in his head that he still had the unused soap in his hand. He wiped it off on the towel and then used the rest of the towel to try to dry himself. He got back into his clothes, brushed his teeth, and then combed his hair with his fingers. He needed a shave, but he did not want to face his face.

He took up all four notebooks from the top of the plywood dresser. He left on the overhead light and pulled the door closed behind him. But he did not go to the car. Instead, he walked around to the front of the building, already feeling cold, already smelling the faintly resinous tincture in the early evening air. As he made his way along the edge of the pool, he saw a family grouped in canvas chairs. They were sitting so that Garrison would have to cut through them in order to get around the pool and onto the path to the office. As if on signal, all their heads turned at once to regard his approach. Did he look so strange? Perhaps it was the sweaters and the jacket. Perhaps it was because he'd been two days without a shave. Or was it that they could see in his face what had been taking shape in his head?

He came abreast of them, and then, excusing himself, Garrison walked a jagged figure through them. They blocked his way. They blocked the way of anyone who might want to get from the rooms back there to the office, to the coffee shop, to the street. But they said nothing. They didn't even move their legs out of the way. As soon as he passed them, he heard the man mutter, "I don't want to hear one more goddamn word about no goddamn swimming."

At first he thought, My God, a father who speaks to his children that way. He loathed men like that, fathers like that, fathers who were brutal with their children, regardless of the provocation. It was unthinkable to Garrison to behave in such a way—with Andy, with . . .

Jesus Christ Almighty!

He reeled with it, the violence of the irony. "Oh, Good Christ," Garrison said aloud, and refused to finish what he was thinking.

There were vehicles of every description strung out in

a line in the drive that led into the motel—campers, pickups, vans, the characterless cars driven by route distributors and salesmen. Inside the office, road-weary men were jockeying for position at the desk, all trying to catch the eye of the skinny, bearded man whose nonchalance suggested he was enjoying the commotion, the life-and-death authority it gave him. Garrison could see him slowly flipping through a box of cards, the ripe lips shaped in a falsely thoughtful pout. Garrison stood at the rear, near the door, tall enough to be seen over the heads of those in front. When he was noticed, he shouted, "Later!" and in reply the beard moved and one small eye winked.

In the Ford, he set the four books on the seat beside him, and left by the back exit, turning south.

He had nothing particular in mind. Except that he had to start doing something, move in closer to the thing he had to deal with, somehow or other make contact, find out what he had to know.

It was not until his headlights caught the mailbox that he realized he'd missed the clump of mesquite trees. He swung the car around and cruised back, watching the low growth that edged the highway, then cutting a hard left when he saw the hidden entrance, almost missing it a second time.

He had no trouble finding the bunker. He could see it as soon as the Ford crested the hill, lit up as if it were radioactive or stood in the night under its own private sun. Spotted at equal intervals and situated at ground level, a dozen or more sodium lights encircled the bunker, their powerful beams trained on its concrete shoulders and illuminating the thing as if it were some clumsy juggernaut at rest, a space vehicle, brooding and lumpish, being readied for lift-off into the moonless night.

The effect was stupefying, the thing just out there on the blank mesa, mute, angry, a broad-backed animal perhaps, sullen, trapped, a grid of shrieking floodlights pinning it to the stark earth.

Garrison let the Ford go into neutral and coasted the rest of the way toward the flats, his eyes fastened on the mad vision ahead. He dimmed the lights and tapped the accelerator, coaxing the car into the same position from which he'd watched earlier in the day, reaching it and then shutting down engine and lights. A great silence captured the car, forcing its way through the vents to squat beside him on the seat.

Peter. This close. A lost piece of his heart within reach. Just off across the way, there, inside that queer dwelling. Peter. After thirteen years.

It was a school night—past eight o'clock. The chances were he was in there. Incredible. Thirteen years.

Garrison saw the Land Rover. It still stood just beyond the line of piñons. And behind it there was another car now, something that looked like a Jeepster.

Breaker's car?

Was Breaker inside? Did he live with Willa? Were they just student and teacher, or were they also lovers?

Garrison lit a cigarette and then put it out because the smoke kept getting in his eyes. His eyes—everything seemed to get in them now, drift across them and stick, as if glue had been smeared under the lids. He rubbed at his eyes and blinked until he could see better. But there was nothing to see, nothing but the concrete hump, lifeless in the weird blue light, the round black windows, the smooth land dropping off sharply into a kind of trench just in front. What was it? A waterless moat? To protect Willa from what? Why would anyone want to live like that? And the night lights. It was fantastic!

He stared until his eyes hurt. He tried to imagine what was going on in there. But how could you guess about what went on inside a crazy thing like that?

He saw headlights flash in his rearview mirror—and when he looked, he saw the car itself nosing down the hill. It didn't give him much time. He watched in the mirror as he fired up the Ford and then moved it evenly up the road beyond the paving. He kept his lights off, but he could tell from the tires that he was driving on dirt now. There was a bend ahead, wasn't there? He could miss it, get trapped in the sand. He concentrated on his tires, the feel of the earth beneath him, shutting down again when he judged that he was far enough away from the entrance to the bunker. But when the car passed him, he turned the Ford around and drove back, using his dims to find his way to the cattle guard. For a long time he stared at the porthole windows, and that was what he was doing when it happened, when he saw Peter. But it wasn't in a window that Garrison saw him. It was in front of the bunker, and his son was coming toward him.

It *was* Peter. It had to be. Garrison saw the high shoulders canted forward, Willa's smoky hair, Willa's slouch. Garrison had expected to see a boy. What he saw was a young man, remarkably tall and rangy for fourteen, materializing suddenly, noiselessly, like a ghost emerging from underground.

The boy was heading straight for the cattle guard and the Ford, white trousers, white windbreaker, something long and glittery in his hand, his head down, his stride strong and loping, the hips and the high square shoulders, like Willa's, thrusting forward.

Garrison tried to turn away. But he couldn't. He stared, transfixed, heart ramming.

His son.

He could not breathe. He tried to swallow. But his mouth and throat were sand. Everything inside him pounded. He gripped the wheel to steady himself, to keep himself from throwing open the door, running, lifting that long, lanky, body, holding it, holding him. *Peter, my God, my son!*

It was a flashlight. Garrison could see it now. The case long and silver. And then Peter turned it on. Just as the

boy reached the perimeter of the security lights, he
snapped on the flashlight, and then he veered sharply to
his right, correcting his course away from the cattle
guard and toward the road behind Garrison, toward the
point where the pavement ended and the roadway started
up in dirt again and turned a steep bend.

Garrison worked the rearview mirror, slowly angling
it to keep Peter in view. He saw the beam bouncing, the
figure all in white. The boy had made it to the road now,
and was tracking it on around toward the bend.

That body, so close, his son. He had diapered it,
bathed it, pressed his lips to the soft belly, breathed the
fragrance of his own flesh reborn.

Peter.

Garrison turned the key in the ignition. Headlamps
off, he wheeled the car around and let it inch along after
the bobbing gleam of light, the figure of his son glowing
as it moved on up ahead.

He thought of the last entry, the book dated *1979*, that
dark square of smeary type pasted on the last page.

*Dr. Steinmetz was so proud of his discovery. He
wanted to show it off to Mother. So the visit to his dig
was arranged. It wasn't far away, a dry riverbed on the
mesa outside of Grand Junction. Bones. Just a few of
them. Fragments. Steinmetz was beside himself, so eager to impress Mother. But she'd brought Jim and me
along, and Steinmetz didn't like it. What did I care?
Breaker or Steinmetz! Both are fools! And what was it
but a few shards of paltry bones! Yet Steinmetz declared
it the find of the century. Relics of Brachiosaurus, he
claimed, the largest of the dinosaurs, mightiest creature
ever to walk the earth. Breaker was awed. Such a puny
mind! But Mother wasn't. She winked at me. We both
know what size is. What is an eighty-ton beast to the
mass of the planet itself? And the planet is as nothing to
the galaxy. And the galaxy? A mere pinpoint in the cos-
mos! And that pathetic catch of bones? One atom of my
brain is vaster than Steinmetz's eighty-ton worm. And all*

*those billions of atoms together? They burn with one
immensity of thought. Get him! Get the beast who sired
me and then left me! Get the filth who soiled Mother! He
is mere flesh, a sack of guts, some quarts of blood, a pile
of bones!*

The road was starting to climb now, a long gradual
rise, the figure in white no more than forty yards ahead.

It would be easy to do it now. To do it without ever
knowing him. To end it now. Finish it. Finish it and save
Andy, all the unanswerable questions answered.

Garrison pulled the knob on the dash all the way out,
and the headlamps kicked into full illumination. With his
left foot he reached out and toed along the floor until he
felt the button. He pressed it down, heard the click, saw
the lights jerk into high. He gripped the wheel and
pushed the pedal down, felt the Ford rushing forward,
saw the figure in white look back as the car approached,
swung wide to the side, and then sped safely past.

It took Garrison more than an hour to get back to the
Oasis without returning the way he'd come. He was still
trembling when he stepped from the car, dropping the
keys when he tried to lock the door, then dropping them
a second time when he tried again, the composition
books spilling from under his arm when he stooped to get
the keys. When he bent to snatch at them, he noticed that
he was crying, and then he remembered tears leaking
down his face as he'd driven past Peter.

It took him a long time to find his room key. He stood
there, smacking at his pockets, feeling nothing. When he
got the door open, he saw he'd left the light on. He
stumbled across the room and fell onto the bed, and then
he raised himself and dragged himself back to the door,
closing it and going to the wastebasket to get the half-
empty quart.

He screwed off the bottle cap and swallowed all he
could, coughed, almost vomited, and crawled back to

the bed. When he thought he could talk, he lifted the receiver and dialed the desk.

"Jack? You busy?"

"Never too busy for you, Mr. Farrar."

"Can you talk?"

The man seemed to understand.

"It's cool, Roger. You just go ahead, whatever it is."

Garrison took a breath.

"I'm a little short," he said. "You know how it sometimes is. You think you could maybe lay your hands on something for me?"

"You need some shit, Roger? Is that what you're saying?"

"You think you could manage something?"

"Name your dream, my friend."

"Yes, well," Garrison said, thinking. "I don't know. Whatever'll take the edge off."

"Hey, Roger, you leave it to me. Fix you right up, my man. You want to come on out to my place tomorrow sometime? Got a very groovy scene out there."

"Thanks," Garrison said. "But suppose I catch you at the Buckdancer Cafe. About noon. You think you could have something by then?"

"Hey, my man, you're talking to Jack, you know? Don't you worry none. You're in old Jack's hands now. You dig, man?"

Garrison lowered the receiver and leaned back against the headboard. He saw the bureau drawers grinning at him in the ragged glare of the overhead light. And he felt the pain start, the snake feeding, the hole opening inside him. But in his agony, Garrison did not cry out. He was thinking about something, a solution. It seemed to make sense. Yes, yes, of course it did!

It was the perfect way out. It was amazing that he hadn't thought of it before.

Good Christ, the thing had been staring him in the face! It was easy. All he had to do was let Peter do what he wanted. And once the boy had done it, then Andy would be safe!

How simple it was. It was heaven-sent.

Garrison thought about it and thought about it—and then tipped the bottle to his lips. Not long after he'd emptied it, he fell into a deep and dreamless sleep. But sometime between the last of the liquor and the beginning of sleep, he understood he'd solved nothing, absolutely nothing.

Because to die now would be never again to see Andy, to give Andy not one day of the little time that was left.

11.

HE WAS AWAKE within three hours, lashed by pain, his eyes opening to blinding light. He checked his watch. It was almost one-thirty. He rolled wearily to his feet and flipped open the valise on the opposite bed. He found his razor but no shaving cream. He went to the bathroom and shaved with soap. He'd have to be clean-shaven.

It wasn't until he got to Grand Junction that he found a bank that looked like it might be able to handle it. He parked out front and tried to sleep. But every time he started drifting off, he saw a figure in white moving in darkness, headlights illuminating an utterly expressionless face.

Just after dawn, Garrison got out of the car and went looking for a place to get coffee, some food. He found an all-night cafe, and he drank coffee until he thought he could hold down something solid.

He sat there for as long as he could, and then he paid and went back out into the streets, shivering in the early-morning cold. He made his way back to the car, stopping to look into storefronts, killing time when time was all he had left.

It felt strange to be using his name again. He signed the forms and collected a thousand dollars in cash and a thousand dollars in travelers checks on his American Express gold card. It all went smoothly, especially when the bank officer who had to okay the transaction turned out to know the name.

"You're not him, are you?"

"Who?" Garrison said, already knowing what was coming next, pleased because it could only help.

"My wife and I make it to the Big Apple once a year. By golly, I guess we've seen at least three of your shows. You *are* that Garrison, aren't you?"

Garrison pulled off the dark glasses and smiled.

"Vacationing, Mr. Garrison?"

He nodded. "With my family, yes."

"Running a little short, I imagine."

"That's right," he said, thinking, *I'm a little short. You know how it sometimes is.*

"A lot to see in these parts," the bank officer was saying, his hand on Garrison's elbow, guiding him across the floor to one of the teller's windows. "Big find right near here last year. Bones of the biggest dinosaur ever. You ought to take your family over for a look. They got it marked."

"Thanks," Garrison said.

"Miss Kranes here will help you." The man nodded at the woman behind the glass, and then he slipped the forms through to her. "Martha, take care of Mr. Garrison, please."

"Many thanks," Garrison said, extending his hand.

"No trouble at all," the bank officer said, shaking Garrison's hand. "A pleasure to serve you. The wife'll get a big kick out of this. We get East around Christmas every year. Never miss the shows."

"Thanks again," Garrison said, smiling as the bank officer moved off, wondering if the man might call the Oasis Inn to check. He'd had to give a local address. Did the Oasis Inn look suspicious? Did it make sense that he'd be staying at a place like that?

He took the cash in twenties, the checks in fifties. It seemed to take forever to write his signature into the blanks while the teller recorded the numbers.

Outside, it was much warmer now, but a hard wind

was blowing from the west. He let it turn him east and left the car behind, making his way along the street until he spotted a hardware store. Once inside the store, Garrison moved decisively, as if he knew exactly what he wanted. He went directly to the glass case where the handguns were displayed, beckoning impatiently for someone to come help him. He took off his sunglasses with a flourish, tapped the case, moved his feet, trying his best to exhibit annoyance, haste, but confidence, a man whom no one would think to challenge.

"This one here," Garrison said, pointing when an elderly man finally hurried over, wheezing and beaming agreeably.

The man positioned himself behind the counter, looked at what Garrison was pointing at, and then peered apologetically into Garrison's face.

"That one there?"

"Yes," Garrison said, tapping the glass directly above the gun.

"That no-account thing?" the man said. "It ain't good for nothing but plinking at tin cans."

"That's just what I want it for," Garrison said, still pointing. But the conviction was going out of him. Had he made a mistake? He knew nothing about guns, had never owned one, or cared to. Guns scared him, especially the kind you held in one hand.

"This here's just a twenty-two Buntline," the man said, unlocking the case and reaching in. "Now, it's a fine firearm, mind you, I'll warrant you that. No, I don't mean to downgrade it none—but the fact is it's more a starter weapon for some kid doing target-shooting."

"How much?" Garrison said, unable to turn back now.

"This here?" the man said, hefting the gun in his hand. "Hell, it ain't but a hundred twenty-eight dollars."

"That's fine," Garrison said, reaching for his wallet. "I'll pay cash."

The man looked up at Garrison as if he'd said something strange.

"Ammunition too," Garrison said. "Shells, I mean."

The man turned away and abruptly turned back, slapping two boxes of cartridges on the counter. "Shorts," he said, as if angered now. "Two boxes okay?"

"You bet," Garrison said, counting out the bills.

"I'll see your ID first," the man said. "You're not local, are you?"

"No," Garrison said. He fingered his driver's license out of his wallet. "On holiday. Just doing some camping, is all. Here," he said, "here's my license. I'm staying at the Oasis, down in Cortez. Just up here to do some banking and shopping. Not much of either one in Cortez," he added, disgusted with himself for saying too much.

The man took the license and examined it as if it had been soaked in lethal substances. "Going camping, you say?" He turned the certificate over and then he turned it back again. "Long way from home, ain't you?"

"That's right," Garrison said. "Just figured it might be wise to have something with me out there." He waved toward the door as if indicating a wilderness.

Again the man looked at Garrison as if something puzzling had been said.

"Mister," he said, "just let me put you to rights on one thing. This here Buntline ain't going to do you one lick of good up against nothing unless you get right in close. Now it's a good piece of shooting equipment, I don't take that from it. Fact is, it was this very kind of firearm them Manson kids used on them people out Hollywood, if you remember. But for varmints that are likely to come up on you, it don't have near the range and hit you'll need. You let me show you something else that's more in line with what you're looking for."

"No, no," Garrison said, protesting, smiling, doing his best with this, "I'd be nervous around anything really powerful. This'll be fine, I assure you."

"Suit yourself," the man said. He put down the gun and the license and reached under the counter, producing a book that was wider than it was tall, and flipped it open to where a rubber band divided the pages. "Sign first," he said, spinning the book around and showing Garrison where to write his name.

"Pen?"

The man slapped his shirt pockets. "Ain't you got none?"

"Afraid not," Garrison said.

"Well, hold on just a damn minute," the man said, and slapped his shirt pockets again. "Oh yeah, here she is." He pulled a ballpoint from his trouser pocket and handed it to Garrison, and then put his finger on the blank rectangle at the end of the long line of spaces that would have to be filled in.

Garrison signed. The man turned the book around and began copying from Garrison's driver's license.

"Holster?" he said when he was partway down the line.

Garrison shook his head. "No, I don't think so," he said, and moved to the next case and gazed down thoughtfully at the hunting knives and hand axes, appearing to study them with great interest.

The weight of the thing! Of course, the two boxes of cartridges added to it, but as light-caliber as the pistol was, it was the weight of the thing, its physical density, that made the paper bag feel like a deadly package. Garrison held it in his hand and walked toward the door, conscious that he carried something whose power was conclusive. It was like the reptile that coiled and glided inside him, malignant, autonomous, arbitrary.

He headed for the car, walking into the wind now, the bag crackling as dry gusts blew against it. But the weight pressing into Garrison's hand rode his palm like a stone, impervious, solid. He felt curiously elated, as if he had somehow caught hold of his own destiny again, retrieved

strings that had slipped from his grasp. He leaned against
the wind and moved up the street, feeling the density that
rested in his hand. It was like a charmed object, a thing
that could render simple the most intricate problem, cure
the incurable.

He saw the Ford, sun flashing off its light blue finish
like electricity made visible. Garrison quickened his
pace, almost ran. Why did he feel so strange? It was as if
he had been changed, as if he were no longer the person
he'd been, but was altogether different now. It wasn't
that he'd been changed into anyone in particular. It was
just that he wasn't exactly Ben Garrison anymore. He
was no one. He was anyone. He was a man with a gun.

All the way back to Cortez he felt he was being
watched, tracked, pursued. He imagined phones ringing,
descriptions relayed, hurried notes being jotted down. A
tall man, silvery white hair, clean-shaven, sportcoat, turtleneck, dark corduroy trousers—and sunglasses, yes,
sunglasses. He imagined himself the center of a wide-
spread alert, the call racing on ahead of him as he fled
from town to town.

Just before he reached the outskirts of Cortez, he
pulled off to the side of the road and took the gun out of
the bag. He held it, the alien metal, and it filled him with
a kind of dizzy lifting feeling, as if the gun were rising
and, like an airborne magnet, it carried him with it.

He shivered slightly, returned the Buntline to the bag,
and stuffed the bag under the seat. He checked his
watch—almost noon—and then pulled back onto the
highway.

He felt lightheaded, exultant. His mind was clear,
made up. Telephone Andy, call him at school, talk and
talk until everything got said, until the good-bye was as
good as a good-bye could get. Then find Peter—and
make him do it. Before cancer does it and it's too late.

But before Garrison reached the Oasis, the pain found
him again, bolts of lightning that kept striking his spine

and left it scorched, frayed. He caught his breath and gripped the wheel and held on, praying for this agony not to be his last. And then he felt an awesome grabbing, something tearing inside his chest, what might be small claws ripping flesh away from flesh, cords of sinew yanked up by the roots.

He had to pull over to the edge of the road to wait the spasm out. The bones in his hands ached from their fierce clenching. When he could manage the car again, he passed the Oasis by and kept going south. He had to have something. If he was going to be able to handle this, he had to have something.

He parked across the street from the Buckdancer Cafe, checked the time again, and got out.

He felt better now, much better. It was amazing—he almost felt . . . exhilarated, relieved. Get something to quiet him down, then talk to Andy. And after that? Put the gun in Peter's hand.

The place was jammed with people eating lunch. Garrison stood just inside the door. All the stools at the counter were occupied, but no skinny, red-bearded man sat on any of them. Garrison scanned the tables, the booths. Nothing. No Jack.

It was easier to wait outside, warmer, less chance of someone trying to talk to him. He pushed through the door, went back across the street, and leaned against the Ford, smoking, looking south toward the mesa, the red dust rising in the distance.

Jack wasn't alone when Garrison saw the car coming. He could see the girl's head snap back as the white '67 Mercury convertible banged up over the curb and then swung violently into the lot next to the Buckdancer. The girl sat in front, in the passenger seat, her thin arm propped on the door, her hand resting on the roof of the car.

Garrison turned away and started to get back into the Ford, willing to forget it, sorry he had ever considered it in the first place. He could deal with the pain. He could deal with everything. But Jack was already calling.

"Hey, Roger! Hey, man, how's it hanging?"

Garrison turned back. He saw them crossing the street, the chaotic red beard working as if the man were chewing something, the girl squinting in the sun, the slitted eyes almost closed, the small teeth bared in a pinched grin.

Jack had his hand out, and when Garrison took it, the younger man used his other hand to grip Garrison's shoulder in greeting, as though old and devoted comrades were being reunited.

"Great to see you, Roger. It's great to see you, man. You know Lynn. Hey, Lynn, you know my friend. Roger, right?"

"Hey, Brother Sunshine, how do?" the girl said, shielding her eyes, her tight mouth grinning enthusiastically.

The man Jack spit something into his palm, sucked at his teeth, and spit again. "Old Lynn here, she didn't know you was an associate of mine. Small world. Now that's the truth, ain't it?"

Garrison nodded. It was crazy—these people, the gun in the car.

"Hey, Brother Sunshine, you looking fucking awful, man. You sick or something?"

Garrison studied the girl, the pinched face, as if features had been doled out to her by a miser.

Jack laughed. "Roger? Like Roger's going to get right, you know? He just needs a taste, a little lavender in his head. Am I right, Rog?"

"I could use something, yes," Garrison said. "Where is it? Is it in your car?"

The red beard started working again, that chewing action. Jack screwed up his face as if in deep thought. He turned to look up and down the street, a man who might be conducting a survey of the flow of traffic.

"For crying out loud," he finally said, fixing Garrison

with his small quick eyes, "be cool, man, be cool." He
sighed, and again he checked the empty street in both
directions. "Dig, man, this ain't your Boston or your
Barstow, you know. I mean, hey, it's *uncivilized,* you
dig? They got fuzz here you would not *believe.* Indian
fuzz, man. You any idea what those sonsabitches is *like?*
So be cool, my man, be cool."

"It's all right," Garrison said, turning, pulling the
door to the Ford open again. "Forget it. I changed
my mind."

He felt Jack's hand on his shoulder, the bony fingers.

"Hey, man, *relax.* It's just we got to do this thing
right, you know?"

Garrison turned back to him; he was trying to figure
out which girl this one was—the one who had been
behind the wheel, or the other one. Did they look so
much alike or was he was beginning to forget things, get
things all mixed up? He stared at her, trying to remember, and then he had to blink and rub his eyes to try to
clear them of the patches of fog that seemed to condense
and cloud his vision much more often now. She wore
skintight blue jeans that she'd somehow been able to roll
above her calves, and she had on what seemed to be a
boy's basketball jacket, bright red satin that Garrison
was sure would reveal writing on the back if she only
turned around. Her feet were narrow and the toes were
long and slim, and he couldn't help noticing the lovely
network of veins that wriggled in a delicate tracery
across the instep. She wore some sort of Japanese
thongs. He didn't know what they were called but he
didn't like them on women, and these he thought particularly ugly because they were finished in some kind of
cheap black material that was supposed to look like velvet. Yet her feet were really quite remarkable for such a
hard-looking bit of a thing, that ill-tempered, jammed
face that came at you like a piece of lead pipe.

When Garrison started listening again, he heard Jack
saying something about bone, that he hadn't seen

any bone yet, so what was everybody getting in an uproar for?

"No uproar," Garrison said. "Not interested anymore, that's all. But don't worry about the money end of it. I guess I can handle that part of it okay."

"Sure you can!" Jack said, stopping to chew again and then to spit into his hand, sucking at his teeth and checking the street. "I mean, like dig, man, I could *tell*, you know. The way you carry yourself. Hey, Roger, don't get me wrong, my friend, I know you can handle it all right. Hey, did I say otherwise? But there's *Eric*, see? And he's my main *man*, and what he'd like you to do, you know, is to come on out to the place and like work the deal out there. You understand what I'm saying?"

"Skip it," Garrison said. "I appreciate your effort, but I don't have time for this. Yes or no. Here or nowhere."

The man put his hand out to touch Garrison's chest, and the girl turned away, as if she feared to see contact between men.

"Mr. Farrar, hey now—don't get *uptight*, you know? Hey, man, don't *do* that. It's cool. I'll talk to Eric, okay? I'll see can he make an exception. Believe me, I understand. Like dig, old Jack is *with* you, man—he understands what you're saying. But just between you and me"—and here he reached for Garrison's arm to turn him away from the girl, lowering his voice as if to suggest the girl must be spared the least indiscretion—"my man Eric's got him a very heavy scene out there, you know. Old Lynn here, she's just a *part* of it, you understand? Now if Eric takes a liking to you, the way *I* already have, well, like he can put you in a room with five more like her, you know what I mean?"

Garrison saw the small eye wink, and then the man turned to check the street in both directions, winking again when he fixed his attention on Garrison once more. "You hear what I'm saying to you, don't you? Like one

at a time, they might not be so much—but, hey, five at
once? You understand what I'm saying?"

"Not interested," Garrison said.

"Hey, Rog, believe me, I understand. You got more
important things on your mind. Believe me, man, I can
dig it, you know?"

For a moment Garrison was startled. But he let the
remark pass.

"You speak to your friend," Garrison said. "See
what he's willing to do for me." He had his hand in his
pocket, one of the twenties folded in his palm. He took
his hand out. "Meanwhile, this is for your trouble. I'll
be in touch."

He nodded for Jack to get out of the way, and then got
in behind the wheel. He pulled the door closed, started
the engine, heard the girl shout, "Hey, Brother Sunshine! Hang on a little!"

Garrison faced forward as if he he had not heard. But
Jack still had his hand on the door, and he kept it there
until the girl had stepped in beside him and taken his
place at the window.

She leaned in, squinting and grinning.

"How about you wheel me up to the motel so I can
catch me a swim?"

"Can't Jack drive you?"

The girl looked away as if she had to verify her facts.
"Him, he's going on back to the place. Like he don't
start his shift till five."

Garrison pushed in the lighter, fumbled for his cigarettes, stalled.

"I hadn't thought of going back. There's some things
I've—"

But when he looked up, he saw that she was already
moving around the front of the car, motioning for him to
unlock the door.

"Says you promised her a ride once."

It was Jack. When Garrison turned, he saw the red

beard stuck in at the window again, the wispy bristles alive with the action of his jaws as they methodically worked whatever he was chewing.

"You bet," Garrison said. "I did."

"Yeah, like for helping you to find that goddamn funhouse. So tell me, Rog, what the hell's it like inside the goddamn thing? I mean, I've seen some shit, man, but that pad is fucking out of sight, you know?"

"Look," Garrison said, letting the emergency out, "I'll give the girl a lift and you go talk to your friend. Fair enough?"

The man winked again. He held the folded twenty up to his nose, sniffed it, then held it above his eye in a kind of salute. "Hey, Mr. Farrar—don't get me wrong now. I'm like at your service, you know? You understand what I'm saying?"

"That's nice," Garrison said, and touched the accelerator.

Jack smiled, jumped away from the car, then skipped to the center of the street, holding one hand up against traffic and using the other hand to give Garrison directions, gesturing extravagantly to the street and to the car. But there was no traffic coming and a child could have managed the U-turn.

It was only a mile or so to the motel. He wanted to make it in silence, to get there and get rid of her with the least fuss possible, to call Andy and go find Peter. Garrison set his jaw and stared ahead, eager to be free of the girl and alone again so he could take a real look at the thing that was stuffed under the seat and would presently end his pain, his fear, his life.

Look at me. You don't know me, but do you see the resemblance? Of course you do—because I'm your father. Now look at this. Take it. Use it. You'll never get another chance.

It was crazy. It was absolutely lunatic. Would even a total psychotic take the gun and do what you asked? And a boy like Peter, a boy who seemed to hold everyone but his mother in contempt? How could you arrange a thing like that, contrive a set of circumstances so it would just happen naturally? It seemed impossible, a task requiring enormous ingenuity, planning, timing, subtlety. He wasn't a man like that—and even if he were, he was also a man dying, a man in pain, a man with no time for the strategies of a tactician. It would be like a game, and it would be Andy's life they'd be playing for. And if Garrison lost?

"Come on, Brother Sunshine, how about it?"

It was the girl. She'd been talking to him, pushing at his arm, and he hadn't been listening.

"What? How about what?"

"A swim."

"Me? You crazy? In this cold?"

"Cold? Shit, you call this cold?

She reached her hands behind her neck and stretched her legs out, showing him her breasts, her strong young body. For the first time he noticed that she was wearing a kerchief, and that it stuck up high on her head as if it covered wet hair drying with rollers in it.

She saw him looking at her.

"You starting to think about what you see, Brother Sunshine?"

"How old are you, anyway?"

"Old enough."

"Old enough?" Garrison said. "My Christ, I haven't heard that expression since I was a kid myself. Yeah, I guess some things never change."

The girl moved in her seat, adjusting herself so that the line of her hip and leg was better displayed. "That's what Eric's always saying. Like how you can always count on human nature being what it is and never getting any different."

Garrison didn't agree. He liked to think that mankind kept improving itself, that the human spirit kept striving to rid itself of meanness and all the rest of the vanities that dragged man down. But now he wasn't so sure anymore. What was the point when you were dead at thirty-four? What was the point when you had to leave behind what you loved, without having used up all the loving that was in you?

He stopped the car in front of the Oasis, and left the engine running.

"Here you go," he said, and waited for her to get out.

But the girl stayed where she was, and stretched again.

"Hey, come on, man, let me bring you out."

She had her hand on the door, but she wasn't leaving yet.

"Thanks, but let's drop it," Garrison said. "You may be old enough, but so am I."

She moved her hand from the door and unzipped the red satin jacket all the way down. It fell away to show the top of a bathing suit.

"I could make you forget all about age, Brother Sunshine. I could bring you out. Like it's this talent I've got. Ask anyone."

There was something about the girl's words that made Garrison dizzy with feeling, something about them that crawled inside him despite himself. But it was ridiculous. He wasn't here for anything like this. And yet, in a way, the girl seemed to be a part of it, a part of what he *was* here for, as if her brazen sexuality went with all of it, the crazy composition books, the crazy bunker, the crazy security lights, Peter in white, the crazy marriage, the gun, the cancer, sixty days.

Days? Perhaps hours. Perhaps only hours were left.

"Really," he said, his voice breaking. "I don't think so, okay?"

"Yeah, sure," the girl said. "Hey, I know, man. It's okay. Just let me use your room to dry off after I get out. That's no big deal, is it? I mean, I was shitting you, you know. I mean, it really is sort of cold."

He wanted to object, find an alibi, give her a flat no.
Where the hell was she going to go if he hadn't been
here? She was using him, drawing him on—he knew
it—and yet he couldn't exactly say no.

He looked at his watch. After one. The high school
probably wouldn't let out for a couple of hours yet. But
he'd have to call soon to catch Andy at school.

He looked at the girl. He wanted her to be able to see
from his face that what he was saying was all he was
saying—that she could use his room when she got out of
the pool, but that was the extent of it, and then she had to
clear out, that he had an errand to run, and it was in the
opposite direction from town, so no more rides, no more
nothing.

"Hey, like that's okay," she said. "Don't worry."

He told her his room number, and then he reached
across her and pushed open the door. When she turned
away and started for the pool, he saw the back of her
jacket. There was something written on it.

One word.

Eric.

He drove around the block and used the back entrance,
pulling into the space in front of his room and reaching
down under the seat before getting out and locking the
car. He could feel his exhaustion now—and hunger.
He'd hardly slept. How long had it been since he'd really
eaten a meal? It was then that he remembered he'd been
counting days. This one, which one was it? The fifty-
fifth? Fifty-fourth? But it didn't matter anymore.

How long ago it all seemed now. The tests. Flood's
voice. McIver, Dillon. New York.

Oncology, oncologist.

And his eyes, this haze that from time to time spread
over his vision. It was getting worse. Like a coat of glue,
like shellac. Did it come from the same source? Was it
like the continual ache that ran from shoulder to shoul-

der? Was it all wired to that thing down there? Even his pain didn't seem to make sense.

He double-locked the door. He went to the bed and dropped the bag. The bedclothes were just as he'd left them. No maid had come to clean up. Good. He didn't want it any different. He didn't want to be reminded of order, routine, the things which signified that life goes on. Besides, he didn't want anybody in here.

And then he remembered the girl—she was coming.

How soon? It was a mistake. He'd been stupid again, done something that made no sense. Was that it? Was he losing his mind? Was that where the cancer was now, in his brain?

He hurried. He saw his fingers trembling when he parted the mouth of the paper sack to look down and see inside. He half expected the gun to have transformed itself into something else since the last time he'd looked, its power to perform magic going to work once daylight was shut out.

He sat down on the bed. He slipped his hand under the sack and upended it. The contents spilled out like a judicial statement, a verdict of death, the fall of a three-word benediction intoned at graveside.

The barrel was absurdly long, but it wasn't a big gun. And yet it looked massive. It was like the machinery that had been used to test him. It was like those gleaming contrivances at Columbia Presbyterian and Sloan-Kettering. Things with a place for him to lie down on. Cold shiny surfaces that moved while other things were buzzing and humming and clicking, globes with snouts and nozzles that cruised back and forth over your torso as if powered by distant motors whose operators sat before a console housed deep beneath the surface of the earth. The gun gave him the same strange feeling, a sense of his own frailty, his own puny mortality in contact with a huge, implacable force. He remembered how it always was whenever he came away from those hospitals, a feeling it took him hours to shake. It was as if he'd just been for a cruise in a submarine where he was the only man aboard.

As an actor, he'd had guns in his hand. A few times. Real guns. As a director, he'd sometimes handed them to actors, shown them how he wanted them to hold the things. Real guns, just as genuine as this one. But this was different. What it *meant* made it different. And where it was. Because this was no stage. It was a squalid motel room on the edge of the most spectacular desolation in America. It was a place where something like this could really be happening, a father gazing at the instrument that could save one son from the other. But what if Peter wouldn't do it, would not use the gun? What then?

The answer came to Garrison, and it drove the breath from his body.

He had no choice. In the very act of fathering, nature had chosen for him. Didn't it happen to all parents? If not like this, then in small ways, daily acts that, in the end, added up to the same thing? Even in the happiest of families, parents were made to choose between children. It happened all day long, so much that they never noticed. Or if they did, they'd never admit it. A slightly better serving of food, the last cookie in the jar, a hug that lasted for a fraction of a second longer, a look that said, *I love you more.*

Parents knew it. Children knew it. It was a truth kept secret more utterly than any other. It was the deepest secret of all. It was the primal terror between parents and children, the one truth no one dared acknowledge.

Garrison took the gun into his hand. He broke out the cylinder. He studied the empty chambers. He put his nose close to them and smelled.

You sacrifice one child so that another might live, might thrive. Animals did it by instinct. Dogs sat on puppies until they were dead. Sows ate their young. It was nature's plan. There was no shame attached to it, no crime. It was necessity.

Peter wanted to murder. Andy wanted to live.

Only Garrison stood between them. For the time being.

Necessity.

He reached for one of the boxes of cartridges, skidded the cover off, filled each of the chambers. He rubbed his fingers together to feel the waxy stuff that had come off on them, and then, with a motion of his wrist, he returned the barrel to firing position and shifted the Buntline to his left hand. He sniffed the hand that had held the thing.

He raised the hand that now held the gun. He studied his wrist. Turned it in the light. Saw it for the first time, the body transformed by the thing it was joined to. His flesh and the blue-black steel. It was like leaving your mortality behind, like becoming a thing that motors powered. A gun could do that. It could change a man. It was like holding death in your hand.

He let himself back down on the bed. He lay there, staring at the ceiling, considering the iron logic, the Buntline in his hand. It was still in his hand when he sat up again and pulled the telephone onto the bed. No. He'd decided. He wasn't going to call Andy. He was going to see him again! There was another way to solve the problem. Oh, Jesus— There *was*.

She answered on the first ring.

"Joanie? Honey? It's the Hollywood kid."

"Oh Jesus, Ben, where the hell are you?"

"Guess."

He heard her sigh, but he could tell from its exaggerated duration that she meant it playfully.

"All right, don't guess," he said. "You're a lousy guesser, anyway. Where I am is in Colorado. But if I wanted to, I could be in Utah or Arizona or New Mexico. All I'd need is a few more feet on this telephone cord. Now can you guess? Or do you give up?"

Again he heard her sigh, but doing it humorously,

letting him know she was poking fun at her annoyance. He'd done what he wanted, gotten her to forget her anger.

"Give up?"

"Give up! Why should I give up when I'm having all this fun? How about we play Statues when we finish Geography?"

Garrison laughed. "What do you say to the Four Corners area? How's that for being somewhere?"

He heard her sigh again, this time not so good-naturedly. "*Where* are you, darling? Exactly where?"

"Honest, baby, no one's exactly anywhere here. I mean, it's kind of noplace. But there's a town about twenty miles from where I am, a sort of intersection called Cortez."

"Is that where you're *staying?* And what in the name of sweet Jesus are you *doing* around there?"

"What I'm doing around here," he said, and let his shoulders go back against the headboard, "is checking out locations with these nuts I'm with. It's a Western. The thing they wanted to talk to me about—I'm supposed to let them know whether I'd like to use this particular terrain or something else, which is crazy, because what the hell do I know about the possibilities, but that's anyhow what I'm doing."

"Why didn't you tell Andy when you called? I've been frantic. I tried the Beverly and the Beverly Wilshire, and when that was no dice I started pestering Steve—and he's being very evasive. It's not like Steve to be that way. Ben, what's going *on*, honey? Are you all right? Is something wrong?"

"*Nothing's* wrong, baby. It's just these crazy movie people, is all. Honest, I would have told Andy if I'd known at the time. These guys are totally mad, you know? One minute they're talking about having lunch in London, the next minute they want to know if you play tennis—because if you do, then how about everybody flies into Palm Springs for a few sets and then bay scallops at Melvin's. You know. I'm telling you, sweetie, it's incredible. They're total crazies, these people.''

There was a silence for a time. Was she buying it? If she wasn't, then what *did* she think, what *was* she imagining? That he was with a woman? He remembered the girl. It made him sit up. For the first time, Garrison realized he wanted the girl. He didn't know why, but he did.

''You should have asked Andy to get me out of the shower.''

''So you could catch the cold you missed by staying in there?''

Once more, a silence.

''You're sweet.''

''Thanks,'' he said. ''At least I'm not the worst guy in the world.'' He heard what he said, and he was willing to understand that it was not true.

''Ben, tell me how I can reach you. What number are you at? Where are you staying?''

''I told you, baby, not anywhere. We're just driving around. I'm calling from a gas station.''

''Well, where will you be tonight?''

''Search me. I think they want to go on down into the Painted Desert and then cut back up to Monument Valley, which is where they shot all those John Ford Westerns, or a lot of them, anyhow. Then up to Bryce Canyon and Zion and Kanab.''

''I can't believe this,'' she said.

''Me neither.''

''Is this how they spend their money?''

''It's their money,'' he said. ''How's my old man, is he okay?''

''Happy as a clam. He got a hundred percent on his spelling test yesterday. First time this year. Mrs. Flynn drew one of those smiling faces at the top of his paper and he's positively thrilled, only he thinks it might be babyish to show it. But you should have seen him when he went off to school this morning—pretty puffed up, and I think he was even swaggering.''

"You say swaggering? My old chap is *swaggering?*''

"Swaggering.''

"Ah, God,'' Garrison said, "what a guy.'' And just as he said it, he heard someone banging on the door. The girl! Could Joan hear the noise at the door? Hadn't he said he was in a gas station?

"Honey, they're hollering at me to come on. I've got to say good-bye.''

"For God's sake, Ben, I haven't talked with you in *days*. Just tell them to wait. They'll wait.''

The banging was louder, more insistent.

"I can't, baby. We're talking about some pretty unreasonable characters. I've got to go.''

"I mean it, Ben. I've got some of your time coming, too.''

He shouted at the door. "Hold on a minute!'' And then to Joan he said, "Baby, *please*.''

"Will you call me first chance you get?''

"Promise. Now say good-bye. I love you, darling. I love you very much. I love you and Andy with all my heart. Tell him, okay?''

"Of course. Be careful, darling. You don't sound right to me. I don't care how important this movie job is, it's not worth killing yourself for.''

The banging started up again.

"I promise, baby. I love you. Kiss the old chap for me. I'll call as soon as I can.''

"Ben?'' Her voice was suddenly urgent.

"Yes?''

"You're my fella, you know. If you want to tell those movie types to screw it, it's okay by me, you know.''

"Sure, baby. I know. Now hang up, honey, because I've got to go.''

He waited until he heard the line click dead, and then

he lowered the receiver and started for the door. She was banging again, hitting it with all her might. He was shouting at her to wait a second and he had one hand on the doorknob and the other on the latch when he remembered the gun.

"Hold it!" he yelled. "Be right with you!"

He went back to the bed, snatched up the gun and the boxes of cartridges, and stood there uncertainly, his eyes sweeping the room for the fastest place. The bureau! He yanked open the bottom drawer and gently laid everything inside.

When he got the door open, she had one hand to her crotch and she was jogging up and down, her clothes in her other hand. "Jesus Christ, man," the girl shrilled into his face, and then pushed into the room and past him. "I got to take a goddamn *piss!*"

Garrison shut the door and watched the small muscles in her back as she dumped her clothes on the second bed, cursed, and then disappeared into the bathroom. She didn't bother to shut the door. He heard the fast rush of her urine and her soft moans of relief.

He fitted the latch into the locked position. But he stayed by the door, trying to think, trying to deal with what he felt.

He wasn't surprised when she came out of the bathroom with nothing on. Nor did he make any effort not to look at her or to seem indifferent.

"Changed your mind, I see. Is it a fact, Brother Sunshine?"

He didn't answer. He just stood with his back against the door, looking at her. She moved a few steps closer, and then she flopped down onto the second bed, a kind of formless, girlish drive.

"You got something to drink?"

He shook his head.

"Anything to smoke?"

"Just these," he said, pulling the pack out of his pocket.

"Shit," she said, and reached her arm out to show she wanted one. "I meant *smoke,* man."

"Stand up first."

"Huh?"

"Stand up."

"Why the hell should I?"

His voice was husky when he answered. "I want to see you," he said.

She grinned knowingly, and then she made what she must have thought was a sensous gesture of the lips, pooching them out like a bad actress hoping to appear seductive. Garrison could see that she saw herself on stage now, moving languidly from the bed and then, slowly, with pathetic grace, getting to her feet and raising herself on tiptoe. She held out her arms and then brought them forward slightly, bending them, putting her hands behind her neck, pointing her elbows toward the ceiling. She turned very gradually to one side and then the other, so that he could see her breasts in profile, the buttocks, the belly, the calves. It was only then that the full force of what he was seeing struck him—she was a girl.

"How old are you really?" he said.

"Old enough to take whatever you got," she answered, her elbows still pointing at the ceiling, one knee bent forward, the calf molded, the leg tensing on the ball of the foot.

He saw that she did have rollers in her hair—and it was odd—because they somehow made her more appealing, as if in her indifference to these things she proved the authority of her eroticism.

"It doesn't matter," he kept repeating as he moved across the room to her and knelt in front of her and pulled her belly to his face. He tasted her taut young skin, and it tasted of the pool, of chlorine. For a long time he held her this way, his tongue moving over her belly, touching, tasting.

She let her body move with it, and Garrison understood she wasn't acting anymore. Her hands were in his hair now, and her fingers urged him on. No, he thought, it doesn't matter.

She lifted one leg until she got it over his shoulder, and he brought his tongue down to where she wanted. All the toughness seemed to have gone out of her as she moved against him now, and with one hand she helped him, using her fingers to help him get to where they both wanted. His hands pulled at her buttocks and lifted her so that she could let herself go back and lower herself to the floor.

He heard her murmuring, her voice throaty, "God, man, beautiful, beautiful—oh, angel, angel." When he looked up, he saw her looking down at him, her eyes wide. He raised her buttocks so that she could see better, and so that he could see her eyes and keep watching them until they closed shut hard.

She asked to stay. In a way, he almost wanted her to. But it was impossible. He checked the time, and tried to hurry her. He could see that she was doing her best, sitting on the edge of the bed, pulling on her jeans, but he wished she'd stop talking and leave. "Hey, man, no kidding." She was still pleading with him, asking to stay. "I really don't want to go back there. I mean, that dude Eric, you just don't know. Let me crash here awhile. A couple of days. No shit, I won't be like in your way or anything."

"It won't work," Garrison said. "Look—is it Lynn?"

The girl nodded, smiled.

"Look, Lynn," Garrison said, "you didn't ask for it, but I'm going to give you some money. Use it to get yourself on a bus to Barstow. I don't know, but maybe it'll help. Because I can't. Not now. You don't understand. But I just can't help you now."

The girl nodded. She was standing now, doing up the buttons on her jeans, pulling into her red satin jacket.

Garrison was disgusted with himself. He knelt before her again to lift each thong to the foot she raised. He touched them, her feet, the fine tracery of light blue veins.

"Come on," he said, checking his watch again, "you've got to get out of here." He put four twenties into the pocket of her jacket. "Try to get yourself back to Barstow. You think you can do that?"

The girl raised her eyes to him. "Don't worry," she said. "I can do it."

"Okay," he said. "Now hurry. Please."

She went into the bathroom and came back out with her bathing suit.

"It's cool, man. Don't worry."

He bent to her and kissed her face like the child she was. He let her out the door, got quickly into his clothes, and wrapped the loaded Buntline into his second sweater. Then he bundled it under his arm and pulled the door shut behind him.

It was almost two-thirty. The high school couldn't be more than five minutes away.

12.

THE GROUNDS WERE virtually empty. Surely, if school had already let out, there'd be kids around, stragglers, those that were waiting for a bus, a lift home. Garrison sat parked across the street, the sweater balled on the seat beside him. What if the coach saw him, called the police—and the police came, asked questions, checked the car?

You the one I told to get more pounds in his tire?

Had he done it? He didn't remember. It seemed he had, but he couldn't be sure. Everything before this moment was a century ago. Even the girl. What had she smelled like, tasted like, felt like inside? He couldn't remember. He couldn't remember anything now. Except what he'd come here for. He stared at the building, and waited.

Should he get out and check the tire?

He wanted to light a cigarette. But he was afraid to move, to make the slightest motion.

Shorts. What were shorts? Were there also longs? Were shorts as good as longs? Which killed better? Could you kill with shorts at all? The Manson gang, what had they used? Longs?

He had to stop this. It was driving him crazy. Or maybe he already was crazy. Of course he was crazy. You had to be crazy to be doing this. To kill your own son? No matter what your reason! Yes! The pain had made him crazy.

He blinked his eyes. The lids wanted to stick together, stay closed.

Where? Where would you do it? Between the eyes? In the heart? Up against the roof of the mouth? How did a father do this thing when he had to, when he had no choice?

Garrison was blind with confusion. He wanted to run. He heard a bell going off, like an alarm. He grabbed the sweater and put it in his lap. He started the engine.

All right. What *was* this? It was nothing. Just a father off from work early, here to pick up his son.

There were kids everywhere now, a storm of them. They came out of the building in waves, or like spurts gushing from a tube. Pulsations. So much noise. The shouting.

Garrison blinked again, rubbed his eyes. The colors—so many colors against the colorless backdrop of the building—and everything in motion. But then he saw him. It was easy. That tall figure—and just as before, white, the same white trousers, white windbreaker, unzipped now, the front hanging open over a white T-shirt. The long, loping stride, the wide shoulders held high and slightly forward. Everything white except the boots.

The boy was so close that Garrison could see them, even tell that they were rough-out leather. Hiking boots, climber's boots, something like that. They were there, right at the curb across the street. Peter was standing there as if waiting for something, a bookbag, a small backpack or knapsack, slung over one high thin shoulder.

Garrison dropped his hand to his lap. And just as he did this, a Volkswagen without fenders and the front bumper removed screeched to a stop at the curb. Garrison heard boys shouting, two in front, one in back, and he saw Peter get in, and then another boy came running from across the street, from somewhere in front of Garrison's car, and he ran around to the other side and got in too, the Volks speeding up the block before the door closed.

Garrison watched in the rearview mirror, and he was about to start up and follow the Volks when it suddenly turned and headed back, passing him and cutting around a car in front before he had time to pull out.

The Volks drove south, straight through town. Garrison let it stay well in front, and when he understood where it was heading, he dropped back even farther and kept his distance until at last he saw it veer to the side of the road and pull up to the thicket cf mesquite trees. He stopped, saw Peter get out, saw the Volks drive off, continuing on up the highway in the same direction.

He stayed where he was. He looked at his watch, counting off the minutes. When he got to eight, he started up again, drove ahead to the mesquites, and turned in. Peter was nowhere in sight. Good. He'd made it beyond the hill.

Garrison went slowly, letting the car crawl at a walker's pace. He wanted to keep the dust down and to maintain the same distance, time the Ford's motion to the boy's loping stride—so that when the car came over the hill, the figure in white would come into view already well along the double row of ruts and on the way into the bunker.

He had no plan, not even a rough idea of what he would do next. He had only the gun, the convulsion that was potentially in it. The gun would make the plan.

He took his hand from the wheel and placed it on the sweater, let it close around the shape of the thing within.

It was loaded, wasn't it? Hadn't he done that? Of course he had! He had a sense of having done it just before he called home. But shouldn't he look? Just to make sure?

Instead, he reached into his pocket and spilled aspirin into his lap. He didn't count. He felt along the folds of the sweater and chewed whatever he could find, whatever had come out. He thought pain was coming. But it didn't.

He braked at the top of the hill and looked out toward the flats. Peter wasn't there! He wasn't on the rutted path that led from the road to the bunker. Was he inside? Was he already inside?

Garrison blinked. The sun was gigantic. He took his hands from the wheel and rubbed hard at his eyes. He pressed the gas pedal just enough to stir the Ford into coasting speed. And then he saw him, far off to the right, all the way into the bend and heading along the road where it was dirt again and curved off behind the bunker and disappeared out of sight.

Garrison fed more gas to the engine.

He took the sweater from his lap and moved it to the seat beside him.

He added pressure to the acclerator, and the Ford responded, crunched heavily toward the cattle guard, gaining speed, the bright orange rectangle boiling up into the windshield.

The road was making a slow turn to the left now, and when it straightened out, Garrison could see his son, eighty, ninety yards ahead—the bookbag, or whatever it was, a dark spot on his back. To his left, Garrison saw the land opening up, an abrupt flattening that seemed to whirl away toward the horizon like a great spinning disc of sand. He saw Peter turn now, turn and start to run, cutting left into the vast terra-cotta expanse, an immense plate of aridity sailing into the sky, everything brown and red and yellow spinning and blending into one mute color, a hue as ancient as earth itself, and above it all, as if only here was where it was, the raging globe of the sun.

Garrison hit the gas, closing the distance to where he'd seen Peter make his turn. He saw the stanchion when he got closer, a plaque of some kind on it, a small sign. But he couldn't see what it said, not until he'd stopped the car and gotten out, the sweater in his hand. He crossed the road, running, saw enough of the raised metal letters to read MESA VERDE NATIONAL PARK. But Garrison wasn't thinking about where he was, only about the figure in white that he could see running on ahead, the dark spot jerking up and down as the boy slowed to a steady jog.

Garrison ran. He put his head down and he ran. The sun was furious, a torrential shower of searing rays that ricocheted off the pink sand and attacked his face. Yet there was no heat in it, just a burning that singed his cheeks and stopped his breath. He raised his head and saw the white flag with the dark spot sixty yards in front and as many yards off to his right.

He adjusted his direction, aimed for a parallel course, but the pace was too fast for him, and with the thing he held in his hand, it was impossible. He slowed to a trot, jammed the gun down under his belt, jerked the belt a notch tighter, and tied the arms of the sweater around his neck. He tried to run again, but he was already winded, and the ache was back, the blunt digging that worked its way down under his collarbone and tunneled from shoulder to shoulder. He stopped to catch his breath, and for a few seconds he rested there, crouched over, head down, hands on his knees. He could feel pinpricks of sweat, a rash of them flowering over his chest and back. But he was cold, terribly cold.

He straightened up, still gasping for air, shading his eyes to see how much distance he'd lost. He looked, caught a glimpse of white in motion, and then nothing.

The boy had vanished.

But where could he have gotten to, when everything seemed so flat?

Garrison pushed the butt of the gun down deeper, tried to swallow to wet his throat, and then broke into a run again, aiming on the diagonal toward the spot where he guessed Peter would reappear. But as he ran across what had seemed land that was uniformly flat, he felt it swelling under him into a wide, shallow dome.

When he made it to where he'd thought Peter would be visible again, there was nothing, just the endless mesa, blinding earth, a seamless stretch of tilting planes. In the distance he could see buttes now, abrupt monoliths of sandstone that rose from the desert floor like sentinels, brutal, watchful, standing guard over an infinite silence.

Garrison turned in a circle, his eyes narrowed against the huge light. There must be arroyos out there, canyons and washes and ravines, all those chasms where the earth would drop away and a man could vanish. Or a boy.

The cave! Breaker had discovered the books in a cave! What was it the letter had said? *A hideaway in a nearby national park, which he has turned into a kind of . . .*

A kind of what? Garrison couldn't remember. But he remembered the night before. Of course. That was where he'd been headed. The cave!

Garrison started up again, moving at a trot, unsure of his direction, finding the land more complicated now, a thing that suddenly vaulted and fell and shot away into drunken, warped planes as if sections of earth had cracked apart and the shards had then come to rest at bizarre inclinations that bore no coherent relation to one another. Nothing seemed to go with anything else, and yet moments ago it had all seemed so solid, so logical, an enormous steaming sheet soaring toward the rim of the world. Again he turned in a circle. But there was no flash of white, no sign of movement anywhere—just the sweat crawling over his torso and the massive pulse of the sun and the curious sensation that he was the last man on earth, abandoned to noiseless extinction on a slag field of angry prehistoric rubble.

He wanted to sit down. He wanted to sit down and die right now. Why go on? Why try? To kill what you loved to save what you loved? It was insane. It was a punishment worse than his own agonizing death. Wasn't it enough to die at thirty-four?

The backpack! A bit of dark moving against the flaring light! Garrison blinked. There! Like a target marked off on a fiery curtain.

He saw Peter, a hazy shape of white revealed against a backdrop of red rock as the boy darted in front of an escarpment a hundred or more yards distant.

Where had it come from, that strange formation? It was like nothing Garrison had seen so far—no geometry to it, but instead the calculus of an inflamed imagination, as if the surf of a breaking wave had collided with a crosswind and in that instant the water had turned to stone.

He couldn't figure how the boy had managed to get up there. The thing looked entirely inaccessible from here. Again Garrison swallowed, but it didn't help. His throat was parched, a desert forming inside him. He gulped air, shoved the gun down again, and set off at a hectic walk, eyes fastened on the figure of his son moving in a half-crouch along the distant ledge. Garrison lunged forward, tripped, fell heavily. He scrambled to his feet and slipped again, recovering quickly. But this time, when he jerked his head back to see where Peter was, the boy was gone.

Garrison stood poised, listening. The silence was like a noise. He turned, looked behind him. Where was the car, the road?

The hell with it! He ran toward the freak outcrop, running on rock now, a shamble of sandstone slabs that overlapped like ice floes jamming through a narrow lane of water. He jumped from level to level and back again until he made it to a jagged gully that cut a clear route to the outcrop. He was on sand again, tripping and slipping on the powdery stuff until he completely lost his footing and fell headlong, the long barrel of the pistol jabbing its angry snout into his groin as he struggled to get back on his feet.

The land ahead lifted toward the outcrop, and it was all scrubbed clean again, no rocks, just a slanting plane of cracked earth with seams and crevices jittering off in all directions, like veins gone crazy, a system of blood vessels deranged by electric shock. He leaned into the sharpening incline and climbed, astonished at the effort he had to exert to keep himself from sliding back. It was like trying to navigate in a funhouse, surfaces shifting as soon as you touched them, the logic of line and vector overturned, a trick the desert could do without mirrors. The land seemed to reel in front of him. He slid to his stomach and held on, jaws clenched, sucking air through his nose. He felt the gun pressed to his belly, and for an instant he didn't know what it was doing there or how he had gotten here, clamped to the earth as if riveted in place, the sun coming to rest on his back like a girder.

He raised his head, judging the strength it would take to get to the outcrop. And what if he could? What then? Would he be able to see Peter from there? Or would it just be more of this maze, a crazy-quilt of shattered geography, empty of everything except the spectacular forces that had created it? The cave! Suppose Peter was already in it?

Garrison heaved himself to his feet, listed leadenly to the side, went down on one knee before he could achieve forward motion again. He went ten yards, twenty yards, but then gravity grabbed him and started to haul him down. It was when he looked up for something to dive to, something to stop his downward slide, that he saw the boy watching, squatting on a slab of rock that leaned against the bottom of the outcrop.

Garrison dropped to his knees and held on.

"Hey!" he shouted. "Over here!"

He knew that Peter saw him, heard him.

"Hey!" Garrison shouted. "Can you hear me? I'm lost!"

The boy was looking right at him, just squatting there. Garrison raised his arm, swung it from side to side.

"Over here!"

He saw his son stand, turn away.

"Wait up!" Garrison screamed. "I'm lost! Can you help me? Please!"

He raised himself as much as he dared, used his shoulders, struggled to move himself forward, inches, feet. It was a distance of not many yards to the end of the incline—and when he thought he was near enough, he flung himself out and grabbed for the lip of the thing with his fingers, caught hold, and pulled himself the rest of the way up. He eased himself over the edge, and then jumped into a kind of grotto and started climbing again.

When he could manage it, he stood for a while and tried to catch his breath. Then he shouted again, shouted for help. He saw Peter turn, move his arm, but not in greeting. Instead, it was meant to wave him off.

"Hold on a second!" Garrison yelled.

He climbed, jumped to the desert floor once more, then leaned forward to launch himself up another incline, its long smooth face like a leer of contempt. But Garrison kept moving forward, shouting as he gradually covered ground.

"I'm lost! Can't you see I'm lost? Hey! Please!"

He saw the boy turn away again.

Head down, Garrison dug in and shoved himself up, scratching at stone that came away in his hands.

It went through his skull like a steel rod.

"Go back!"

Peter's voice. The voice of his son.

Go back!

Garrison looked, saw the boy wheel his arm through the light again, emphatic now.

"Get away from here!"

"I can't!" Garrison shouted. "I don't know which way is back!"

He saw the boy turn on his heel, adjust the straps of his backpack, reach for a handhold on the outcrop.

"Please!" Garrison shouted. "I'll die out here!"

He saw the figure in white in motion, long arms and legs moving for purchase on the outcrop.

"You hear me?" Garrison screamed. "I'm in trouble! Come back!"

The boy kept climbing.

"For Christ's sake!" Garrison screamed. "I'll give you a reward! Just help me!"

The boy was up on the outcrop again, squatting on the ledge, looking back down.

"You hear me?" Garrison yelled. "I'll pay you!"

"How much?"

Garrison got down on his stomach. He shaded his eyes, saw his son seated on the ledge now, the long legs hanging over the side, ankles crossed, arms folded.

He didn't answer. On his belly he skidded himself to the top of the thing he held to, clambered over, dropped to sand again, looked up into his son's face. Part Willa's, part his own, and part something of Peter's own invention.

"I said how much."

Garrison saw the tooth, and thought of all the other things Willa had stamped him with, things you could not see.

"I'm dizzy," Garrison said. "Just give me a minute."

He bent over, tried to smooth his breathing, steady himself.

"I don't have all day."

"Sorry," Garrison said. "I'm knocked out, is all."

He wanted to sit down, lie down, go to sleep. Sleep— that was what he wanted. He wanted it more than anything else. Sleep or death—an end to this.

The gun! Was it visible?

Garrison turned back to the thing he'd just climbed, spread his legs and reached his hands out to lean against it, like a Sunday jogger stretching muscles before his run. Then, with his back turned, he dropped his hands down to make sure the sweater covered the handle of the gun. He buttoned his coat before he turned around and faced Peter again, the boy still sitting with his ankles crossed, his arms folded, his expression as blank as the clothes he wore.

Garrison smiled and took a step closer to the base of the ledge. "I'm bushed. And I guess I got a little scared back there. Sorry. Sorry I had to yell at you."

He saw that the boy wasn't really looking at him, that his gaze was fixed on a point back where Garrison had come from, or maybe it didn't see outward at all.

"It didn't bother me in the least," Peter said, his voice toneless, as if he were talking to himself. "You said you'd pay. How much?"

"You bet," Garrison said, stepping into the shadow the outcrop cast. The sun was lowering now, its descent blocked by the wall of rock Peter sat on. How soon would it turn dark? What if Peter had kept on, vanished again? The road, the car—Garrison had no idea in which direction they lay. "Just trying to collect my thoughts," he said, looking up, smiling, trying to force his son to look down, see his eyes, see the love that was in them. "Would five dollars be all right?"

The boy didn't answer. He banged his heels against the side of the outcrop, and Garrison had to step back fast to keep the powdered rock that came away out of his eyes.

"Not enough?" Garrison said, looking up.

He saw Peter use the heels of his hands to raise himself and then draw up his knees and push against the ledge, hoisting his long body up, a maneuver he executed more with power than with grace. He was squatting on the ledge again, hunkered down but still looking off to somewhere in the distance.

The car? Could he see the car from up there? Did he recognize it?

"No good?" Garrison said. "How about I double it, then? Make it ten." He drew himself up to his full height. He could see the staring eyes—frost-blue like his own—the prominent cheekbones, the slight crinkling around the corners of the lips, like brackets, that Garrison knew in time would deepen to sharply etched tucks. But how was it that Peter did not notice? Had the boy never seen a picture of him, or had cancer already worked so great a change? If he ever looked in a mirror again, would he see his face erased?

No, the little lines around Peter's lips would never deepen to tucks. It took time for that to happen, and there wasn't going to be any time. Without thinking, Garrison moved his hand to the middle button of his jacket. They were already inscribed onto him, the habits of a man hiding a weapon.

"You were a fool to come out here with all that crap on." The boy made a sound like a laugh, and Garrison saw the tooth again, the dwarfed incisor that Willa hid with a characteristic closure of the upper lip, as if she held a bolus of chewing tobacco against her gum. Peter let it show, only it didn't show much. "But you'd be a fool without it, too."

Garrison nodded. "Yes, yes, I suppose you're right. It's not my element, I can see that. Just an impulse, is all. Driving by, and it looked so pretty. Thought I'd do it, come out here and walk around. I should have known better."

"Where's your car?"

"Don't know." Garrison tried to smile. "That's just the trouble."

"You don't understand me. Where did you *leave* it?"

"Oh," Garrison said. "Sure," he said, moving his

feet a little, trying to position himself so that he could see Peter better. "All I know is that it's on a dirt road back there—right opposite some kind of concrete structure that's got the park's name on it."

"You didn't go through the booth?"

"Why, no," Garrison said. "I didn't see anything like that. There some kind of entrance you're supposed to go through?"

Again the boy ignored his question.

"What were you doing on the road?"

Garrison looked around, as if the answer were about to issue from the rocks behind him.

"Just driving," he said. He reached into his pocket for his cigarettes, his lighter.

"What *is* your element?"

"Pardon?"

"You said this isn't your element. What is?"

"Oh, I don't know," Garrison said. "Streets, buildings." He laughed. "Maybe not. Hell, maybe the truth is I don't have an element." He lit a cigarette, cupping the lighter against the wind that was blowing now. "People, maybe. How's that? Maybe it's people that're my element."

"Jesus fuck," the boy said, shaking his head.

"What's that?"

"Nothing," the boy said. "Forget it."

Garrison stepped closer. "You got something against people?"

"I said skip it," the boy said, his voice flat, his face still lifted to some distant point.

"Well?" Garrison said, and again he looked around as if the terrain were coaching him, telling him what to say. "Will ten be enough?"

The boy said nothing. He sat staring off, his position unchanged. It made Garrison think of Willa, the way the boy appeared not to hear your questions or value them enough to answer.

"What's your name?" Garrison said.

For a while he held his head up, waiting, and then he looked down, still waiting. But all he heard was the meaty silence of the mesa.

"Mine's Farrar," Garrison said. "Roger Farrar."

He heard the boy laugh, or do something close to it, a kind of snicker, but a breathier sound than that, something he seemed to produce by raising his tongue against the passage to his nose and forcing out air in a short hard burst.

"Something wrong with my name?"

"It sounds phony," the boy said. "Like a name somebody made up."

"Somebody did," Garrison said, dropping his cigarette and stepping on it. "My mother."

"Roger Farrar," the boy said, savoring the syllables, reciting them as if their absurdity should be obvious to anyone.

"It's a pretty lousy thing to poke fun at a man's name," Garrison said. "Especially when he doesn't even know yours."

The boy got to his feet, his motion so sudden that Garrison was pierced with a quick stab of alarm. But when Peter jumped to the ground beside him and was standing there—*so close, his son's body so close*—Garrison wanted only to lift his arms and reach, reach and draw his child close, hold him and make everything all right. Or not lift his arms, but instead lower his hand, reach under the sweater.

"Mine?" the boy said. "Yes, of course. I'll give you two hints." His eyes rested on Garrison's face as if he saw nothing, saw instead back into his own head. "My mother is a world-famous anthropologist. A *cultural* anthropologist, not that I expect you to know what that means. Her best-known works are *The Dream System of the Havasupai,* Yale University Press, and *The Syntax of Linguistic Play Among the Ute Indians,* Cambridge University Press, which is a book that's won three awards but which Mother turned down. Every single one of them. And do you know why?"

Garrison shook his head. He wasn't really listening. He was watching his son's face, reading it for signs.

"Because to accept an award from someone, one must believe that person to be superior to oneself. Mother knows there is only one person that is superior to her. And do you know who that is, Mr. Roger Farrar?"

"I'll bite," Garrison said. "Who?"

"Me."

"And your name?"

"Guess."

"Couldn't begin to."

The boy snorted, the same airy sound that seemed to come chiefly from his nose. "I didn't think so," he said, and then made the sound again. "*Your* element."

"Hey, come on," Garrison said, resisting the impulse to raise his hands to his son's shoulders, touch him, struggling against the enormous pressure building in him to hold the boy, embrace him, make him stop whatever he was and be something else, something that helped people when they cried out. "Let's be friends, okay? I mean, I'm not such a bad fellow. Just a guy who got himself lost."

The boy stared, his eyes glazed over.

"What about your old man, then? What's *he* like? He an anthropologist too?"

The blank face stiffened.

"That is why I agreed to guide you back. Because of what he is like. You will pay me a certain sum, and it will be added to the money I have, and when I have money enough, I will undertake a trip to go see him. It will be to reward him for what he is like."

There was a long silence, and in it Garrison heard his son's breath issuing through his nostrils. But mostly what Garrison heard was the fall of his own heart.

"Really?" he said when he was able to speak. "Where's that? Where is he? I don't understand."

The boy looked at Garrison curiously. Perhaps he was seeing Garrison for the first time.

"What earthly business is it of yours? Let's move it," he said, turning away, grappling for a handhold on the outcrop, pulling himself up and then looking back and motioning for Garrison to follow.

"Hold it," Garrison said. "I thought you were taking me back. Isn't it the other way?"

The boy's face was without expression, and he offered no reply.

"You want more than ten? Is that it?"

"Fifty," Peter said.

"All right, fifty," Garrison said. "But it's the other direction, isn't it?"

"When I have finished what I came out here for."

"What if it's dark by then?"

"I have a flashlight," the boy said, his voice flat, mechanical, a machine simulating speech.

"Suppose it doesn't work?" Garrison said as he labored to find footing and push up.

"Don't be afraid," the boy said. "Unless it is fear that is your true element."

"I'm not afraid," Garrison said, reaching for something to hold to as he shoved himself up. "Not for myself, anyway." He clambered onto the ledge and lay there on his belly, trying to catch his breath. At length, he rolled over and looked up into his son's eyes, saw them lidded against the infernal light pouring from deep in the western sky.

"Exactly," Peter said, his words scarcely audible. "But you mustn't worry about me, Mr. Farrar. I know the way in the dark."

13.

It TUNNELED INTO a monolith of sandstone rock.

Think of the face of a feeding shark, the chin resting on the desert floor, the brow more than a hundred feet above, and in the middle, flopped open under the overhanging snout, the mouth of the cave itself.

It was huge. And with the sun behind it and the face of the monolith all in shadow, you could see where the eons had laid down their different stripes, lines of earthen colors that swept in lateral arcs across the roof of the gaping throat.

There was a wooden ladder leaning against the lower lip, except it didn't reach all the way there. The rungs went to just above the chin, where the rock notched in to form a little shelf. Garrison could see it was from there that one had to claw and crawl to make it the rest of the way. It was almost straight up.

"Stay here," Peter said, and started for the ladder.

He was already on it, going hand over hand, halfway up, when Garrison roused himself and quickly covered the ground to the foot of the ladder.

The boy turned, looked down, snarled, "No!"

But Garrison had started up and he kept going.

"It's private!" the boy shouted.

"No problem," Garrison called back. "You just go on ahead and make believe I'm not here. I'll wait for you up there at the top of the ladder. Fair enough?"

The boy did not answer. He turned back to his climbing, and by the time Garrison stepped off the ladder,

Peter was nowhere in sight. But how had he made it the rest of the way so fast?

Garrison leaned out as far as he dared, trying to see up into the mouth of the cave. But it was impossible. The entrance was almost directly overhead.

He took a breath and then started inching his way to the top of the shelf, turning himself around slowly when he got there, rotating his body by small degrees until he faced away from the monolith. He drew his knees up carefully and dug in with the heels of his shoes, pushing hard to keep himself from skidding back down. What he sat on was an oval of rock less than six feet the long way, graded to more than a thirty-five-degree drop. If you slid off, then you went all the way—unless you could somehow catch on to the ladder without knocking it back off from the face of the rock.

From where Garrison sat, the mouth of the cave was at least twenty feet over his head, a climb that meant clinging with one's fingertips to a near-vertical plane of powdery sandstone. Was that how Peter had done it? And done it so fast that Garrison hadn't even seen him make the ascent? It had to be. There was no other way. Unless there'd been a rope ladder or something of the sort, something that Peter had pulled up into the cave after him and that Garrison just hadn't noticed at first.

He yanked the Buntline out from under his sweater, broke it open, checked the chambers, slapped the cylinder back into firing position, and then stuck the pistol back down inside his belt. He looked at his watch—he had to blink hard to focus the hands, the numerals. It was close to six.

The desert was losing its color now, the coppery pink changing into something that glowed darkly, like ingots of base metal. And it was cold, and getting colder.

He got a good grip with his heels, and then risked the slow removal of his jacket. When he had it off, he undid the second sweater from around his neck and, very carefully, a little at a time, he pulled it down over the first one and got back into his jacket, flipping up the collar and lowering his head to his knees.

For a long time he sat this way, waiting—waiting for what?

The wind was rising now, smacking at the face of the big rock. Garrison could hear it howling across the mouth of the cave, a groaning mournful sound, a trombone let all the way out into one long note that dragged across the bottom of some grotesquely vacant span.

I will undertake a trip to go see him. It will be to reward him for what he is like.

Yes, he would do what he said. He was that kind of boy. And when he found no father to kill?

Garrison stared at his watch again. The crystal disk stared back like a man with a neon monocle. He lifted his vision to the fabulous mesa land before him, and saw it humming in the spreading fire of sunset. It looked like a zone succumbing to lethal subterranean energies, the pressure of subatomic particles in furious motion. He heard the wind again, the hollow rush of its breath as it blew across the open mouth of the cave, and then another sound, an almost human sound, as the rocketing air probed deeper into the cave's throat and made it moan as if rock could suffer pain.

Garrison listened for the sound again, heard it, and was again amazed. It was extraordinary, the music of natural forces and formations, a virtually human song, like an incantation, as if a lone Indian stood within the cave and called aloud to his gods.

Yes, Garrison thought, *I should pray.*

He would find his way back alone. He would have to. For Andy's sake. *Dear God, for Andy.*

For a time, Garrison's lips moved silently, shaping the names of his sons, and then, with earth and light disappearing before him, he began, "Dear God in heaven—"

It was Peter! That sound. It *was* human.

The boy was chanting or crying. Up there, somewhere

up there inside that thing, the boy was calling or sobbing. It couldn't be the wind!

Garrison leaned away from the niche that held his back. He stayed squatted down and let his heels creep out, edging himself down along the shelf. Moving quickly now, he made a full turn and faced the wall of rock, took a breath, closed his eyes, and stood up. He put his hands to his mouth, cupped them, and shouted with the wind.

"Peter! I'm coming, son! It'll be all right!"

He reached out his hands, grabbed what he could, and started up.

He climbed as if teeth were snapping at his feet, his mind empty of everything except his intention to reach Peter, protect him from whatever it was that had made him cry out. Rock powdered in his hands, and when it didn't powder, it tore at them, and his hands slipped and grabbed again, and when his hands didn't hold him, his feet did, and he just kept going up, hand over hand, grabbing with his chin, his knees, until somehow, without thinking, without knowing what he was doing or how he was doing it, he had his arms where he could use them to heave himself the rest of the way up. He lay on the lower lip of the cave, gasping, his face and hands ruined. He reached down for the gun, pulled it free, and then rolled away from the edge and stood up. He held the gun out in front of him, and with his other hand he rubbed at his eyes.

The neck of the cave was dark, but, farther in, glimmers of light like fireflies winked on and off. He could hear Peter—a sound like wailing, only it had words in it. But at this distance, Garrison couldn't make them out— nor could he see where they came from. Crouching, his arm held stiff in front of him, the gun poised for what might come at him with a slither or a rush—snake, puma, wild boar—he moved forward, rubbing his eyes to see better, to clear away the paste that seemed stuck to them.

"Pete! What's in here with you, son? Tell me! I've got a gun!"

He couldn't see what was around him. He could only see the brightening arrangement of the daubs of light that flickered up ahead. The floor of the cave was angling steeply down now, and from the hollow report of his footsteps, Garrison could tell that he was entering a cavernous space. The air, too, was suddenly colder, and the whimpering chant that issued from the boy was a chorus of sound now, echoing and reechoing snatches of speech that reached for Garrison's heart and turned it inside out.

Daddy, oh Daddy. Please, Daddy, I promise to be good.

Garrison's shout was like the voice of the cave itself.

"Peter! Where are you, son! My God, son, I'm coming!"

He hurled himself forward, heedless now of what might be underfoot, arms outstretched like a child seeking help. And as he ran, the figure in white picked itself clear of the darkness, the image sharpening, filling in. Trousers. Windbreaker. Face.

Garrison slowed, stopped, and then, lifting his feet and letting them down as quietly as he could, he came closer, tiptoeing, until he stood almost directly over the seated figure of his son.

For a time he stood there, looking and listening, paralyzed, and then he slowly lowered himself into a squat in front of the rigid body, the staring, sightless eyes.

I love you, Daddy. Daddy, Petey love you so. He won't be a bad boy anymore. Oh, see how good he is? Don't go away, Daddy. Please? Please don't go away.

The legs were crossed Indian fashion, the arms draped so that the hands rested on the thighs, palms out. The back was arched, the face as stiff as wood. In one hand lay a stick, like a splinter from a shipping crate, the head

of a very small bird stuck to the end that pointed away
from the boy's body. In the other hand a tiny pouch sat
on the open palm, the thin black cloth cinched by what
looked like a shoelace, the cloth too slack to be holding
much of size. A semicircle of candles mounted in brown
paper bags weighted with sand stood to the rear of the
boy, and just inside the crescent of light, Garrison could
see a large alarm clock standing on the cave floor.

"Peter?" he murmured, searching the blind eyes.
"Son?" he said, and pushed the gun back under his belt
and pulled the sweaters down over the butt.

"*Anasazi!*" the boy screamed, just as the alarm clock
shrieked to life. His eyelids closed and Garrison saw
them squeeze as if pressing away a vision. When they
opened, the hand with the pouch came up at him and
punched at his chest, a soft, weary blow strong enough
to knock Garrison off balance. It rocked him back on his
heels and the momentum carried him all the way over.

"Get away from here! Get away!"

The boy's voice was wild with wrath, and yet the
volume was subdued, almost a whisper, a hiss. His face
was twisted in rage, the lips curled in contempt.

"Filth! Corruption! Get away!"

"Sorry," Garrison was saying over and over, his
hands raised in front of him in a gesture of apology.
He got to his feet and backed away, his hands still lifted
in conciliation. "No harm done. I'm sorry as hell,
honest."

"No harm? Is that what you say? No *harm?*"

Garrison kept backing slowly, arms held wide in testi-
mony to the sincerity of his regret.

"I thought I heard you calling for help."

"*I?* I, calling for help? Don't be absurd! I do not call
for help—of that you may be certain."

Garrison was too far away to see the boy clearly now,
too far away to tell exactly what he was doing. Something with the stick and the little black bag? He could
see Peter crouching beyond the half-circle of lights, but it

was impossible to tell what he was doing. And then Garrison saw him come forward and stoop to extinguish the first of the illuminated paper sacks, going noiselessly from one to the next like an altar boy.

"I won't be able to see!" he called when he saw Peter bend to the last of the candles.

"I will," the boy said softly, and then blew the candle out.

It was a darkness the skin could feel. Garrison reached into his pocket for his lighter.

"What are you doing?"

"Just getting my lighter."

The boy's voice was much closer now. "That won't be necessary. Trust me," the boy said, and then Garrison heard his breathy laugh. "How did you get up here, Mr. Farrar?"

"How?" Garrison reached his arm out to see if he could touch something, orient himself, feel something, a reference point. He felt weightless, dizzy, a thing careening in space. "I climbed, is how. How the hell did you think I did it?"

"It is a difficult climb. Difficult and dangerous. What motivated you to try such a thing?"

There was nothing behind him. He took a step back and tried again. "I thought you needed help. You sounded like you were in trouble or something."

He heard the laugh, a kind of rasping of air, nasal and sneering.

"And how long were you present before the alarm went off?"

"What alarm?"

"The alarm clock."

"How long?"

"How long."

Still nothing, no wall, no surface that said, Here is where you are. "It went off just as I got here. Hey, what the hell is this, anyway? How come you're making such a big deal over nothing?"

"Over nothing?"

"That's right," Garrison said, and this time he took the lighter out of his pocket.

"You have something in your hand. What is it?"

"I told you. My lighter."

The sudden brightness was like a bomb going off. He shut his eyes against it, and when he opened them, the beam of the flashlight was still there, a prod jabbing into his face.

"Quit it!"

The light stayed where it was.

"I told you it wouldn't be necessary. You can put your lighter away now."

"Then take that damn thing out of my face!"

"Just as you say," the boy said, and directing the beam to one side, he stepped past Garrison and led the way out.

All the way back, they went in silence, the boy in front, Garrison struggling to keep up. No, if he had done it, then he would never have made it back alone. Even in daylight, chances were he'd never have figured it out. But that wasn't why he had not acted, had not used the gun.

All the way back, he kept replaying what he'd seen and heard in the cave. What did it mean? A trance of some kind, something so deep that the boy never heard Garrison declaring himself.

Peter? Son?

He wanted to do it again now—catch up, reach for the high square shoulders, turn him around, say, *Peter! Son!* But instead Garrison walked and climbed in silence, exhausted, in pain, feeling neither fatigue nor agony but instead confusion and a terrible dread. The things the boy had said as he sat there dreaming aloud, wasn't that the real Peter, a child suffering with loneliness, a child crying out for love? Wasn't that why Garrison hadn't used the gun? Or was Peter the other boy, the boy who enjoyed his power to impart fear, the boy for whom torment seemed a delight?

And there was something else, something Garrison had noticed just before they'd made it back to the mouth of the cave and to the rope ladder that was there all the time, there where Peter had yanked it up after him to make sure that he wouldn't be followed. Just before they'd gotten to the rope ladder, Garrison's eyes had adjusted to the dark.

He'd looked to the side a little. Not much at first—because he was afraid to take his eyes from the path of light in front. But when he did, he saw them clearly enough—all along the side of the cave nearest him, one after the other, each one held to the sandstone by a single nail driven through an eye, pinned there in a line, every one of them spiked to the stone—pictures of men, magazine ads for things like whiskey and sailboats and vacation spas. A totem to what? Paternity? And what was in that little black pouch?

Anasazi. It was what Peter had screamed there at the last. Gibberish vomited from the bottom of a trance? *Anasazi.* A name? A curse?

He saw Peter stop, sweep the spear of light in a short arc, and then strike out again, correcting his course a shade to one side. Moments later, Garrison could see the stanchion, the car.

"That's it!" he called ahead, knowing it wasn't necessary, wanting only to break the long silence, roll back the night with words.

But the boy said nothing. Nor did he give a sign that he had heard. He did not quicken his pace nor slow it, but instead continued on in the same loping motion, passed the stanchion, crossed the road, and then circled the car, training the flashlight over it and here and there pausing to look closer.

"That's it, all right," Garrison repeated, still looking for words to turn this around, to stop whatever seemed to be happening.

"Unlock it."

"It's open," Garrison said, and crossed the road.

"Open?"

"Yes, of course," Garrison said. "There's nothing in it. Why should I lock it?"

"Perhaps you neglected to lock it. Perhaps you were in too great a hurry."

"In a hurry? To go sightseeing?" Garrison pulled open the door and turned on the headlights. "I'm starved," he said. He got in and started the engine. "Pretty damn thirsty too. How about you?"

The boy stood away from the opened door, said nothing, his flashlight playing on the undercarriage of the car.

"Buy you some supper if you like."

"You a tourist?" the boy said, still studying the car.

Garrison could feel the Buntline stabbing at him now that he sat. It was still stuck under his belt, and it dug at his belly and groin.

"I guess that's what you'd call me."

The boy was bent over, apparently looking more closely at something.

"Don't you think it unusual for a tourist to be using this road?"

"Hey, look," Garrison said, "I've had enough of this, okay? I'm offering you supper. Do you want it or not?"

The boy stood up and came closer.

"You owe me fifty dollars," he said, his voice almost a whisper again. "And I suggest you see to that tire."

"You bet," Garrison said. "Look," he said, "I'm going to give you sixty because twenties are all I have."

"Fifty," the boy said.

"Okay," Garrison said. "Take sixty now and give me the change tomorrow."

He held out the bills, saw Peter shift the flashlight from his left hand to his right hand and then reach for the money with his left hand.

"Look, pal, I don't feel so well. I'm staying at the Oasis Inn. It's a long ride, and I've got to get started. How about you? Can I drop you off somewhere? Buy you some supper?"

"Poor Roger Farrar," the boy said, and with his knee he pushed the door closed.

"Don't you want a lift somewhere?"

"Good night, Roger Farrar."

Garrison turned the car around. But before he pulled away, he reached over to lower the window on the passenger side.

"The Oasis Inn!" he called. And then, to make it stick: "When you get ready to give me my change! Unless, of course, your word is no better than your manners!"

He watched him in the rearview mirror for as long as he could. But then the road bent toward the cattle guard and the light behind him winked out. The porthole windows of the bunker were in darkness when he passed the double row of ruts. But the security lights blazed a great circle of crazy day, a hole punched out in the dominion of the night.

He looked for the Land Rover, the Jeepster, the Sprite. But he was going too fast to see anything beyond the piñon trees standing in a line, and the grim, humped form of the half-sunken dwelling that slumbered sullenly nearby.

14.

IT WAS TAPED to the door so that he had to lift it to fit his key into the lock, a yellow sheet of paper torn from a pad of telephone message forms. He couldn't see what it said until he got inside and turned on the light, and when he did see, when he flipped the form over to see if anything might be written on the back, he went to the telephone and dialed the desk.

"This Jack?"

He heard the wheedling voice, saw the wispy red hair ringing the moist, naked mouth.

"At your service."

"Explain this, mister. And do it fast."

"Oh hell, man, don't go getting all bitchy on me now. It's *cool*. You're safe. Old Eric just wants to like have a little chat, you know? Otherwise, he figures he might have to make a call to a few people. Hey, man, *relax*. You can *trust* Eric, you know? We ain't about to tell anybody. Come on, Ben—we're your *friends*. Now you know the way out to the place, don't you?" Garrison heard the chewing sound, the wet sound of the man sucking his teeth. It sounded like the man was chewing a rubber band. "I mean, you been out there, right?"

Garrison sat down on the bed, his mind racing for the thing to do next.

"How did you find out?"

He heard a sigh of satisfaction, and then the voice again, high with enthusiasm for the tale.

"Well, it was just putting two and two together, you

know? I mean, this lady calls up. Very class chick, I can
hear. Says she's calling every goddamn motel in the
Four Corners area, starting with Cortez—because she's
looking to see if her husband is maybe registered, and
even if he isn't, what she wants to do is leave a *message*
in case he shows up, you know? And she goes, like his
name is Ben Garrison, but you can't miss him because
he's this real handsome dude with this real silvery hair
even though he's only a young guy, you know? She
says, hey, Ben Garrison, the famous director, right?
Now I ask you, did it take a pretty ace cat to put it all
together? You with me, Ben? So meanwhile, I give old
Eric a call, right? I say to myself, hey, man, how come
Bennie is strung so tight? And like he's using this other
name, you know? And then there was old Lynn telling
me how the dude was asking how to find the crazy professor woman. You see what I'm saying? And then
there's that ace chick in New York calling everywhere in
sight, knocking her brains out with the special operator
and all, how she's got to find this guy who's so famous
and everything. Well, shit, old Eric, he just thinks you
might want to keep everything real cool, you know? So
what he wants is for you like to hustle your ass out there
to the place and just shoot the shit with him, see where
maybe your needs and his needs are moving in the same
direction. And there's this other thing. Like he wants
you to know no hard feelings for fucking with his
woman. He's cool, you know? Bitch come out there to
get her things and cut, and old Eric, he really squared it
with her. So it's cool now, you understand. Hell, man,
we're from Barstow. We *got* this town. You understand
what I'm saying?''

Garrison passed his hand in front of his eyes and then
dropped it gently to the bed.

''You forced that girl on me. Was it your friend's
idea?''

''Man, we didn't force shit on you. Hey, my man,
you're a big boy. Like you got total control to dick or not

to dick. But listen, Bennie, the girl's cool. She really likes you, you know? Eric just had to straighten her out. So relax, man. We're reasonable. We understand these things. It's just a little complication, is the point. You and Eric'll work something out. It's what, man, nine? Clock here in the office says nine something, right? By ten o'clock, you'll have it all under control. You understand?''

"What did you tell my wife?"

"*Nothing,* Bennie, *nothing.* Old Jack just said thanks for calling and hope to see you out West one of these days. Sounded like a real foxy chick, man. New York, you know? Hey, I can dig it. Famous director? Now, Lynn, she's nothing special—no class, right? But, shit, that's *quim.* Eric finds 'em. I tell you, the man's got a gift. So you go talk to him, hear? Hell, he'll likely throw the whole goddamn infield at you for the right kind of consideration. You know, enough bone? Which reminds me, seems there's this talk around about you hanging out at the high school. Now what Eric figures is this. The crazy goddamn professor lady's got this *kid.* You following me, Mr. Garrison, sir?''

Garrison slammed the phone down. He looked at the square of yellow paper, the message written on the back.

Dear Ben: I would be most honored to make your acquaintance. Yours most cordially, Eric. P.S. Please call by at your earliest convenience. I believe you know the way. No need to worry about missing me. I am always here. Sister Lynn looks forward to seeing you too.

He balled it in his hand and squeezed hard.

Leave the motel? No. Tomorrow was Saturday, no school. Peter might show in the morning. He could risk it until morning. Jack, Eric, whoever they were, they wouldn't act for a while. First they'd wait him out, sweat him. Meanwhile, he'd made contact and set up a second meeting. Tomorrow. He could hold out until morning, maybe until noon. Then break for somewhere else, anywhere else. With Peter. Get the boy away from here, away from where they might start looking.

Andy! He'd completely forgotten. Was he sick, hurt? Joan could only be calling for *that!*

But Ben didn't call Joan. He called me. Why didn't he call Joan directly? I didn't know at the time, and he certainly didn't volunteer anything. But now that I know what had happened just before he called, I guess he figured he'd blow it, give it all away. God knows, he was in a state when he talked to me. He'd never have been able to handle it with Joan.

As soon as he got me on the phone, he started giving me instructions. First, the number he was at—a phone booth, I later found out, because he didn't trust the switchboard at the motel. Then he said I was to call Joan, do it that instant, see if there was any emergency either with her or with Andy, but to do it in a way that wouldn't alarm her, just putting myself on the phone with her to see if anything developed. As soon as I knew everything was all right—or wasn't all right—I was to call him right back and give him a report.

I called back minutes later, told him everything was fine, nothing out of the ordinary, that she was only trying to get in touch with him to tell him to take it easy. I could hear the sound he made, the release of breath, the relief. He was in a bad way. On the verge of hysteria, I think. He wanted to make sure I called Joan in the morning and told her I'd heard from him, that he was scouting locations in Utah. I was to make sure there wasn't something else she'd been trying to reach him for, without letting her know that *he* knew about her call to him. Then I was to call him at the Oasis Inn in Cortez, Colorado, and let him know what she'd said.

What was behind Joan's trying so hard to reach Ben that night? It turned out it wasn't anything that mattered

in the long run. McIver had called and asked for Ben,
and when Joan said he was on the Coast talking to people
about a movie, McIver went crazy, started screaming
threats, told Joan he was going to see to it they lost every
dime they had, that Ben Garrison had locked assholes
with the wrong boy. He told her that, just to begin with,
he was going to get a goddamn injunction against any
goddamn film with Benjamin Garrison's name on it, and
so on and so forth. All Joan was trying to do was to get in
touch with Ben to tell him she didn't give a damn what
the family had to go through for him to do the work he
wanted to do, that she and Andy were with him all the
way. End of report.

But I never got it through to Ben. When I called the
Oasis Inn that morning, eleven o'clock New York time, I
was told there was no Benjamin Garrison registered
there. It didn't matter that he'd forgotten to give me the
name "Roger Farrar," because Roger Farrar wouldn't
have been there the next morning, either.

But we talked more that night. It was just before he
went out to the commune, if that's what you call it. Not
that Ben mentioned any of that at the time. He only said
how glad he was everything was all right at home and
how I was to find out more in the morning, and to keep
on calling Joan every so often, say I'd heard from him,
reassure her, do my best to give him the time and distance he had to have.

For what, I wanted to know, did he need time and
distance?

It wasn't that he was willing to put the problem of
Peter before me, to see what I'd say, what I might recommend. It wasn't Ben's way to shift the question to
someone else, not when the question went to the very
heart of what Ben was as a man. But he let me know
there was trouble, that it had to do with Peter, that it
somehow involved Andy's future safety.

I remember saying, "Look, without telling me more

than you want to tell me, answer me this—is there any way to be sure that Andy's welfare is threatened?''

"There's no way to know for sure," he said. "And besides, I hurt and it's hard to think.''

I said, "Then let me help you think. Tell me what I need to know so that I can think aloud with you. Ben, tell me. For God's sake, man, let me help.''

"I can't," he said. "It's not your trouble. It's mine.''

I said, "Ben if it's your trouble, then it's Joan's trouble. So at least discuss it with her.''

"No," he said. "It won't be her trouble. I'll see to it that it won't be. Not any more than it has to, anyway.''

And then he tried to change the subject to other things that were on his mind—the list he'd given me, had I been working on it?—and so on. I tried to quiet his anxiety about all that, to convince him there was nothing to worry about, that he could count on me to handle everything just as he'd asked and just as I thought he would want me to.

It was then that he said to me, "Hey, Steve, you've been a good buddy to me for a lot of years. Hey, good buddy, I know you wanted to give me your coat that time. I know you did.''

Just that. No more. There was a silence on the phone. I let it stand, waiting. It was he that ended it, the words so hushed that he may not have meant them to be heard.

"I don't know. I can't think. And even if I could, it's too far over my head. It's bad—but there's nobody else who can do it. I'm the only one, and I don't know enough. All I've got to go on is what I can guess. But who can ever know for sure? I'm just a *man*. Who can tell me? Oh, Steve," he said, "I hurt so much. Oh, God, I'm really hurting now, you know?'' And then his voice got loud, very hurried but very clear. "Swear you'll take care of my people—that you'll do all you can. And swear you'll make them understand.''

He didn't wait for me to swear anything. He knew he

didn't have to. He'd said what he needed to, and then he hung up.

I rang right back, of course, but he was gone. Or he was there in the phone booth and was not going to answer.

What choice did he have? He couldn't risk their making good on their threat.

He drove straight there from the phone booth, and when he got to the road that led to the trailers, a girl was waiting out on the highway, another one just like the two he'd seen so far. She waved a kerosene lantern at him when he slowed to make the turn, and then she got up on the hood of the car, like a harbor pilot sent out to bring a ship into port.

He didn't need her to show him the way. And besides, there was no missing the asterisk of trailers and the tall pole with pennants on it rising from the trailer in the center of the spokes. Once you were on the right spur road, you had to drive straight ahead. But the girl on the hood kept swinging her lantern as if she guided the Ford through treacherous shallows.

He rolled down the window and shouted for her to get off, that he couldn't see with her up there. The girl nodded, but she stayed where she was, swinging her lantern in still wider arcs, frantic sweeps of light and shadow that made the name on the back of her jacket jump in and out of the dark. It was like a sign going on and off—*Eric Eric Eric*.

Without warning, she slid from the hood and Garrison had to brake hard. She came around to the open window, held the lantern to his face, said, "Good," and then slapped the roof of the car.

He saw other girls now, ten, twelve of them, some with flashlights, some with lanterns. They stood in a group to one side of the trailers, and if they noticed him, they gave no sign.

"Out!"

It was the girl who had ridden in on his car.

Garrison slid from behind the wheel. The door was still open when he felt someone taking him by the arm, someone who'd come up from in back as if from hiding. It was the other girl, the one he'd seen the first time.

"Where's Lynn?"

"I don't know no *Lynn*," the girl said as she steered him toward the trailer that stood in the center of the starred formation.

"The one with you. I gave you a lift, remember?"

"This here's the way," the girl said.

The man who stood at the door of the trailer was tall and fat and black, tall enough to have played professional basketball, fat enough to no longer be able to, and black enough to pass for a pure-blooded African.

"Welcome, Benjamin, welcome," the man said. "I give you greeting," he said, not moving from the doorway to let Garrison enter, but instead blocking the way until the girl had kissed his hand and announced, "You are in the presence of Eric."

The black man stood aside and spread his arms.

"I am Eric," he said. "Please, Benjamin, make use of my property, all that you see, and know that we are brothers."

The black man bowed and held out his hand to indicate that Garrison should move with him to the back of the trailer. But Garrison kept to his place near the door.

"As you will," the man said, smiling. "Now then, shall we proceed straight to the heart of the matter?"

Garrison nodded.

"You understand, Benjamin, that coming here is an admission of guilt. Why are you trafficking with that Stafford child?"

"Mind if I smoke?" Garrison said.

Eric smiled. "I counsel against commercial tobaccos,

but I will make an exception in your case. Yes, you may smoke in the presence of Eric.''

Still smiling, the black man turned away and moved toward the rear of the trailer, inclining his head toward what seemed to be a pile of blankets. Garrison followed and saw the foot. It wore a thong sandal fashioned out of a material made to look like velvet.

"Now to business, sir," the black man said, turning back to Garrison. "You will find me eminently reasonable, for I am a man of peace. Civilization is my watchword. Do I wish to hand you over to the appropriate authorities? On my honor, I do not. Observe, for example, my continued protection of this woman whose harlotry is like a gob of spit in my face. Did I chastise her as she deserved? Or did I not feed to her the fatted calf despite her vileness?''

The huge man bent to pull away the blankets, but whatever was revealed, Garrison couldn't see. He only saw the foot move a little, as if the mere lifting of the blankets was a torment to the body that was under them.

The man laughed and clutched his crotch and shook the heavy genitals his tight trousers displayed.

"Oh, yes. Eric fed this hussy the fatted calf, all right. Right up her ofay rosebud. Wouldn't you say so, sweet sugar?''

The man still leaned toward the girl, cocking his head to one side, one hand cupping an ear as if he hearkened to a distant answer. And then he turned on Garrison and roared with laughter.

"Yeah, fill your lungs with cancer if you like, you honky shit. I know you messing with that Stafford kid. Now how much bone you got on you, and don't fuck me with no jive!''

Garrison didn't light the cigarette that he held. Instead, he put it in his pocket and got out his wallet from his breast pocket with his left hand. "Almost a thousand dollars," he said, and with his right hand he slowly drew the Buntline from his belt, raised it, pointed it at the big belly, and fired off the first round.

The man Eric just stood there, staring, amazed, unchanged except for the small hole in his leather shirt. Garrison walked up to him, raised his arm higher, touched the tip of the long barrel to the cleft just under the nose. But he did not fire again.

The black man seemed to be smiling. He took a small step forward. Garrison could feel the gun pushing into the groove above the roots of the man's teeth.

"Motherfucker," the man said.

He put his hand to the barrel and moved it to one side. "Look what you done to me, you motherfucker," the man said.

He gave a shallow sigh—and then, still smiling, he collapsed.

It was deserted outside. Not one of them was in sight. There was no time to get the girl dressed, to go looking for her clothes. He covered her with a blanket and carried her back out to the car.

It wasn't until he was at the highway and had to turn one way or the other that Garrison realized he couldn't go back to the motel. But he turned left, toward town, and then left again at the mesquite trees, and he didn't stop until he saw the stanchion in his headlights, and even then he drove another two hundred yards to make sure. When he shut off the headlights, night closed in like a crazed mob, the darkness so dense it was like a noise. He turned in his seat to see if the security lights ringing the bunker placed a glow somewhere in the distance. But there was nothing, just the crowding weight of the desert night and, over and over, in his ears, the quick, brittle snap of the Buntline firing—a simple, unvarying code, strict, impeccable, precise.

"He really put it to you, didn't he?"

The girl lay in the space between the seatback and the door, her legs up on the seat, her body curled tight.

When she answered, it was the voice he'd heard the first time—mocking, belligerent, tough.

"Well, you put it better to him, Brother Sunshine."

Garrison leaned his head against the wheel. "God forgive me," he said, but his voice was just breath, nothing in it but air, and then there was something harsh and gagging right behind it, the bile rising fast in his throat. He banged open the door with his shoulder and heaved himself into the road, coughing a long, watery mess as he fell.

He lay there for a long time, trying not to think, trying to pull the night inside him and blot everything else out.

Sleep. If only he could sleep.

When he thought he could get back up again, he dragged himself to his knees. But then a wide, thick blade drove a wedge between his organs, and then, into the space the blade had cleared, a frenzied nozzle sprayed short, bright bursts of ice pellets. He went back down and stayed there, even when the pain had passed.

He slept like that, in the middle of the road, while the girl drew her knees up higher and dozed off for an hour. She didn't look for him when she woke up. Instead, she pulled herself over behind the wheel, turned the key in the ignition, and drove away.

15.

COLD WOKE HIM sometime before first light. He came
awake with his arm up, reaching, flailing the air to
snatch at the covers that must have worked their way to
the foot of the bed. Why couldn't he reach them? He
tried reaching with his feet, scissoring his feet in the dirt
road to catch the edge of the blankets and tease it up to
where his fingers could get at it. When nothing worked,
he opened his eyes to see where the blankets had slipped
to. But it was too dark to see anything, and so he lifted
himself on one elbow and started feeling around for the
switch on the table lamp.

Had someone moved the bed? Moved the bed and
opened the door and the window? It was freezing. It was
like sleeping outside on the ground.

It was then that Garrison understood—and remembered. He closed his eyes and tried to figure out how
he'd gotten down here on the floor of the car. It was so
hard—and he could feel the hump over the drive shaft
digging at him, jabbing at his belly. He turned a bit to
ease it away. But it didn't do any good. He put his hand
down to feel why the thing was jabbing at him like
that—and then he felt the gun.

He pulled it away and laid it down next to him on the
floor of the car. The girl must be colder than he was—
nothing on, just a blanket to cover her. Had she opened
the windows to get some air? He sat up, thinking to close
them.

He'd forgotten. And now he really remembered. He

remembered throwing himself clear of the car to keep up with the string of acid that had been tied all the way down there inside him and that someone had started yanking on, pulling it out of him so fast it was going to rip something loose if he didn't catch up.

He wasn't in a room. He wasn't in a car. He was nowhere. He stood up, looked for the direction the car was in, and when he couldn't see anything, he put his hands out in front of him and moved around in the darkness, feeling the air. At last he gave up and got down on his hands and knees and kept crawling in one direction until it got softer, and then he stopped and let one shoulder go down and followed it with the rest of his body, gingerly coiling into himself, trying to make of himself a small warm ball, and sleep. In the morning, when the light came up, he'd see the car. That was the big thing, the only thing he was going to think about. He wasn't going to think about the other things—because maybe they hadn't really happened. None of it had happened, not Eric or Willa or Peter, or even the voice of Dr. Charles Flood.

Garrison drifted into sleep again, face to face with a small, honey-haired boy, eyes closed, as his father's are, because he is sleeping too. Will he wake if his father bends to kiss him and to raise the blanket higher, to nip it up to just under his chin?

Lavender. It is the color of his quick bright breathing . . .

No, not lavender. Lavender was all red. Red lips moving. Because someone is chewing. Rubbery wet sounds as if sucking down a tooth. Tooth stuck too high in the gum. Won't come down because it can't get over the bone. Fix it. Bang it. Once. Very fast. Very hard. Like something snapping. *There.* Good. Solved! Something else? One thing? Two? Three? Four, five . . . too many to count. Don't count, clock counts. Hear it ticking in the empty rooms. Look under the beds, the beds, the beds—closets, closets, closets. That's where they are! In all the closets! When the alarm goes off, they'll pop right out. Surprise, surprise! But first think of the word that says the game is over. The word . . . lavender. No. Dawson? Edwards? Eagle? Ott? The word . . . they'll come out giggling and happy if he can think of the word. It isn't fair! They told him the word and they warned him to remember and now look what he's done, he's forgotten it, an easy word, a hard word, *carcinoma!* Carcinoma? Pancreas? Like that. Onco . . . a hard one, one . . . he's . . . never . . . heard . . . before. "Not *fair!*" he shouted in his sleep.

Something was pushing at him.

Stop it! Trying to remember the word. Just give me a minute, a . . . little . . . more . . . time . . .

"Hey, Garrison! Hey, Roger or whatever the hell! Come on, Brother Sunshine, get the fuck up!"

Anasazi!

He had it and then he lost it. But he stood with his legs spread and his arms up ready for when its wings turned it around and sent it gliding back at him again. Ana—

"Okay," Garrison said, and breathed through his mouth and dirt came into it and he started choking and couldn't stop. The girl was pounding him on the back, using her fist to do it, and it helped but it wasn't helping enough. He crabbed his body along the sand, scrabbling for air because he was going to suffocate if he couldn't stop it from going out and get some new air in.

Garrison caught a small breath and held it, and then he caught a second one and held them both, struggling to his knees to make it easier. His eyes were closed, and when he tried to open them, the lids wouldn't move, crusted shut as if permanently closed.

"My eyes!"

The girl quit pounding on his back and took his head in her hands. He could feel her turning him back and forth, examining his face, checking to find the best use of the sun, and then he felt her fingers lightly brushing across his eyelids, soft, almost tender strokes that swept carefully outward from the bridge of his nose. "Just dirt, man. You got all this shit in your eyes. Hold still." She kept brushing at his eyes, deftly, lightly, murmuring how it was all right, just try to open them now.

The light was mammoth. The desert at dawn, all that color and space, was like a crash of cymbals that sounded in his eyes.

"Jesus Christ Almighty," Garrison said. "My God, my God."

"What?" the girl said. "What's wrong?"

He looked at her and saw her face backlit by the scattering fire of the rising sun. "Nothing," he said, and then he noticed. "Where'd you get those clothes?"

"Went back," she said simply. "Like that's what I'd gone out there for in the first place, you know?" She was kneeling in front of him, her hands flat on her thighs. She leaned down a little to look up into his face.

"He didn't do that to you, did he?"

"Do what?"

"You got like scratches all over your face."

"No," Garrison said, remembering the climb to the mouth of the cave. *Anasazi.* He looked at his hands, saw the dried blood. "No," he said, "it was something else."

"Yeah," the girl said. "Like there's always something. So what now, lover man? You understand you offed the fucking dude? I mean, like what the fuck are you going to *do?*"

He got to his feet.

The gun!

He ran into the road, turned slowly, eyes stinging in the orange light.

"In the car!" the girl called. "Stuck down between the seats. That's how come I knew you were around here somewhere. Hey, can't we get the feedbag on?"

"I don't know," Garrison said, and started for the car. It all came rushing in on him now, the thing he'd done, how it changed things, cranked everything up into high gear. *Speed*. Whatever he did now, one thing was sure—it had to be fast. He pushed the door open for the girl to get in. "I don't know," he said again. "Just sit a minute and let me think."

"Yeah," the girl said, "that's the thing to do. We'll figure something out." She moved over and sat close to him, her leg against his and one arm up on the seat behind him.

"But just so you know I think you did right to waste that goddamn coon. Fucking jiggaboo had it coming, man. I'm telling you, like you don't know the half of it. Those chicks out there, he made them fucking *zombies*, man, feeding them all this shit in their arm and like doing this number on their heads?"

Garrison wasn't listening. He was trying to think, but it was hard to figure out where to begin. The girls—they could identify the car. And wouldn't Jack know anyway? The room—he'd left the composition books in the room, and on the cover of every single one of them was the name Peter Stafford. They'd get the name Garrison from Jack. He'd tell them New York, the big-shot director. *Joan!* The police would get in touch with Joan! And Willa! They'd *all* know! *Peter* would know! They'd stop him, lock him up until cancer finished it. And then there'd be Andy and Peter all alone!

"Like he liked to do you in the asshole, you know? Big fucking dirty spade. Had them all scared shitless, rocked right out of their fucking gourds, man. I'm telling you, man, it was like being in a goddamn concentration camp, only he didn't need no fucking iron bars. You did right, man. You ought to get that other fucking creep, that Jack. Like it wasn't just that the cat was doing a gig for him, you know. I mean, working that goddamn motel. I mean, the fucking fag was like *gone* on Eric. You know what I'm saying? No lie. Used to make us *watch*. It was sick, man—I'm telling you, it was weird."

"I want you to do something for me," Garrison said.

"Stop talking now and listen. It's important. You've got to do it fast."

"Anything, man," the girl said. She pushed up to raise her knees to the seat, turned toward him, pressed her lips to his hair, spoke softly into his ear. "I'd do anything for you, no shit. You saved my fucking *life*, man."

He started up the engine and turned the Ford around. As he covered the distance back to the stanchion, he tried working it out in his head, what he'd say to Peter, what he'd do next. It seemed to make sense. And if it didn't, then it didn't. Because it was his only chance.

He told the girl. He told her what to do.

"If the woman answers the door, then you say you've been attacked or something and you need a glass of water, or you've got to use the bathroom, or something like that. Just as long as you don't give her the idea it's so bad that she's got to call the police. If it's a man, then you do the same thing, okay? And maybe once you get in there, you'll see the boy—tall, as tall as I am, dark sort of hair. His name's Peter. No, forget that! Don't use his name. But maybe he'll come to the door, and if he does, then it's no sweat."

And then he told her what to do.

"Can you do it?"

The girl nodded emphatically. "Farrar, right?"

"Right," Garrison said. "And here's where I'll be. You see the post over there, the sign for the park? Right here. All clear?"

"I got it," the girl said, and nodded solemnly. "Don't worry, man. Like I really owe you and I know it, you know?"

"Just do your best," Garrison said.

He drove her to the cattle guard, let her out, turned the car around, and headed back to the stanchion.

He saw her coming. She was alone.

He leaned over and popped open the door. He could see he was doing everything fast, speeding up routine motions. He was a man running now. He understood it would be this way from here on out, that now to the finish he was a murderer, a man on the run.

"Freaks!" the girl said, getting in and rolling her eyes in exasperation. "The whole fucking world is just freaks on top of freaks. What kind of people live like that, you know? Like in a fucking *hole* in the ground."

The expression reminded him.

"That's what you called it—" He was about to say *yesterday*. But Garrison was suddenly aware that he didn't remember when the girl had said it, and then, with a shock that made his heart race, he understood that he'd lost track of the sequence of events. What else had he forgotten? Something that would trip him up?

The front left tire! That's right. Peter had said it needed air again.

"Well, that's what it *is*," the girl was saying. "A big bathtub upside down. Fucking nutty as Eric's place, him and his fucking flags."

"What's it like inside? Describe it to me, the layout."

"Nothing," the girl said, moving up close to him again, fitting her backside in tight against his. "Just rooms. A big letdown, a drag if you want to know the truth. It's just like anyplace else, only real dark. Oh, man, I'm so hungry," the girl said.

"He's not coming, then. The boy."

"Him? Oh, sure. He said he'd be along in a while. Sonofabitch was eating and wouldn't give me any, you know?"

Garrison felt between the seats and got the gun out and stuffed it in his pocket. But the barrel was too long and he couldn't get it all the way in.

Front left tire. Reload the pistol. He had to start making a list. He had to *think*.

"You see the woman? Or a man?"

"I didn't like see anyone but the kid. And I didn't hear

anyone, either. So what are we going to do, you know?
You got it figured yet?''

Garrison shook his head. "We'll just wait, is all," he
said.

"Yeah, man, but I could like eat my arm, you
know?''

He got out his cigarettes. "Here," he said. "Sometimes this helps.''

He got out and checked the tire. It was down, all right.

"Hand me out the keys," he said, leaning in at the
window.

There was a spare in the trunk. He banged it with his
fist. It was hard. He lifted the rubber mat and saw where
the jack was. He found the instructions pasted to the lid
of the trunk. He slammed it down and got back in behind
the wheel.

She pushed close to him, put her hand on his belly,
moved it to his fly, and started to undo the zipper.

"Why don't we make it while we're waiting?" she
said, reaching in, taking him in her hand, then using two
fingers and her thumb.

"The boy'll be here any minute," he said.

"Shit, man, you wasted a guy. So what's the big deal
if you get caught balling?''

She had her head down, looking at him, as if she
needed to check the progress she could feel her fingers
making.

"You got a nice one," she said, and made two little
kissing sounds. "I seen some guys is awful.''

"Later," he said. "The boy." He tried to move her
hand away, but she had her chest against her arm now
and her shoulder in his belly.

She looked up at him, wetting her thin lips with her
tongue, the same girlish posturing to appear seductive.
Yet it was just this, the flagrant gesturing, the graceless
directness, that made Garrison want her.

"I'll just give you head," the girl said, lingering over

the words, licking her upper lip with a pointed tongue. "Like it's protein, right?"

"Please, not now," he said, and pushed her away. She smacked the door open and looked back at him before getting out. "Shit, man, I'm *scared,* you know?" He saw her face break, the effort to stop the tears.

The girl turned away and headed off, cutting a wide circle around the car. Garrison watched her go, the red satin jacket, the jeans rolled to midcalf. His eyes followed the slow path of the red—and saw white—the windbreaker. And then the rest, coming at a trot.

Garrison watched, fascinated. It was like a dance, the slow red, the fast white, and behind the march of the two colors, the immense orange of the shimmering desert.

He reached under the seat and got the box of shells. He opened the gun, heard the crisp snap firing in his head, the modest sound of death. He removed the single spent casing, fitted in a new cartridge, pressed it in tight, closed the cylinder, and then bent down and put the Buntline and the box of ammunition back under the seat.

When Garrison looked up, he saw Peter just yards away.

"Thanks for coming!" Garrison called as he got out of the car and moved around it to the other side. "I don't think you'll be sorry."

The boy stood off from the car at near attention, his long dusky hair combed wet against his skull, a sharp part dividing it almost in the middle. He wore the same climbing boots, but he'd changed to dark brown twill trousers and a checked flannel shirt, and he had the arms of a thick gray sweater looped around his neck and the white windbreaker zipped all the way up.

"That will be for me to decide," he said, looking off to where the girl still wandered in a circle.

"Of course," Garrison said, stepping closer, reaching for a cigarette. "All right, it's this. I need you to hide me. And get me food. I was thinking that maybe I could use your cave."

"What about her?"

"Her too, if that's okay."

"How much are you proposing?"

"Fifty a day. A hundred a day. Whatever you say."

The boy eyed him. His arms were folded, and he undid them, bent quickly to snatch at a small stone and fling it a short distance away.

"Serious trouble, I take it," the boy said, not looking at Garrison, studying the ground as if considering another stone, looking for the best one.

"It's just as the girl said. It couldn't be worse."

"You killed someone?"

"Maybe," Garrison said, amazed to hear his answer. "I don't know. Maybe I did."

"Why?"

"The girl," he said, nodding his head in her direction.

"How?"

"What difference does it make? The point is, I'm in trouble and I need a place to hide for a while. Yesterday you implied you had no use for people, so I figured my having done what I've done wouldn't bother you too much. And the other thing you said was how you were looking to get money to make a trip of some kind. So it works out for both of us. You're a logical person. You can see that I'm right."

The boy bent down again and lifted some sand into his hand, and then tossed it straight up as if testing the direction of the wind.

"My cave is private. Who was this man you say you killed?"

Garrison looked off to see where the girl had gone. He needed time to do this right. Talking to Peter was like playing chess—or draw poker. You had to watch every move, take nothing for granted. "Dirt," he said. "Just dirt." He looked back at his son. "The girl's hungry," Garrison said. "Me too. So? Do we have a deal?"

The boy reached into his pocket, took out a penknife, pulled open a blade, and began using it to clean his nails.

He was smiling, but only slightly, yet it was enough to reveal the stunted tooth, the miniature incisor that rode too high on the gum.

"How did you know where I live?"

Garrison grinned, trying to cover up his surprise.

"Easy. You said your mother was a famous anthropologist. The girl knew. She lives around here. She told me."

He saw Peter glance in the direction of the girl, as if by looking at her he could determine the truth.

"Yes," the boy said, looking back at Garrison, "everyone around here knows about my mother, her house. They think it odd. But that is only because they are ignorant. I suspect that you too are ignorant, Mr. Farrar. But it now occurs to me that you may also be useful. Would you like to be useful?"

Garrison smiled, astonished. The more he heard, the more he saw, the more convinced he was. "Why, yes," he said. "Sure."

"I have something in mind," the boy said. He moved to the car and leaned his back against it, and then, with the same sudden gymnastic motion Garrison had seen once before, Peter hoisted himself onto the hood, and folded his arms again.

"Yes," the boy said, "I believe we might work something out."

Garrison dropped his cigarette and stepped on it. He could feel the snake in him opening its jaws. He wanted to get out his aspirin, swallow a handful of them. But he sensed that he shouldn't do anything but listen.

"You bet," Garrison said, stepping in closer. "What exactly do you have in mind?"

"The girl," Peter said, shifting ground. "Why on earth would one murder for a person like that?"

"It's beside the point," Garrison said. "The point is, I did it."

"On the contrary," the boy said. "Tell me."

He unfolded his arms and went back to working the

blade of the penknife under his nails, his expression blank again.

"I was protecting her. It's as simple as that."

"Protecting her? How would you even come in contact with that sort of creature, let alone with someone who would want to interfere with her?"

"It's complicated," Garrison said. "We don't have time for it now."

"Time," Peter said, slowly shaking his head. "What would you know about time? But of course if you don't wish to tell me, I could always ask her. Or, more effectively, just call the police. Not that I am entirely convinced that you in fact did murder someone. After all, Mr. Farrar, it is not every day that someone who's chased you through the desert, begging you to fetch him back to safety, comes knocking at your door on the morrow to declare he's in the meanwhile dispatched some citizen and needs your charity yet again. Even you can appreciate that, can't you?"

The boy seemed very pleased with himself. He regarded the fingernails of one hand, and then set about working on the other.

"Mr. Farrar? Are you paying attention? Surely you can see how absurd this must all seem from my point of view. For example, what sort of weapon did you use? Show it to me."

Garrison took another step closer, and held out his torn hands. "These," he said.

The boy smiled.

"How ridiculous! You earned those wounds yesterday when you had the audacity to pursue me into my cave. One could not strangle someone with hands like those."

"I could," Garrison said. "I did."

The boy slipped quickly from the hood. He stood inches from Garrison now, and was almost as tall.

"Could you do it again?"

"What do you mean?"

"Murder. Kill. An encore, if you will."

"Why?"

"*Why?*" Peter said, raising the penknife, inspecting the little blade closely, and then clipping it shut. "I'll tell you why, Mr. Farrar. For an eminently better purpose than protecting *that*." Peter nodded at the girl, who had given up her pattern now and was crossing and recrossing the road as if measuring off its width.

"Which is?" Garrison said, for the first time noticing the sweater, noticing how the boy wore it with the arms tied around his neck.

"Protecting *me*. Protecting *yourself*."

"Who from?"

The boy laughed, that curious effect he produced by forcing air through his nose, almost a snort of contempt, but not exactly.

"You protect yourself from *me*, Mr. Farrar, because if you are telling the truth, then I am now in a position to turn you over to the authorities, am I not? And as for whom you will be protecting me from, we will have time to discuss that once we've come to terms." The boy raised his hand and admired his fingernails again. "I trust we are agreed, Mr. Farrar. Frankly, I don't really see what choice you have. Do you? Unless you are lying for some reason—which, of course, the police would doubtless be delighted to determine. We enjoy in Cortez a particularly unhumorous breed of law officer, I can assure you of that."

The pain was shrieking in him now, but Garrison tried not to show it. He gritted his teeth and kept his eyes fastened on his son's eyes.

"I see you are beginning to comprehend the merit of my remarks. Excellent, Mr. Farrar, excellent. We're going to get along famously, you and I. You are the answer to Peter Stafford's prayers. I need you, and you need me. It is the simplest principle in human society. Indeed, mutual need is the very foundation on which civilization is established."

Garrison could speak again now. But he wasn't sure what he should say.

"I'm hearing you right. You want me to kill someone. Is that what you're getting at?"

The boy laughed. "Why not?"

"Who?" Garrison said. He knew what the answer was going to be. But he had to hear it.

There was nothing in the boy's face when he answered. He might have been commenting on the weather or asking someone to pass the salt.

"More dirt."

16.

HE LOOKED AT the sweater, the heavy gray wool knotted around the boy's throat. The space between them was airless, unimaginable—a ferocity that could only exist between father and son.

The boy stared at him, waiting—and Garrison stared back.

"We'll take a trip," Peter said. "You and I. In this car."

Garrison nodded.

"You understand," the boy said. "You have no choice. You understand that, don't you?"

What more proof did he need? He could turn around to the car now, open the door, reach under the seat, get the gun. Or he could put out his hands and take the ends of the sweater.

"I've killed someone," Garrison said. "But you're not afraid of me, are you? I want to know something—I want to know how you can stand here threatening me and yet not be afraid of me."

The boy laughed, breathy, sneering.

"You are not the quality of man who inspires fear. On the contrary, you are the quality of man in whom fear flourishes. You fear me, you fear her, you fear *that*," the boy said, jerking his chin over his shoulder to indicate the great wheeling disk of earth. He looked back at Garrison, leveling his half-lidded gaze on his father's stricken face.

"I am waiting for your answer, Mr. Farrar."

He had only to lift his arms, take into his hands the ends of the sweater.

"It's the way you said. What choice do I have?"

"Exactly," Peter said. "Living is like that. It eliminates the choices."

"Yes," Garrison said. "I guess it does."

The boy smiled slightly, and Garrison saw the tooth.

The unbelievable had happened, was happening. He had come here to save his son, both of his sons, at last willing to believe that he might have to kill one of them to save the other. But events had brought him to this, and events were happening too fast—and he couldn't think, because whenever he tried to slow things down to think, events raced on ahead of him and he couldn't keep up.

How many days did he have left? He'd lost count.

Was he losing his mind? Was that what had made him do what he'd done last night?

Garrison heard the snap of the Buntline firing. And then he heard his son's voice:

"Stay here. I'll be back in less than an hour."

"Yes," Garrison said. "All right." And he lowered his head as if surrendering himself to whatever might happen next, a power as implacable as the cancer that was working away inside him.

He didn't see Peter cross the road. But when Garrison went to open the trunk, he saw the figure of his son already well along into the distance, loping in the hazy light, set on a course not toward home but out onto the blazing mesa.

He guessed the boy's objective.

The cave.

It was hard, working with the tire. His body was empty of strength, and pain filled all its emptied spaces. His palms were shredded from the climb to the cave, the wounds dried now so that it hurt to close his hands.

The girl came to watch, and she helped him where she could, picking up the lug nuts when they fell to the sand, working them back for him into the right fitting in the wrench.

Garrison worked slowly, his motions sluggish, like a man laboring through very deep water, and he let himself listen to her talk, answering when he had to, trying to find some comfort in the simple humanity of her chatter.

"No shit, man, I can't stand it, I'm hungry. Won't the kid give us any food? Maybe what I should do, you know, is hike up to the highway and hitch a ride into town. I'd do it except you'd have to give me some money again—because like, dig it, the fucking nigger took everything off me, the forty you gave me plus everything else, which was only the six dollars I had, but it was like everything, you know?"

"I gave you eighty," Garrison said. "But maybe I'm wrong. Maybe I made a mistake."

"Yeah, well, like it matters a lot now, you know? Forty, eighty, the spade's got it to spend in jungle-bunny heaven. Honest to shit, you really cooled him, man. Out of fucking *sight,* you know? Oh God, you should of seen the two of them, that creepy Jack and him. Make you puke. But it wasn't all bad, you know? I mean, it was a place to crash, and the dude took care of you good sometimes. I mean, like it wasn't *all* bad. And some of the sisters was like family, you know? I don't mean family like *my* family—because they're the pits, the absolute pits, man. My family is. But anyhow, so what do I do now? And where did the kid go? I mean, like I'm starving, and I just want to know. You think I should cut for town? I could bring you something back. Hey, you think I wouldn't come back? Is that what you're thinking? You think I'm thinking about splitting because of what you did? No way, man, *no way.* You ain't the first cat who's into something heavy. Hey, no shit, man, I've seen some *things.* Eric did a girl out there—you know that? He *did.* This little skinny chick, skinnier than me. Said it was God's will how she crapped out, you know? Balled her in the ass and just like closed the door on the chick, no shit. That Jack knows. He was *there*. So what's next, man? I got to know. No shit, Brother Sunshine, I'm getting real jumpy, and I got to hear you say something. Is that it? You're pissed at me on account of I tried to go down on you when you didn't want no head? That's it, right? You can tell me, man. It's okay.''

Garrison shook his head and kept on tightening the lug nuts.

"Yeah, well, good. But so what about the kid? You see him just walk off into nowhere like that? I mean, are we waiting on him for something? If he went to get us something to eat, he went the wrong way, didn't he? I mean, there's nothing out there but just more of what you see right here, you know? So is that it? Like we're waiting for something?''

Garrison nodded and stood up, the earth yawing at his feet. He put his hand against the car to steady himself.

"Can you put those things away for me? See if you can get this stuff in the trunk.''

"The tire?'' the girl said, her small eyes slitted up at him.

"Leave the tire. Just the other stuff.''

He lit a cigarette, leaned against the car, smoked. When he had the strength, he got the tire up, rolled it to the back of the car, and hefted it into the trunk. He saw Peter as he lowered the lid to close it, the boy materializing in the section of landscape the raised lid had blocked off. He was standing motionless, looking in the direction of the cave. And then Garrison saw him raise his left hand as if he had just decided to put something in his windbreaker. Then the boy turned and started for the car, coming at that same long-legged lope, pausing before he crossed the road to stuff whatever it was deeper into his pocket.

But there'd been enough of it showing for Garrison to guess the rest, a bit of black cloth.

"Get in!'' the boy called from across the road.

The sky had turned the color of muddy ice as they headed away from the stanchion—a deep, almost brown color that laid thickly against the reddening mesa. The girl sat in front, her arm resting on the window carriage, her fingers drumming on the roof of the car. The boy sat in the back, his stiff body pressed into the corner just behind the driver's seat, so that Garrison could not see him in the rearview mirror. Instead, he leaned over the wheel and peered through the windshield at the desert preparing itself for rain, all that bland color suddenly vivid, garish.

As they neared the cattle guard, the thought first occurred to him. He slowed down.

"Don't you think you should tell your mother something? Don't you think she'll worry otherwise?"

Garrison had to strain to hear the answer. "Mother flew to Berkeley yesterday, to present a lecture at the university. And as for her worrying about my absence, you needn't concern yourself. Please drive faster."

Garrison saw the Jeepster, but no Land Rover.

"There's no one in your house? No one at all?"

"No one," Peter said.

The girl was suddenly all commotion, as if overcome with a flood of ideas. She pulled her arm in, flung herself around, and hopped up on the seat with her knees.

"What's it like, living in a crazy place like that? Like it must be real *weird*, right?"

The boy didn't answer. Or if he did, it was nothing Garrison could hear.

"I'll bet you get kidded a lot, you know? Hey, they used to kid *me* a lot, too. For being skinny and for having this nothing nose. Shit, man, they just want to rag you— it doesn't matter about what. I'm from Barstow. It's a bigger town than this. Than Cortez, I mean. California, that's where it is. So where did you say your mom was, Berkeley? Where's that? And like what's your name? Mine's Lynn. So what's yours?"

Garrison listened for the answer, heard nothing. He

was still wondering what he would have done if Peter
had said Willa was there.

"Turn left," the boy said as they neared the tangle of
mesquites.

"Where are we going?" Garrison said, checking to
see if he could spot Peter in the mirror.

"Town."

"Far *out!*" the girl said, jiggling in the seat, her face
still turned enthusiastically toward Peter. "Food! Oh,
Christ, am I going to scarf me some food!"

Garrison turned north at the highway.

He looked for Peter in the mirror again. "They'll
probably be watching for this car."

The boy looked out the window as if he had not heard.

"Hey, come on," the girl was saying, "he's Roger
Farrar and I'm Lynn Slansky. So how about you? Like
what's your name, you know?"

"Stafford!" the boy screamed. "Peter! William!
Stafford! Now shut your mouth before your name goes
down on my list!"

"Your list?" The girl laughed and turned to face Garrison. "His *list?* What the fuck does he mean, his fucking *list?* The fucking kid is *bananas,* man—he's strictly
out of his tree, you know?"

"Stop the car!" Peter screamed.

Garrison slowed a little and turned in his seat.

"It's all right," he said. "Let's take it easy."

"I said stop the car! Do you hear me?"

Garrison had never seen anything like it before, such
gigantic fury, but the face masking it so thoroughly
calm, the face even placid.

He drew the car to the side of the road, unsure of what
the boy would do if he didn't.

Peter had thrown open the back door and was pacing
alongside the car before it came to a complete stop, his
hands on the front door, pulling it open, acting with
shocking speed before Garrison had time to react. The
boy reached in to take the girl by an arm, yanked her

halfway out, and then, pivoting, whipped her free of the car and heaved her, like a sack of salt, feet first into the brush.

"This her shit?"

It was Peter screaming, his face unchanged, utterly impassive. Garrison looked and saw that the boy had a bundle in his hand. It must have been the girl's clothes, things she'd stuffed in a man's shirt and stowed on the floor in the back.

"Easy," Garrison said. "Easy now. Yes, I guess they are," he said, getting out on the other side.

As he came quickly around the front of the car, he saw Peter drop the bundle where he stood, kick closed the back door, swing himself into the front seat, and reach back out to slam the door.

"Come on, goddammit!" Peter screamed.

Garrison picked up the bundle and went to the girl. He knelt down and helped her to sit up, and he saw that her face was white with fear.

"You okay?"

"I think so, man," the girl said. She had his hand and she wouldn't let go. He had to use his other hand to get his money out. He laid a stack of twenties beside her.

"You see this?" he said. "There's a lot here. Be careful with it. Go away from here. Try to put it all out of your head. None of it concerns you. You'll be all right, I swear. Get yourself to a bus and just go somewhere. Maybe Barstow. I don't like leaving you like this. Do you understand? Will you be all right?"

The girl nodded. He could see it was taking all she had to hold back the tears.

"No shit, man, I'm scared. It's all too much, too much shit coming down. That kid, I'm telling you, he's like real *off*, you know?"

"I said come on!" Peter screamed. "Now!"

"I know," Garrison said, touching the girl's hair. "That's why you're safer if you're not with us. He's my son and I'm sorry for the way he is. But I have to see to it

that he doesn't hurt anybody else. That's what I have to
do, and what you have to do is just try to forget about
everything. Will you try? Will you forgive me?''

The girl nodded and wiped at her nose.

"Put this in your pocket," Garrison said. "There's
maybe two hundred dollars here. It'll take care of you for
a while if you look after it. Will you promise me you'll
do that?"

"Yeah," the girl said, letting go of his hand to take up
the money. "And hey, man, like thanks, you know?"

"You bet," Garrison said, and touched her hair again.

He stood up, turned to the car, saw his son's face in
rigid profile, the eyes riveted to the road ahead. Garrison
looked back at the girl and smiled.

"In your pocket," he said. "Don't forget."

The boy banged on the horn, a single, commanding
blast. As if it had been a signal to the heavens instead,
the dark sky shuddered violently and its fierce answer
plunged to earth.

17.

THEY LEFT CORTEZ like that, Ben and the boy riding beside him, the frenzied rain hammering at the big blue Ford, Peter demanding that Ben drive faster and faster, and Ben doing it, in a hurry now to bring it all to whatever conclusion God contrived.

At Denver, they got on the Interstate going east, having stopped only twice—once, very briefly, in Cortez, for the minute the boy had asked for, and later, in Grand Junction, for food and gas. From there they drove straight through, stopping only when they had to, Ben doing most of the talking, doing what he could to draw the boy out. But Peter grew more and more silent as the miles sped on to New York, answering rarely, saying less and less, until for hours Garrison's son sat unmoving, beyond hearing, his face stone.

But somewhere near Grand Island, Nebraska, Peter roused himself as if shaking off ropes. "You're going east. I never told you to go east."

"Sure you did," Garrison said. "Don't you remember? You said New York."

The boy said nothing in reply. He folded his arms, settled back against the seat, and closed his eyes.

His hands hurt. His eyes hurt. But nothing hurt like the thing that ripped at his belly. It wasn't a snake anymore. Now it was a nest of serpents, their chewing incessant.

Why not now—while the boy sleeps?

He'd seen the way the boy had dealt with the girl. One day it would be Andy—and the result inestimably worse.

"You asleep?" Garrison said as they crossed into Iowa just after dawn.

He wanted to stop now, rest his eyes. He wanted to pull over to the side of the road and close his eyes for an hour or two. The sun was in his face. But he didn't lower the visor or reach for the dark glasses that lay on top of the dash. He wanted to see Iowa, and remember. But somehow he could see nothing but the sunrise as it unfolded on the hood of the car, particles of brickish grit glittering rosily in the rising morning light. Wherever he looked, he saw pink dust—despite the cloudburst that had showered the Ford before it left Cortez.

"Pretty sunrise," he said. "You ought to see it."

But Peter did not answer.

Garrison glanced at the shelf where his sunglasses lay lodged between the dash and the windshield, and saw how red deposits had collected in drifts. He looked at the backs of his hands, turned to study his son's face, and saw coppery flecks stuck to the skin where it was contoured or creased. He imagined that the air itself might be made of coral motes—as if, when the doors were closed in Colorado, molecules of color had been trapped inside, so that a wavelength of light was captured, and the physics of the high mesa was seized and carried all the way to Council Bluffs.

"I'm from Iowa," he said, not expecting an answer anymore. "From farther on east. Town called Ames. You wouldn't want to see it, would you?"

Garrison looked at his son to see if his eyes were open. They weren't. But the boy had moved so that his back rested against the opposite door now.

"Don't know if I'd want to see it myself. Haven't been back since I buried my mom. Oh hell, I can't say I ever loved it really. Ames or even Iowa. It was a hard life."

Garrison shook his head as if correcting something.

"For my folks, I mean. I lit out when I was about your age. Thing is, I've never been really crazy about any particular place. Except Maine."

The boy's face was lifeless, the eyelids lowered. Perhaps he really was sleeping.

"You ever seen country like this before? Sign up there for Cumberland. Lord God, *Cumberland*. It's like going to an old movie. I had an uncle in Cumberland. Dead now, of course. Like my mom and dad."

Garrison gripped the wheel. With his torn hands, it hurt to do it, but he held tight.

"How about your dad? He's alive, isn't he? Well, sure he is. Isn't that why we're going to New York?"

His hands were bleeding again. He moved them on the wheel and squeezed.

"My dad was okay. Hell, I thought he was tops. Still do. It was awful, leaving them—my folks. But I was a kid. I guess I thought it would be more awful to stay."

The Ford dropped down into a long underpass lit by fluorescent bulbs, a milky wash of sickly colors. When it came out into sunlight again, Garrison had to blink hard.

"Sometimes a kid doesn't know much. I sure as hell didn't. Not like you. Christ, I didn't know *what*. Except how much I wanted to have my own people. You know. A family."

He reached for a cigarette. But then changed his mind.

"Beats me how come I was that way, but that's how I was. Couldn't get married fast enough—and I did it, too. When I was twenty."

He thought he saw Peter move, but when Garrison turned to look, everything was the same, the boy resting against the opposite door as if he'd been tacked in place.

"Twenty. Can you imagine? Smart woman, though. Worlds smarter than I was. Lord, I loved her—but I didn't know what love was until we had a child. A son."

Garrison turned in time to see the boy's eyelids flutter. But that could happen when you slept, couldn't it?

"You hearing any of this? Well, I'm just talking. Jawing is what we used to call it back home. My God, *jawing*. Hell, it's good to think back. You ever think back? I wonder what a smart boy like you thinks about when he can go anywhere with his mind that he likes. Me, I've never been a great thinker. But that's okay. I'm not complaining. Sometimes it's better not to think too much. But I'll bet you don't agree with that."

He saw a sign for Des Moines, and it made something tighten inside him.

"Des Moines," Garrison said. "Ninety-four miles, by God. Ames is just north of there. You think we've got time for a little side trip north? But we're in a hurry, aren't we?"

He thought of Andy, the miles farther on—and he tried to count the days that were left. But it was no use. He'd lost count. He was losing everything.

He rubbed his eyes, and started again.

"I guess I didn't do enough thinking for her. My wife, I mean. She just up and left one day—with my son. Went into hiding. Gone. Just *gone*. You ever hear of anything like that? Great God, how I loved that boy. Still do. Maybe more than ever. But he doesn't know a thing about me. He was only a year old. I don't suppose he knows how I kept on looking for him. I guess he thinks I didn't care. Well, that's natural, isn't it? A boy gets taken away from his father, never knows his dad, never knows what he's like. Unless, of course, his mother told him. But you can guess what she must have said, seeing as how she probably didn't want him missing his dad. Or something like that. Hell, I don't know. You hungry? I could go awhile, but I'll bet you could use something pretty soon. Peter? You awake?"

Garrison looked and saw his son's eyes wide open.

"Hungry, right?"

"This car," the boy said. "It is a rental, correct?"

Garrison heard the Buntline. It was like a stick of wood snapping in his head.

"That's right," he said. "Why?"

"Hertz, isn't it?"

"Yes, I got it from Hertz."

"Des Moines will be a big enough city. I want you to turn it in there, exchange it for another vehicle."

"Turn it in?"

"They might be looking for a blue Ford sedan," Peter said.

"They?" Garrison said. "You mean the police?"

The boy wasn't looking at him when he answered. Instead, he stared straight ahead through the windshield.

"The girl will talk. You were a fool not to have shut her up. Assuming, of course, you haven't been lying to me. But in any event, it is perfectly all right with me if they apprehend you—providing you have first done what I've asked."

Garrison slid his hands to the top of the wheel, and he took hold of it with all his strength.

"Listen to me," he said. "You listen closely now. If I were a killer, then why not kill you? That way there'd be no one to worry about."

"You won't kill me," the boy said.

Garrison swallowed. It was hard to make his throat work.

"I might have to," he said. "Maybe you'll give me no choice."

"No," the boy said, turning to face him. "You can't. Nothing could make you do it."

He was choking. He couldn't breathe. His arms and legs were buzzing, and his face went slack, numb.

"Something could. There's one thing that could."

"No," Peter said, "there's nothing. You couldn't because you're my father."

For an instant he thought he would faint. But he held on, unable to speak, unable to do anything but bring the car to the side of the road and pull off the highway.

He turned off the motor and put his head down against

the wheel, his eyes closed, the blackness they looked out
on turning and turning as he listened to Peter's voice.

"How long did you intend to keep up this farce? It
was you in the stands watching football practice, and it
was I who sent the coach after you. Did you really think
for one minute that you had me fooled? Don't you know
that I led you to the cave? That I staged it all? When I
suggested that your only means of saving yourself was to
commit a homicide on my behalf, did you still not know
that I was playing with you? Are you really so unin-
telligent? When you were watching from the cattle
guard, did you think you were not watched back? What
do they call you? Ben? Benjamin? Benjy? Or Father?
Who calls you Father? Andrew, is it? Do you call him
Andy? He's seven now, correct? *Kill* me? I can't imagine you really thought you could. There *is* no one named
Breaker. I sent you those notebooks, the letter. I did
quite a good job of it too, don't you think? Breaker. It's
more believable than 'Roger Farrar.' Truly, Garrison,
you make me laugh. On your way to New York to
murder yourself for me. Do you appreciate the high comedy of that? And when we would have arrived there,
what then? Had you given the matter any thought? What
took you so long? As I recall, I sent the envelope in June.
I expected you months ago. It's autumn, Garrison, autumn. Aren't I the boy you love so much?"

"The cave," Garrison said, his voice choked. "Was
all that an act too?"

The boy leaned closer, and when he answered, he was
almost whispering in his father's ear.

"I'm very good, aren't I? Everything was made up,
don't you see?"

Garrison raised himself from the wheel. When he
opened his eyes, they were blotted with stains, dark
spots that clotted his vision.

"Why?" he said. "Why did you do it?"

"Oh, I don't know," Peter said. "To amuse myself, I
suppose. A performance. Perhaps you'd like to direct me

one day. You were an actor, weren't you? Though
Mother says you weren't a very good one. Have you
really killed someone? Is that the net result of your little
mission to Cortez? Your family will be very upset. Or
don't they have capital punishment in New York? I suppose we should look that up when we stop in Des Moines
to change cars. It's wonderful what you can find out
from reference books. One can read all about one's father in *Who's Who in American Theater*. Ah, but of
course it was in Colorado that you committed the of-
fense. The girl will talk, you know. That's what I did
when we stopped in Cortez. I knew you'd think I was
calling Mother. *Berkeley*. Willa hasn't lectured at
Berkeley in years. She was in town, at her girl friend's.
Hence, the absence of the Land Rover. Don't you see? I
called the police and told them where to pick up the girl.
I merely had to remark that she was a vagrant and had
information about a possible homicide. So if you really
killed someone, I suppose you'd better start worrying.
But what do you think? About the notebooks, I mean.
They were good, weren't they?''

"The Jeepster. What about the Jeepster?''

The boy straightened up and moved back against the
opposite door.

"What about it?''

"Nothing,'' Garrison said, his head still spinning,
pain starting along his spine now, a sharp nibbling that
rose up his back. "Just wondering whose car it was.''

"Ours,'' Peter said. "But we let the maid use it. Is
there something that troubles you about this? Please believe me, I'd be happy to explain anything that might
baffle you. You are, after all, my father, and I expect
you're going to need my help. It never occurred to you to
get rid of this car, did it? Now tell me, did you or did you
not kill someone? And if you did, who? And whatever
for? Not really because of that little imbecile from the
trailer camp. I can believe many things of you, but truly,
I cannot believe that.''

Garrison lit a cigarette. He drew on it and held the
smoke down a long time. He turned the key in the ignition and fed the engine gas. He drove slowly for the first
half-mile and then he picked up speed.

"Well?" the boy said. "Did you or did you not?"

Garrison saw a second sign for Des Moines. He would
stop there, change cars. He would do just as the boy
said.

He made his mind go blank, and when he finished his
cigarette, he promptly lit another one. He pulled the
lighter from the dashboard, and when he looked to see if
the coil was glowing hot, he saw the smoking Buntline
instead.

18.

THEY MADE THE SWITCH in downtown Des Moines, giving up the big car for a white Pinto, Garrison using his American Express card to pay the charges. But when he put the credit card on the counter, he quickly thought to pick it up again before the clerk came back with the billing. The big Ford was already garaged, and the Pinto stood at the curb, waiting. He could see it through the glass doors. Wouldn't the attendant have left the keys in the ignition? Or stuck on top of the driver's sun visor? Or would they be in the glove compartment?

The clerk had his back turned and he was busy at an adding machine totalling up figures.

Garrison reached his hand to his face. He needed a shave—and there were the bruises. His hands too. And his clothes. He would attract attention, looking like this. His appearance would arouse suspicion. Maybe the clerk was just stalling while someone on the other side of the partition ran a check on him.

He turned toward the door as if appraising the Pinto, and then folded his arms as naturally as he could. He had the Buntline in his breast pocket because there was no place else to fit it—and now he was as worried about its bulk showing as he was about the credit card. But what difference did it make? The number was on the form he'd turned in. They would have talked to Jack by now. They would have talked to Willa. They'd have a license number, a description, the word out to every Hertz office in the country. And surely they would have doped out that he had Peter. But then again, maybe he didn't have him anymore—because he'd dropped him off at a Denny's just inside the city limits.

The clerk seemed to be taking an abnormally long time. Garrison turned back to the counter. Maybe he should grab the card and run. Forget the Pinto, forget everything. Just quietly walk out, go up the block, turn the corner, and run. Or forget the credit card too. He couldn't risk using it again, could he?

But run where? And to what purpose?

Joan would know by now. And wouldn't they be waiting for him in New York?

It was then that the realization first hit him. He had only so many days left to live—fifty? Fewer? He didn't know exactly. But then again, neither did Flood. The point was, if they caught him, whatever time he had left, he'd live it all in jail.

"Just sign and initial where I've checked, Mr. Garrison."

It was the clerk—forms for the old car, forms for the new one.

"I gave you collision insurance on this one, the same as you had out of Denver."

"Fine," Garrison said. "That's swell."

The clerk picked up the credit card.

"I'll just run this through and you'll be on your way. Sorry for the delay."

"That's all right," Garrison said. "I'm in no hurry. Except to get these looked after." He touched his face to indicate the bruises. "Been camping. Sort of bumming around in the woods. Kind of a hobo holiday."

The clerk seemed bored with the explanation. And maybe he hadn't even noticed anything. But Garrison was glad he'd said something.

He waited until the clerk had turned around, and then

he signed his name in all the blanks, folding his arms as soon as he was finished.

All the way back to Denny's, Garrison prayed that the boy would still be there. He'd had no choice. There was no other way to get the gun out of the old car without getting Peter out of it first. But there was the risk of losing him, of never getting his hands on him again.

He was there, standing in front, hands jammed into the pockets of his windbreaker and a smile on his face.

Garrison motioned for him to wait, turned, and drove into the lot and parked. He checked to make sure Peter was out of view, then bent to push the Buntline under the seat.

The boy was still smiling when Garrison came around to the front entrance.

"Feeling pretty good, I see."

"Why not? A pleasant drive, a pleasant meal, interesting conversation as one tours the American countryside. I'm enjoying your company, Father. You're an immensely interesting man. Imagine, my dear old dad, a murderer. Not every fellow has a dad like that."

Garrison said nothing. He took the boy by the arm and steered him back inside. Peter pulled away after only an instant of contact, but it was long enough for Garrison to feel the heft of the boy's strength. He guessed it was considerable.

They got a table and Garrison ordered coffee and a hot beef sandwich.

"How about you? You had enough, or you want something else?"

"Oh, I don't know," Peter said, patting his lean belly. "Maybe a lemon Coke," he said to the waitress, and smiled broadly. "That okay with you, Dad?"

Garrison nodded to the waitress and got out his cigarettes and lit one, and then he took out the bottle of aspirin and poured six of them onto a napkin.

"I see you had no trouble. Nice car. Cute."

Peter grinned agreeably, and then he tilted back his chair and craned his head around as if inspecting the quality of the clientele.

"I don't suppose the celebrated Ben Garrison gets around much to places like this in New York. Or holes up in too many infested hostelries like the Oasis, eh? But of course the celebrated Ben Garrison wasn't a fugitive from the law back in those good old celebrated days."

The boy brought his chair back down suddenly, and leaned his elbows up on the table. He hunched forward, his expression earnest.

"Pillhead, huh? What's the matter, Pop—am I giving you a headache?"

"It's not you, Peter. You're just a dream, the answer to a father's prayers." Garrison started on the aspirin, chewing them up three at a time, not bothering to use the water the busboy had poured.

"Arthritis, then?" Peter said, pleased with his deduction.

"That's right," Garrison said. "Just a mild case, but sometimes I've got to go heavy on these."

"Sure," Peter said, picking up his napkin and methodically tearing little pieces of it off and shaping them into tiny balls. He wet his fingers from the glass and rolled the balls into specks. "You see it all over on the reservations. People who can't afford a better way to handle the old aches and pains of rheumatism and arthritis and your good old degenerative diseases. But a big-shot like you? Aspirin? My, my—how ludicrously low-rent, Father." Peter grinned, obviously delighted.

The waitress brought the food, set the dishes on the table, and then moved the sugar and salt and pepper from the edge to the center.

"Anything else, fellas?"

Peter laughed. But Garrison noticed that it was a different laugh now, not breathy but still vaguely unpleasant, a touch contemptuous, yes, but something more than that. Too loud and even slightly mad.

"Something funny?" the woman said. She lifted the lid of the sugar bowl and looked in.

"Nothing to do with you," Peter said. "No, I don't think we'll be needing anything more, thank you." He looked at Garrison, his face all sincere inquiry. "That's right, isn't it, Dad?" And again the boy laughed, a short loud bark that made the woman turn to look around.

"We're fine," Garrison said to the waitress. "Just a check, please."

When they were alone again, the boy raised his Coke and held it up as if in a toast.

"Here's to us," he said, drank a sip, and put his glass down.

Garrison ate in silence. He was willing to understand that, even as he ate, the police could be coming to get him, that the boy might have called when he'd dropped him off on the way to Hertz. But perhaps Peter didn't really believe the thing had happened. Perhaps he thought everyone else was as busy with fabrications as he was. From his way of seeing things, the killing could be just as phony as the name Roger Farrar. But in any case, Garrison was sure Peter had called them about the girl. Or had he?

It didn't matter. The facts were the facts. He'd done it. Killed. Whether or not Peter believed him. And by now the police would be looking for him because that part of it was real. Looking for him for murder and maybe for kidnapping too.

The FBI. He'd carried the boy across state lines.

Garrison finished his coffee and lit another cigarette. He leaned back in his chair. But it seemed to make him colder. He huddled close in to the table again. When he looked at Peter, the boy was looking right back at him, the smirk still in place.

"I was just thinking," Garrison said. He picked up the check and tapped it against his water glass.

"Oh?" Peter said, widening his eyes in mock enthusiasm. "Tell me your thoughts. I'm very interested in the thoughts of a man who's got his nuts in a vise."

"About how it's really you who's responsible for my killing a man."

"Really, Father?" Peter pouted his lips as if wounded. "But I don't see how."

"Those composition books," Garrison said. "The letter. What did you expect to achieve?"

The boy yawned extravagantly. "Oh, really, Garrison, motivation, motivation! Is that how you talk to your actors? What do you call it, the Method? Stanislavsky and all that? Must I understand my motives to be a convincing actor?" The boy took up his glass of Coke and sipped a little more off the top. "No, I don't think so. As for my own amateur opinion, I think I was really very wonderful. Goodness knows, I persuaded the great Ben Garrison, didn't I? Is there a more demanding test?"

Garrison leveled his eyes at his son.

"How do I know you're not acting now?"

"Um," Peter said, setting down his glass and yawning again. "I suppose you don't. But that, of course, suggests that I am a better actor than you are a director. Wouldn't you say so? In any event, this is a bore, don't you think? What I'm interested in is what happens now. What's your next move?"

Garrison squashed out his cigarette.

"I haven't decided yet. Frankly, I don't know."

"Don't know? Seems to me you'd best make up your mind pretty fast. They're after you, you know."

"Right," Garrison said, still tamping the butt into the ashtray. "But I don't guess you're interested in sticking around for the rest of it. You've played your trick, had your revenge. I bought it all. That's enough, isn't it?"

He heard his son laugh again, and when Garrison looked up from the ashtray, he saw the boy's face suffused with heartiness, as if the mirth inside him were too much to stand. But when the boy spoke, his voice was very quiet.

"I wouldn't miss it for the world. After all, it's my play. I wrote it, don't you see? Go home and miss the final act?"

Garrison pushed his chair away from the table and stood up. When he looked back down at Peter, the boy's eyes were all innocence, all sweet expectation.

"I trust it's all right, Father. If I tag along, that is?"

"You'll miss the football season. You think the Cougars can get along without you?"

Peter got to his feet, and again Garrison was startled to see his size.

"They'll manage. Besides, this is such fun."

"Suit yourself," Garrison said, and moved off toward the cashier. Halfway there, he almost staggered when the pain took him by surprise. But he steadied himself quickly and rode the spasm out. He hadn't learned anything new, but a plan was taking shape. Not a plan so much as a direction. And Peter would move in it.

Garrison had seen to that. He'd set the hook.

"That's clever, that's good," Peter said when he saw Garrison turn the Pinto north toward Ames. "Take the whole show back to the old homestead. Christ, it's like a sleazo novel."

"Then you weren't sleeping, were you?"

"Oh, don't you worry about P. W. Stafford, Mr. Garrison, sir. He's on his toes all the time. P. W. Stafford's a heads-up kid, and don't you ever forget it." The boy stretched out his long legs, reached his hands behind his neck, and threaded his fingers together. "It'll be like a scene out of *Bonnie and Clyde,* right? Man on the run takes a last sentimental look at the old place. I could weep," Peter said, and barked with laughter. "Mind?" he said, and turned on the radio without waiting for an answer.

Garrison closed the vents and tightened the window on his side. He was colder now, cold all the time, and with the increasing cold he felt his strength ebbing, as if he were a sack of something granular that was leaking away through a gash in the middle.

He listened to Peter tune the radio, snatches of farm reports, feed reports, market prices, gospel singers, country-and-western music, the boy switching from station to station and then, with amused exasperation, snapping the radio off.

"This is dumb," he said, leaning back again and shutting his eyes.

"I could give you the fare and you could fly back home."

The boy opened his eyes, interested. "Are you kidding? I told you, I want to be around for when it warms up."

"Fine with me," Garrison said, relieved.

He turned to look at Peter and saw that the boy's eyes were closed again.

"So you want to be an actor. I'm flattered."

"Don't be."

"And you're very gifted. That's obvious. I mean, it's extraordinary the way your whole manner's changed. Even the way you talk."

"Yeah," the boy said as if he were already half asleep, "I'm amazing. You don't know the half of it."

"I'm sure I don't," Garrison said. "And you? Do you? For example, do you know when you're acting?"

There was a silence, as if Peter was giving the question some thought.

"Just drive," he said. "Okay?"

Peter was apparently sleeping when Garrison pulled into Ames. At least Garrison could hear him snoring slightly, and his face had the slack look of true sleep. In slumber, it was a good face, free of the guardedness that hardened it when the boy was awake, and it was difficult for Garrison not to keep looking at it.

Now that he was here, he didn't know what to do about it. There was nothing he really wanted to see—not the farm nor the machine shop, nor the place where his mother and father were buried. Yet being here seemed to matter to Garrison in some way that had nothing to do with heightened memories or with reverence for the past. But how to put his finger on it, the thing he wanted from this place?

He drove slowly through the town, looking more often at the face of the sleeping boy than at things he might remember—Greene's Pharmacy, Four Points Congregationalist Church, Steiger's Feed and Supply, and all the rest of it. He expected change, and he found it. But it didn't bother him. It wasn't *his* place, this place—but then again, neither was New York. He was willing to understand that he'd never really had a place except one place—and even that place wasn't a place so much as it was certain pictures that had stayed in his head from when he was eleven and he'd gone there with his father.

Still, he drove around and looked at everything, and then he turned the car back toward the highway and gassed up before heading southeast onto the Interstate. Peter was still sleeping, or pretending to be asleep. It didn't matter. Garrison didn't much feel like hearing the boy's sarcasm and ironies just now. He wanted quiet for a time. He wanted time to invite his feelings.

He had to get ready for what he had to do.

He'd wait until nightfall. He'd drive east—on to New York and, if possible, to Andy and Joan—but when the sun went down, he'd pull off the highway.

He'd do it at that special hour, that charged, hollow instant between the last of daylight and the start of true night.

He'd wait for then, and then he'd kiss his son and reach under the seat.

There was no other way. The boy was a maniac, demonic. To die and leave Peter behind? To leave Peter to hunt Andy to the end of the earth?

He'd *do* it. He had to do it. It was unthinkable. But there was no other way. And no time to look for one.

19.

He left the Interstate while they were still in Iowa, using the exit at West Liberty, a rural community in the hilly country east of Davenport. It was late afternoon, but the sun continued to burn a bright orange hole low in the sky behind them, and the Pinto lit up with a burnished light when Garrison swung the car around on the off-ramp and followed the feeder road back west into the town.

For a few miles they saw, here and there, harvesting machinery standing idle in the fields on either side of the road, and then the houses at closer and closer intervals until the familiar features of a town began to emerge.

"You could have got gas back there."

Garrison said nothing in reply.

He parked across the street from the first church he saw.

"What now? More *Bonnie and Clyde?*"

"I won't be long," Garrison said.

He shut off the motor and smiled. For a moment he almost reached his hand out to touch him. But when the boy saw the motion, he leaned away toward the door.

"Maybe you want to come along."

Peter laughed. But then he was quickly silent, and pushed open his door.

"Jesus, give me air."

He sat around in his seat so that his feet were on the curb.

Garrison got out.

"You sure?" he called over the top of the car.

The boy reached back in, flipped the key in the ignition, and turned the radio on.

Garrison crossed the street. But when he was on the sidewalk, he turned around and came back. He got in behind the wheel, started the car, cut right at the first corner, and then right and right again, until they were headed back toward the outskirts of town.

"You think you could eat something?"

The boy shook his head.

"Nothing? Not even ice cream? A Coke?"

"Later," Peter said.

"Sure," Garrison said, and he could feel himself tremble.

He saw a Chevron station ahead and he slowed the Pinto and looked at his son.

"I'm going to get some gas now so we don't have to stop so much at night."

The boy was slung down in his seat, and he didn't turn to see the way his father was looking at him.

"And I was thinking that maybe you'd like to call your mother and talk to her. You could do it while I'm getting the car checked."

Peter raised himself in the seat a little and drew up the zipper of his windbreaker.

"Aren't you afraid I'll tell her where we are and she'll send the cops after us?"

"No," Garrison said. He drove the car up onto the apron of the filling station and let it roll forward to the pay phone at the far end. "I'm not afraid," he said.

"And I'm not interested," Peter said.

The attendant, a boy not much older than Peter, stood smiling a few feet off from Garrison's door, signaling for Garrison to lower the window, and when Garrison lowered it, the boy spoke as if making a speech he'd been practicing for hours.

"If you're here just for the phone, sir, it's out of order. But you're welcome to use the one inside."

Garrison turned to Peter.

"Well?"

"Not interested."

"She'll be worried about you. The decent thing would be to talk to her." And then, because he couldn't help himself, Garrison added, "This one time."

Peter turned to him. "This one time?"

"Yes," Garrison said. "I mean, you haven't been in touch with her. She must be worried sick."

"Her?" Peter said. "Willa?"

"I want you to do this for me," Garrison said. "There's a reason."

"Your reason. I don't have one."

"Don't you love your mother? Aren't you concerned that she's probably frantic about you? If I could only see there was someone you really cared for, really loved the way a son is supposed to love."

"What of it?" Peter said. "What earthly difference does it make, what you see or don't see?"

"You won't do it?" Garrison said.

The boy turned away again. "I'm not in the business of doing what you'd like me to do. Besides, I already told you, I'm not interested."

"Sir?"

It was the attendant.

"I guess not," Garrison said.

"Can I get you some gas, then?"

"No, thanks," Garrison said.

"Wash your windshield for you if you'd like."

"Not now," Garrison said. "Thanks."

He waved to the attendant as he backed up, and then he drove back onto the road, his eyes on the divider line as the Pinto covered ground. The white line was hard to see now that the sun had fallen so far behind the trees.

"What happened to your big-deal plan about not stopping for gas during the night?"

Garrison reached forward and set the headlights at dim. Moments later he pulled the knob all the way out.

He rolled his window back up and turned up the collar of
his sportcoat. He watched the odometer now, the counter
ticking off tenths of a mile. It was on 6. When it came
back to 6 again, he'd turn off the road. No, not 6. He'd
do it at 9—because he couldn't handle waiting for it
anymore.

They'd driven on out beyond the tight orderly pattern
of houses now. The yards were getting bigger, the front
porches more spacious, the roadway dipping more
deeply as open fields began to appear, some already
cleared, others partially harvested, neat bundles sometimes glowing as if the sun had grazed them in its descent
and they smoldered at the core.

He looked back at the counter, and his heart jumped
when he saw that it had already passed 9 and was climbing up through zero back to 1 again. Up ahead, to his
left, he saw a spur road cutting between two fields.

There.

What difference did it make where?

He turned.

Peter sat up in his seat as if an alarm had gone off.

The boy looked around, and then he looked at Garrison and laughed.

"More sightseeing? You got an uncle up this road?"

When the counter hit 6 again, he stopped and shut off
the engine and the lights.

It was almost too dark to see his son's face.

"This your escape plan? You going to burrow into the
ground here, or just get out and take a leak?"

Garrison was cold, but he rolled down his window. He
wanted to hear the small night sounds of whatever
moved in the earth in these fields. He turned in his seat.

He faced his son. He could see him well enough to
know that the boy was looking back at him. But there
was no telling what was on the boy's face, whether it
revealed something that Garrison could speak to.

"I love you," he began. "It doesn't matter to me

what you're like. I love you. That's all that matters to
me. It's what should matter to you. Maybe if we had
time, it would. But there is no time. In our case, Peter,
there is no time. It's no one's fault that it's this way. Not
yours or mine or your mother's. I love you. And maybe
in your heart you love me. But I can't take a chance that
you'll never get down that far inside yourself. Your hate
is dangerous. It's dangerous to you, first of all. But it
could go further than that. It already has. And I've got no
way of knowing how far it will go. Maybe you don't,
either. You think you'd be happy if I were dead. But
maybe that wouldn't be enough for you. Who can say
what would ever be enough for you? You blame me. For
all those years when you had no father. I understand that.
But I can't change it. There's no time to change that.
After all the wasted years, here we are. Your father,
Peter. You and me. Your life is the life that came from
my body. You're from my body, too. Your mother did
something terrible. But I don't blame her for it anymore.
She couldn't help herself. And neither could I. I cried
and cried. I looked everywhere. I loved you with all my
heart and soul then, and that's how I love you now. Not
anything could change that. Nothing you could do, nothing you could say.''

"Nothing I could say?" Peter said. "All right," he
said, his voice a third voice, a voice Garrison had not
heard until this moment. "You want to talk to me. You
want to get it all out. I respect that. But I don't respect
you. You know why?"

But Garrison wasn't listening anymore. He was trying
to force himself to bend forward, reach down, put his
hand down and get what was under the seat.

"Because you're a coward. Because you're weak."

His right arm was in his lap. He tried to move it, let it
go toward his knees. He did not want to hear the boy's
voice. He wanted to hear nothing but the sounds of
things buzzing and ringing in the fields.

"Because you wouldn't fight her," the boy said.

He couldn't hear anything but the busy thrumming of all that frantic life out there. He didn't want to hear anything but that. His fingertips were almost touching the floor.

"Yes, I made the whole thing up. But not for the reason you think. Maybe I couldn't deal with the real reason. Maybe it was something I just couldn't get at until I saw you, until I was with you the way we are now."

He didn't want to hear what the boy was saying. Talk would only make it worse. It was over now, finished. He had to get his hand a little farther down and do it. First kiss him and then do it and then end it here for himself too.

"Do you hear what I'm saying?" Peter said, his voice very clear in the small dark car.

Had he moved his head closer?

"Do you hear what I'm trying to say? Dad? Daddy?"

He heard Peter move, move closer.

"I wanted you to come out there and fight her. I wanted you to do what you've done. Take me away from her. I wanted you to know what she's done to me. But you didn't even come inside. I stood there waiting at the window, watching you parked out there. But you never even came inside to get me. Why did you give me a fake name? Why did you go to that motel and hide there? Why didn't you come inside and tell her what she is and take me with you? But you were afraid of her and it's the truth. All those years you were trying to find me? Well, it was the same with me. When I got old enough, when I began to see things, understand, that's what I did, too— tried and tried to find you. And then when I finally did, I didn't know what to do about it. How to make you pay attention. Those things I wrote, they were crazy, yes, but I just didn't know how else to do it. I was afraid. I was afraid to cry out for help. I'm still afraid. I want to say I love you right now—because I *do* love you—but I'm afraid to say it. I'm scared that if I say it, you'll go away. Daddy?''

He could feel his son's hand on his knee.

Garrison didn't say anything. He put his hand on top of that hand.

They sat that way for a very long time—while Ben Garrison cried. And with his head pressed to his father's chest, Peter Garrison murmured, ''Daddy'' and ''I love you,'' but in the darkness, he smiled.

Garrison did not to see that smile. He saw what he wanted to see, what he desperately sought to believe. His mind was blind with confusion, a thousand eyes all blinded by the light that poured from his heart.

The apron lights were out at the Chevron station. But there was a light on in the office, and Garrison could see the young man inside, straightening up and getting ready to close down.

He pulled the Pinto close to the door, tapped the horn once, and got out, waving when the young man looked up from his work. Peter got out too, but he did not follow Garrison inside.

''Sorry,'' the young man said when Garrison stood in the open door, ''the pumps are locked up. There's a Gulf five miles east off the Interstate, and we've got another Chevron all the way into town. Doesn't shut down until ten.''

''That's all right,'' Garrison said, letting the door swing closed behind him. ''Just wondering if I could take you up on that offer to use your phone.''

The young man nodded at the telephone on the desk. ''All yours.''

''It's long distance,'' Garrison said. ''Okay if I get the charges and pay you when I'm finished?''

''No problem,'' the young man said.

He was Windexing the display case, but when Garrison said, ''Honey? I wake you?'' the young man put down his things and went outside. Garrison saw him pause to light a cigarette, pocket the match, and then stroll over to Peter, who was standing at the edge of the road looking out at the empty field that lay opposite the service station.

And then he heard Joan say, "Don't say where you are."

For a while he said nothing, nothing except "Joan," trying to make his utterance of the name say everything he couldn't say, a summation of what was no longer expressible. He just kept on saying *Joan* and *Joanie* until Joan started talking.

"They were here when I got home. I dropped off Andy, stopped off at D'Agostino's for a few things, and when I got home, they were waiting for me. They stayed until late this afternoon. But I don't think they ever really went away. I'm sure they're out there watching the house. Ben, darling, don't say anything. Be careful, darling. The phone."

"It's okay, baby," Garrison said. "I know it's hard to believe it, but trust me, it's okay. Now tell me how the old chap is. Was he around for any of this?"

"I called the school. I told them to hold Andy there and that I'd be about an hour late. So, no, don't worry, they were gone when he got home. He doesn't know anything. And he's fine, dearest. And you, darling, how are you?"

Garrison let himself down into the desk chair. He was exhausted, and it was hard seeing now. Everything was getting cloudy again, worse than ever, images fuzzy, blurred as if their perimeters were erupting in all directions.

"I'm all right. Just tired, is all." He tried seeing through the glass, seeing where Peter had got to. But either it was too dark out there or Peter and the attendant had moved out of view.

"I called Steve, honey. He knows."

"Good," Garrison said. "You keep talking to Steve."

"He didn't tell me anything. But he didn't have to. I think I know most of it."

"It's different now," Garrison said. He moved the receiver to his other ear, and rubbed at his eyes. "It's better. I think it's going to be okay, baby. I mean . . ." But for a moment Garrison wasn't sure what he meant. And he had no way of knowing how much Joan knew. "I had a child a long time ago. A wife. It's not anything I can talk about like this. But it's okay now. I mean, the thing I was worrying about, the thing that made me go to Colorado, lie to you, all that—I think it's not anything to worry about anymore."

"He's with you, Ben? Your son?"

"He's with me," Garrison said.

"I'm glad, darling."

"Yeah," Garrison said. "Andy's asleep?"

"Hours ago. Please don't worry. I'm going to keep everything absolutely normal for him. If there's something in the papers here, he'll never see it. Promise me you won't worry about him."

"I promise," Garrison said, his eyes closing with pain and fatigue.

"Ben?"

"I'm here, baby. I'm okay. Just sleepy, is all."

"Will you promise me you'll try to get some rest as soon as you hang up?"

"I promise," Garrison said. He felt drugged. He raised himself in the swivel chair and tried to wake up.

"There was a girl with you. She says she saw you do it. Steve says they have her in jail out there. Darling? Are you awake, dearest?"

"I hear you, baby. She's just a girl, is all—a frightened kid. It doesn't matter. Just try to believe that. Where I am with things now, that's all that matters—that and you and the scout."

Her voice seemed to be fading—or else his hearing was. But a sudden shower of sparks exploding up from his belly into his chest stunned him back to life again, and he slammed his fist against the desk to strike out at the agony. In the dim light he could see a smear of blood where his fist had touched the wood.

"His name's Peter," he heard her say. "It's a nice name."

"He's a nice boy," Garrison said. "Deep down, he's a wonderful boy. There's not anything to worry about now. Do you believe me, honey?"

"I believe you, Ben. I trust you, darling. I know that whatever you did and whatever you're doing, it's the right thing. I love you, my darling."

"Love, baby, love," Garrison said, and he lowered the receiver slowly, hesitated for an instant, then, kissing the air, hung up.

He couldn't keep going. He knew he couldn't make another mile. Not without a little sleep. Besides, why keep pushing it? There wasn't anywhere to go now. Now that they were watching the house and probably watching Joan, what was the point of pressing on to New York without stopping for rest?

He'd sleep. He'd get a little sleep. And maybe in the morning, an idea would come.

He struggled up from the chair and rapped on the glass, and then he lifted the receiver again and found out the charges. When the attendant came, Garrison paid for the call and dragged himself out to the car.

Peter saw him coming and he came to help.

Garrison let him do it, and it was a wonderful feeling, letting himself go and leaning on his son.

It took all he could do to pull himself in behind the wheel.

"Better shove over," Peter said, and moved in to take his place.

"You can drive?"

"Not legally. But I can handle anything Detroit makes."

"Just for a little while," Garrison said, his eyes closing despite himself.

He could hear Peter talking with the attendant, the young man softly suggesting a guest house back in town, saying he'd call up so they'd have something ready. Garrison could barely hear the young man say, "Is he all right?" But Peter's answer was loud in Garrison's ears.

"My dad? He's just very, very tired."

It occurred to Garrison that he had never heard anything so beautiful—and with his heart soaring, after what seemed centuries of vigilance, he let go all the way, and fell into a deep, abiding sleep.

When he woke up, he saw Peter sitting at the foot of the bed, dressed, smiling, the room bathed in a wonderful light that made the boy's smoky hair shine russet at the fringes.

"How long did I sleep? A week?"

Peter moved closer and rested his hand on his father's chest.

"It's almost noon."

"God," Garrison said. He sat up and gently pulled his son against him and then hugged him with all his strength.

"I thank God for this," Garrison whispered.

"Yes," Peter said.

The old woman downstairs was waiting for them when they came down, the two of them smiling ferociously, Peter stepping in front to say, "Mrs. Chambers, this is my father, Mr. Steiner—William Steiner. I'm afraid he wasn't quite up to these introductions last night."

The old woman came forward and put out her hand.

"You got yourself one fine boy there, Mr. Steiner."

"Thank you," Garrison said. "I think so, too."

He put his arm around Peter's shoulders, and the two of them followed the woman back through the house into the kitchen. The room was radiant, sunlight issuing immaculately from the surfaces that glistened all around them, brass and copper and polished iron and the walls themselves a brilliant enamel tile.

They sat at a large table of scrubbed pine while the woman bustled from refrigerator to stove and back again, getting out eggs and sausages and milk and butter and hurrying to pour hot coffee into a big brown mug and set it before Garrison, who sat watching and marveling and feeling totally renewed.

"Second breakfast for you, son?" the woman turned and said.

"No, thanks," Peter said. "Except I guess I would like another of those biscuits if you don't mind."

"Mind?" the woman said, and beamed.

"So you've been up awhile," Garrison said, testing his coffee.

"That boy?" the old woman said. "Land sakes, since first light at least."

Garrison lifted the heavy mug to his lips and tasted the coffee again. He could feel it, the serpent eating at him now that he was awake. But he felt something else much more keenly, a spacious sense of well-being that made him want to sing and grin and hug every living thing in reach.

"You're from Iowa, your boy says," the old woman said when she had at last fed them all that they could hold, and had taken up a place at the table to visit while she brewed herself tea.

"Born here," Garrison said.

He lit a cigarette and looked around.

"Oh, use the saucer there, for pity's sake. Never bothered Mr. Chambers none, and it sure don't make no difference to me."

"Sometimes I think I should have stayed," Garrison said.

"Oh, well," the woman said. "Some do, some don't. A place don't matter all that much. But I'm not saying anything against West Liberty, mind you."

"It's lovely here," Garrison said.

"It's pretty, all right."

"It's the prettiest place I've ever seen," Peter said.

"Why, thank you, son," the old woman said. She glanced with pleasure at Garrison. "I could just steal that boy. Always knows the right thing to say, don't he? Son, you'd charm the birds right out of a tree."

Peter smiled, wet his finger, and used it to catch up the buttery crumbs on his plate.

"Only place I've ever seen that was prettier—" Garrison began softly. But then he realized his mistake and grinned sheepishly at the old woman. "You're awfully nice," he said.

"Go ahead, Dad."

It was Peter.

"Finish your thought. I'm sure Mrs. Chambers doesn't mind, and I'd like to hear."

"Why, sure," the old woman said, wheezing a little as she got up to turn off the light under the teakettle and pour herself a cup. "I reckon I'm old enough to know there's a whole lot of places on God's green earth that could give West Liberty cards and spades."

Garrison looked at them, his son smiling expectantly, the old woman sitting with pursed lips, her eyes wide with real interest.

"Just a place," he said. "And I was just a kid. Eleven. It's probably not anything, really. Forget it."

"Oh," the old woman scolded, "don't be so stingy, Mr. Steiner. The boy wants to hear."

Garrison studied his son, the eyes so dark and earnest. He thought of Andy's eyes, the lightest blue, the face from which they looked out on the world so willing, so full of wonder.

"A father ought to share these things with his son." The old woman shook a spoon at him. "No, you go on and tell us now, or I'll turn you out without a second cup of coffee, hear?"

"Just a fishing lodge," Garrison began. "There's a

lake there. Two lakes, actually. Big Lake and Grand Lake, and I think the town's called Grand Lake Stream.''

"In Maine?" Peter said.

Garrison nodded, surprised. "That's right. In Maine," he said, inviting the memory, trying to bring it back, snippets of images, flashes of colors and soft dark shadows and the gliding smells of things woodsy and how the air felt, cool and watery in summer.

"Maybe it was how the whole thing happened," he began again. "My dad always saying how he'd take me on this fishing trip, and one time he just did it, loaded me into the old truck and off we went. Said where did I want to go, and I didn't know, I just thought of the farthest place away, which was Maine. Not that I even knew where it was. I mean, to me it was like Persia or something.

"My dad could have driven off to someplace fifty miles away and said it was Maine and I'd never have known the difference. But he didn't. Funny," Garrison chuckled to himself, embarrassed. "I mean, after all that driving, what I remember best are just flowers and stones." He shook his head and tapped the ash of his cigarette.

"I remember how the light was when we got there, and my dad saying, 'Yes, sir, this here is it—Grand Lake Stream,' and how it sounded to me, that word *Grand*.

"It was just an intersection, two dirt roads, a gas pump and general store right there where they crossed, and the lakes on either side. We drove around and drove around, and while we were doing it, we suddenly saw this place. A fishing lodge, I guess. It was set way back from the road, up on a hill behind one of the lakes. Big Lake or Grand Lake, I don't know which. This big white building, green shutters all over it, and the darkest, greenest grass I've ever seen.

"What I remember next is going up the walkway to

the big porch out front, and all these little white stones
that lined the path all the way up. They were painted
white, is all—but to me they looked like stones that
came that way. Maine stones, I think I thought.

"I can hear the screen door I went through to get
inside, and feel the coolness in there, and then I know I
went through another screen door and out to the back,
and what I saw out there was three more pathways like
the one out front, white stones spotted along their borders the very same way. Like big marshmallows that had
been put out for a party on the lawn.

"I know my dad was walking with me and that we
took the path that went straight out. And that's all.
That's all there is. It's just that we walked that path all
the way to the end.

"You know what?" Garrison looked at his son. "It
wasn't anything but a path with white stones along its
sides. And little yellow flowers between them sometimes. But it was a great thing in my life."

There were tears in Garrison's eyes when he finished,
and he finished because he couldn't go on.

The old woman fiddled with her teacup and cleared
her throat.

It was silent a long time, and in the silence Garrison
could hear the old woman now and then sigh.

When his eyes cleared and he could see again, he
looked helplessly at the big brown mug gripped tight in
his hands, blood seeping from the scabs he'd cracked
open as he'd talked.

The old woman said, "It's a better place than this."

Peter said nothing, and if Garrison had looked, he
would have seen in that instant something hideous in the
boy's face. But it vanished quickly behind a small perfect smile.

"I think Dad's crying," Peter said softly, reaching a
hand to the old woman's bare arm and giving it a deft,
comforting pat.

*   *   *

Garrison bought iodine and peroxide and bandages and more aspirin in town. For a moment he thought about getting shaving things. But then he realized it would be better to let his beard grow. At the sundries store he got a cap to cover his hair, and he got another one just like it for Peter, billed caps that said CAT across the front.

"For Caterpillar, the tractor," the salesgirl explained. But she didn't have to. Garrison remembered.

They went back to the drugstore and bought toothbrushes and toothpaste before getting back in the Pinto and heading out to the Interstate.

"Where to?" Garrison said, hesitating at the signs that directed traffic east or west.

"East, of course," Peter said. "I want to meet your family."

"I don't think that's possible,"

"Not possible?"

Garrison shook out some aspirin and chewed them up, and then he lit a cigarette to kill the taste.

"They're being watched. At least my wife is."

"Joan?"

Garrison looked at the boy with curiosity again. But then he remembered—*Who's Who in American Theatre,* it was all in there, his history right back to his birth in Ames.

"But what about Andy? Isn't he in school?"

For the first time Garrison realized what might be possible.

"We could get Andy," Peter said. "There's very little chance the police would be watching the school. You've got to try it, Dad. No matter what the risk." Peter smiled, revealing the dwarfed tooth up high on his gum.

It gave Garrison a strange feeling to see that tooth, a momentary twinge of terror, as if an unspeakable abyss had just opened and closed inches in front of his feet. But he threw the feeling off, his heart leaping with happiness again.

"Andy, of course! God, yes!" he said, starting up and turning onto the ramp that would feed them around into the traffic going east.

"Sure, it's worth the chance," Peter said as he settled back comfortably for the hard drive ahead. "And then I've got another good idea after that one. We'll get my brother and go north."

"North? At this time of year?"

"Of course," Peter said. "Don't you see, Dad? Grand Lake Stream. Just the three of us, the way it was with you and *your* dad. Just the three of us at Grand Lake Stream."

Garrison wanted to shout aloud. It was incredible. It was like a wonderful thing happening all over again, a prayer against all odds answered, the great dream of a lifetime coming true and then doing it all over again.

20.

ONCE THEY GOT past Chicago, it was turnpike driving all the way, the road unraveling in front of them as if it existed only for the motion of the small hastening car and for the speed and comfort of the two passengers in it. With all the horror behind him, there lay ahead for Garrison only a kind of delirious tranquility, the prospect of a long enchanted moment before cancer brought it all to an end.

He looked at his son, his heart smiling as he let his eyes feast on the boy's peaceful face. It was wonderful. It was perfect—and if it hadn't been for Peter, it wouldn't be happening.

Of course. *Grand Lake Stream.*

Andy and Peter together at last. His sons. The three of them where smooth white stones dotted clean-swept paths that unwound gracefully through the moist dark grass, nothing but little yellow flowers to make the mystery of the pageant more unimaginably complete.

"It's just the thing," Garrison said, and glanced again at the sweet face of the sleeping boy, grateful for what God had given at last. "It's the only thing, the perfect thing," he murmured to himself, turning his attention back to the road and the darkening sky that spread before them to the east.

They stopped twice during the night for Garrison to rest his eyes and doze off at the side of the road, first in Ohio and again, later, just after they got their ticket for

the New Jersey Turnpike. He awoke refreshed and drove
the rest of the way exhilarated.

When they made their approach to the Lincoln Tunnel
the next morning, Garrison was singing snatches of old
show tunes, Peter grinning joyously and now and then
awkwardly humming along.

"I hear you say you'd like to see a helluva tunnel?"
Garrison shouted, and thumped his hand against the
wheel.

"That's what you heard me say!" Peter shouted back.

"I didn't get you wrong now, did I?" Garrison sang
out.

"No sir!" Peter yelled. "Show me a tunnel and a
half!"

"You got it!" Garrison announced as the small white
car dipped down into the flickering bath of fluorescent
light.

"All *right!*" Peter howled aloud, sitting up high in his
seat and looking around with serious appreciation.
"Can't say it competes with the Grand Canyon, but as
New York tunnels go, it's A-okay!"

Garrison smiled with deep delight.

"Ah, God, just wait till you two guys get together."

The traffic moved smoothly for a Monday morning,
and in no time at all the Pinto came out into the bleak
morning light of Manhattan, turned north and headed
uptown along the West Side.

"It's a weekday, isn't it?"

Peter held the back of his wrist to his forehead as if
divining the date through metaphysical powers. Then he
glanced at his calender watch, laughed, and said,
"Right!"

Garrison laughed too, though it all made him a little
uneasy, the way the boy seemed increasingly to be mim-
icking his own style of horseplay and speech. But why
shouldn't he? Wasn't this the boy's way of showing his
affection? It was natural for a son to want to do things the
way his father did them. Andy, for instance—the way he

favored the expression "You bet," just because Garrison had the habit. There wasn't anything wrong with it. It was the way a son was supposed to be, wasn't it?

Garrison blinked and nodded happily.

"School days!" he proclaimed, and then he started humming the melody until Peter joined in with the words.

All the way uptown and then across to the East Side, they sang the song together, starting it up again as soon as they finished.

School days, school days, dear old Golden Rule
*   days,*
Readin' and writin' and 'rithmetic,
Taught to the tune of a hickory stick . . .

A weekday. He'd forgotten time, and he was glad of it. Back there on the mesa, in the cave, time had somehow gotten brittle and cracked apart, minutes and hours shattering into rubbery lengths of terror and slumber, the undulating trajectory of a nightmare. But now it was all different, and there seemed to be no time at all, just this ceaseless, weightless, delirious drifting, they way it was when he'd walked that path, an everlasting dreaming between two rows of round white stones.

Maine stones, Garrison thought, and laughed to himself as he sang along with his son.

Readin' and writin' and 'rithmetic,
Taught to the tune of a hickory stick . . .

"You better wait here," Garrison said when he found a parking place on Seventy-third. "It's the next block. But maybe they're looking for a Pinto by now."

"Good thinking," Peter said. "You think I should maybe get out and keep walking around the block?"

Garrison checked his watch. Nine-thirty, a little after.

"I don't know. You think you should?"

"I'll think about it," Peter said. "You go ahead—and listen, Dad, watch your step, okay?"

Garrison grinned, trying to cover his nervousness.

He shouldered out the door, and for a while he stood uncertainly at the curb, steadying himself against the roof of the car. Then he pushed off and headed down the block.

The building was between Madison and Park on Seventy-fourth Street, a small converted church, a sweep of wide marble steps leading up to the elegant etched-glass door. Garrison pressed the buzzer, and as if it were connected to the woman herself, he saw the principal, Mrs. Lamming, promptly appear from one side, her gray hair done up in the style of a Gibson Girl, her bearing patrician as she looked quizzically through the glass at the tall, spare man who stood there, his face bearded and haggard, his rumpled clothing misted with pink dust, a workman's cap on his head, an insignia that preposterously read S.C.

Garrison pulled off the cap and called through the glass.

"It's me, Mrs. Lamming! Andrew's father! Ben Garrison!"

The woman smiled benevolently and gestured to the black man standing just to her rear. He wore the uniform of a private security service, and when he came forward to work the special locking device, Garrison recognized him.

"Howard, how are you this morning?" he said as the guard held open the door.

"Just fine, Mr. Garrison, thank you. We ain't seen you around here in a while."

"Been rehearsing," Garrison answered cheerily, and turned to greet the woman.

"Mrs. Lamming."

"Mr. Garrison. Forgive me for not recognizing you."

Garrison stared blankly, suddenly unsure of himself.

He remembered the bandages on his hands, and he raised them and chuckled.

"Rehearsals. Full rig. No time to get out of my stuff."

The woman appeared to be waiting for a further explanation. Or was it that she'd already been alerted?

"Sometimes the boss has to get up there and do it himself. Anyway, the thing of it is," he hurried on, "Mrs. Garrison forgot Andrew's dental appointment this morning—and now she's in her dance class, so she called me at the theater to ferry him over."

He waited.

"Oh?" the woman finally said. She smiled sympathetically. "We can't have that, now can we?"

She pulled a watch from one of the big patch pockets sewn to the front of her smock.

"He's just finishing up assembly. I'll tiptoe in and see if Mrs. Flynn can fetch him out."

"Thank you," Garrison said. "It'll only take an hour. I'll have that scholar back in a jiffy."

"Very well, then," the woman said. "If you'll wait here, I won't be long."

"Hey, old thing!" Garrison called when he saw the boy coming, and because he saw Mrs. Lamming right behind him, Garrison rushed forward and grabbed his son up, muffling the boy's surprise with kisses and hugs as he carried him quickly to the glass door and stood waiting for the guard to unlock it.

Outside, Garrison moved hurriedly up the sidewalk with the boy still in his arms, not letting go of him until they had turned the corner toward the next block over. When he finally set Andy down on his feet, Garrison got down onto his knees, and the boy flung himself forward, kissing and kissing his father's lips and cheeks.

"Papa, Papa, Papa," the small boy said over and over.

And for a long time, all Garrison could say was "Hey, old thing, it's good to see you," and then he felt the tears flooding up from his chest, a wild commotion that he couldn't turn back.

"Don't cry, Papa."

"It's just so good to see you," Garrison whispered as he pulled the boy roughly against him and kissed first one eye and then the other.

"Ear," he said, playing their old game, and when the boy presented his ear, Garrison kissed it and commanded, "Other ear." Andy grinned and turned his head, and Garrison kissed again. His voice still stern, Garrison ordered, "Nose!" And the boy offered his nose to his father's lips, his manner dutiful and very solemn. "Other nose!" Garrison demanded this time, and right on cue, Andy rolled his eyes in panic as if suddenly discovering that he had only one nose, and then together the two of them burst into peals of delighted laughter.

"Henry Henry," Garrison said, hugging Andy all over again. "What a guy my Henry is!"

At length, he got to his feet and took his son's hand, feeling briefly faint but recovering quickly.

"You want to ride on my shoulders, old chap? Or are you too gosh-awful grown up for shoulder-rides anymore?"

Garrison looked down at his son, saw the dark blue school blazer, the heraldic emblem, the gray flannel shorts, the knee socks, the maroon-and-navy striped tie proudly knotted, he could tell, by the boy himself. And he saw the look of fierce independence that Andy tried so hard to capture with his face.

"No," Garrison said, shaking his head as he smiled down at his son, "I guess the old shoulder-ride days are gone forever."

"It's okay, Papa," Andy said, squeezing his father's hand. "Don't be sad."

"Sad?" Garrison said. "Son, son, this is the happiest moment of my life." And then he remembered his hands. "Don't mind these," he said, showing the bandages. "Your old man's just not used to holding on to all those bucking broncos they got out there in California, you know."

Andy looked at him as if seeing everything for the first time.

"Well," Garrison said, touching his own face, "you could walk your legs to stumps, trying to find a razor blade out there in that godforsaken place. Nothing but cactus and horned critters all the way from San Berdoo to Malibu, dagnabit! Anyway, your old dad thought he'd raise himself a little asparagus crop, is all. Want a feel?"

Garrison lowered his face to where his son could reach it.

"Pretty good?"

The boy touched him and then kissed where he touched, and Garrison had to swallow hard to keep himself from letting go again.

"Now then," he said, straightening up and reaching for Andy's hand once more. "What was it I wanted you for? Can you guess? I mean, here I am, all the way back from the Wild West on a moment's notice, just to see my old scout, and I've plumb forgot what it was I had in mind. Let's see now, did I kiss your second nose?"

The boy laughed, and pulled on his father's arm.

"Come on, Papa—stop teasing. I'm almost eight, you know."

"*Eight*, is it! You say eight years old?"

"Come on, Papa," the boy pleaded, tugging at Garrison's arm until Garrison's expression showed that he intended to stop.

"Son, here it is in a nutshell," Garrison began, and he started moving up the sidewalk toward Seventy-third. "A lot of things have happened since I went out there to Hollywood, but that's what always happens when a fellow goes out to Hollywood. Anyway, the point is, they're good things, and I'm happy about them, and I want you to be happy about them, too. You think I can count on you for that, old scout?''

Garrison stopped near the corner and looked down at his son, searching the boy's face for signs.

''You bet,'' Andy said, the boy waiting for what he guessed it was going to be hard to hear.

Garrison hunkered down and put his bandaged hands to his son's waist. He drew the boy closer.

''Yeah, well,'' he began, trying to keep his voice low, but still make himself heard above the street noise, ''it's kind of a grown-up thing, but I know you can handle it.''

''Sure,'' Andy said, doing what he could to help his father.

''Yes, of course,'' Garrison said. ''You see, old thing, a long time ago Papa had another boy, a son, and he lost him. It was terrible and it made me want to cry all the time. But then you came along, and I was happy again. Do you understand what I'm saying? A brother?''

Andy nodded. ''You and Mama had a little boy before you had me, only he died.''

Garrison smoothed his son's hair, silky and honey-colored, like Joan's. ''Not exactly died, but like that, yes. And now the most wonderful thing's happened. I found him. I *found* your brother. And it makes me so happy that I found him. I want it to make you happy, too. That's why I've come to get you out of school, because I wanted to tell you about it right away. You think you'd like to meet him? He's waiting to meet you. You think you'd like that, old thing?''

''A big brother?'' Andy said. ''Are you kidding? You *bet!*'' the boy said.

''What a guy!'' Garrison said. He hugged his son and hoisted him onto his shoulders. ''Just this one more time, okay?''

In answer, the boy clasped his hands under his father's chin, and together they advanced up the block toward the Pinto, Garrison trembling with the huge feeling that was in him, his heart pronouncing a single sentence whose first word was *Please* . . .

It was too much to explain all at once. He knew it would be crazy to try. It was enough just to tell about Peter, and to hope that the rest would somehow fall into place once they got going. But how to explain about the trip? About not going home or back to school?

Please, dear God, let it be right, Garrison prayed as Peter came loping toward them along the sidewalk, his mop of dark hair rhythmically lifting and falling, his taut face stretched in a grin, his hand offered in front of him as Garrison set Andy down.

The two boys stood looking at each other, and Garrison's heart turned fearfully when at last their hands touched. He watched his sons as they stood facing each other, their hands still joined as if neither boy knew how to let go.

He said nothing—because he did not know what to say. He watched them. His sons. He wanted to believe it was a gift, a miracle handed down from heaven in exchange for the price that had been paid.

They left New York like that, Peter still grinning from ear to ear, Garrison driving and Peter in the passenger seat, with Andy squeezed between them.

They sang songs, and it was better that way because Garrison didn't know what else to do. As they approached the New England Thruway, he could see in the rearview mirror the tallest buildings behind him poking thick gray fingers into the grim sky over the city. But in his heart there was only a vision of what lay ahead, a stately building that stood crisp in late-afternoon stillness, the cool green order of its shutters, a hushed presence of velvety surfaces, and the quick bright stippling of yellow flowers. But most of all, he saw a man and his sons moving along a path that wound forever between borders of white-washed stones.

Just before Greenwich, he called Joan and told her what he had done. He begged her not to worry, but he could tell he'd gone too far.

"It'll work out," he pleaded. "You've got to believe me. Joanie, it's the only thing I can do."

He listened to the silence, waiting.

"Honey? Joanie?"

"Ben, he's just a baby. He's *seven* years old. How do you expect to explain all this to him?"

"It'll work out," Garrison said again. "Peter's helping every inch of the way. Don't you see, darling? I've got to make it right, what I've done."

Again there was a long silence.

"Call Steve. He wants you to call him. He says he can help. There are ways. You only shot a man. You didn't kill anybody."

"Not dead?" Garrison said. For an instant he felt as if a sentence of death had been lifted from him. But then he remembered the cancer. "The man's alive?"

"Did you think you'd killed him? Oh, God, Ben, please come home. Please bring Andy back. You're not thinking straight, darling. You're all confused. Let Steve handle it. He begs you to call him. There are things he can do. You have a whole life ahead of you. Don't destroy it by running away and doing something reckless. That man in Cortez is going to be fine, darling. Please, I beg you, don't do this."

When he answered, he spoke very slowly, very softly. He wanted to comfort her, reassure her.

"Joanie, there's more to this," he said. "What I'm doing isn't reckless. You don't understand, but it's the best way. Andy's with me, and he's perfectly safe. He's crazy about Peter. Honest, baby, you ought to see the two of them together. Now, honey, if I came home, there'd be police and maybe jail for a while and things like that. Whatever Steve can do, he can't stop that, and the thing is, I just don't have that kind of time now. Right now all that matters is what's happening right this minute—Andy and Peter together, and me with them, to *see* it. Just the three of us. Can you try to understand that? There's nothing else. This is the only way."

"I don't understand," she said.

"I know, I know," Garrison whispered into the phone. "Trust me, is all. Can you do that?"

"No, Ben, I can't," she said. "You're not yourself. You're talking crazy! For the last time, bring Andy back!"

"You'll see," he said. "Once we get—" But he stopped himself in time. "It's something for me and for Andy and for Peter. Something that the three of us can have. I have to have it, Joanie. I promise you, baby, one day you'll understand why."

"Oh, Ben, *please*," he heard his wife say very softly.

"It's all right," he said, and as though she could see him, Garrison nodded reassuringly and said good-bye.

He stopped for lunch at the New Haven exit, a place called the Three Kings Inn, and while Peter was in the bathroom, Garrison tried to explain. But the boy seemed more and more baffled, and he kept asking questions that Garrison didn't know how to answer—where they were going and when they'd get home and wouldn't the teachers be angry and how come Mama wasn't coming along.

Garrison struggled with answers. But he didn't know where to start. Maybe Joan was right. It was crazy. It was all too much.

"This is different," he said. "I mean, it's just us men, sort of. A camping trip. Sort of roughing it in the woods. Fishing and hiking and things like that." He smiled and raised the boy's hand into his own. "Mama said nope, she just wouldn't like a thing like that, better if only the three of us went."

"Is Mama Peter's mama too?"

"No," Garrison said, panicking. "That part of it's complicated. But I'll tell you all about it once we get where we're going."

"Where?" Andy said. "Where are we going?"

"Way up near Canada," Garrison said, brightening. "A wonderful, wonderful place called Grand Lake Stream. I tell you, old thing, you're going to have the time of your life. No school and cooking out and walking around in the woods and fishing in lakes and all sorts of stuff like that."

The boy looked puzzled again, but he was silent, as if the question that he'd thought of was the wrong one to ask.

"What?" Garrison said. "Hey, Henry Henry, what is it? Come on now, spill those beans, okay?"

The boy seemed about to cry.

"Come on, son, talk to me. Tell Papa," Garrison urged.

"It's just that how are you going to do those things with your hands like that?"

"These?" Garrison said. "Oh, heck, they're fine. Just a little chafed, is all. From playing tennis when I was in California. Thought I'd keep some Vaseline on them to get them fixed up right. Soon as we get to Grand Lake Stream, I'll just whip the darn things off. Okay?"

The boy nodded, but Garrison could see that it wasn't okay, that dozens of unasked questions crowded behind the ones he'd asked, and that there had to be scores more coming right behind those, questions Garrison couldn't answer without Joan to help him—or God.

"Here," he said, spreading the menu so the boy could look on with him. "Let's pick something very special."

But Andy didn't appear to be interested. He seemed listless and uneasy, even a little alarmed.

All right, he'd made a mistake. He'd gone too far. He'd asked for more than was possible.

"Look, son," Garrison said just as Peter came up, the older boy rubbing his hands together with gusto and drawing his chair back to sit down, "eat something, and after you've finished, I'll take you home."

Peter slapped his forehead and rolled his eyes. He

leaned toward Andy and puffed out his cheeks. "What's this?" he said. "Go home? Hey, Andy fella, what's the matter?"

"Nothing."

"He's all right," Garrison said, touching Peter's arm, hoping to restrain him. "Leave him alone."

But Peter leaned toward Andy. "You talking about going home? Just when we're getting started?" Peter laughed jovially. "Hey, Andy, come on, fella, cheer up. Don't you see how this is a great chance for us to get to know each other?"

"He can come home *with* us," the boy said, looking at his father uncertainly.

"*After*wards," Peter said, before Garrison could say anything. "Hasn't Daddy told you about Grand Lake Stream?"

In a crazy way, Garrison was grateful for Peter's help. And yet it made him uneasy. It was as if he were letting Peter take over. But weren't the boy's motives the right ones? Garrison put his hand on Peter's arm again. "Let's order," Garrison said.

"In a minute," Peter said, lifting his arm away and reaching his hand out to Andy. He smiled at the boy, and winked. "Andy? Hey, Andy, don't you see? It's something special for Dad. He's counting on this trip. It's something he's really counting on. For the three of us."

The boy was sunk down in his seat, eyeing Peter and his father.

"It's all right," Garrison said. "We'll eat and then Andy's going home."

He turned and motioned for the waiter.

"Don't you see, Andy guy?" It was Peter again, his voice soft and coaxing. "Don't you see how it's making Dad unhappy? He's planned this. He's got his heart set on it."

"It's not important," Garrison said, in agony for Andy, for the way Peter was bullying him. And yet, if they went back, what then? "Hey, old thing, it's not important, son," Garrison said again.

The boy brought his hands out of his lap and touched the silverware as though to make sure it was there. He took up his napkin and carefully unfolded it.

"It's okay," Andy said, and then, turning to Peter, his small voice just a tiny bit deeper, the boy said, "You bet."

"I hear you say, 'You bet'?" Peter said. "Is that what I heard old Andy say?"

Peter winked, and Andy tried to wink back.

"Could I have a hamburger and a Coke instead of milk? And when we get to the woods, can I help make the fire?"

"Dad?" Peter said, turning to look wide-eyed at Garrison.

But Garrison was staring at the tablecloth as if listening to something else. There was something here that he wasn't getting. He sensed it, but he couldn't say what it was. Was something crucial getting out of his control? Or was he just so desperate that he kept imagining things, kept seeing something ominous when it was all perfectly innocent?

"Dad?" Peter said again. "Can he?"

"Sure," Garrison said, rousing himself.

Peter turned back to Andy and put his hand to the boy's hair, mussed it and smoothed it back in place.

"You *bet!*" Peter assured Andy. But Garrison never heard what he said. He was listening instead to a word that echoed through an ancient chamber. It had no meaning that he knew of. But its four fast syllables were unforgettable.

Anasazi.

21.

THE NINETY MILES from New York to New Haven had been more miles of New York, the city dragging its dreariness after them as far as it could into Connecticut.

But north to Hartford was different.

It was like coming out of ether—and it seemed to go with the mood of things, the way the season began unfurling itself across the windshield, the colors of autumn heated to just below flashpoint.

They sat together in the front seat, quiet with each other now. It was as if, in looking out at the spectacle of the season, some special understanding was passing over them. The air itself seemed to state something—and in their separate silences, Garrison and his sons listened.

It was dark by the time they were rounding Boston. And in the darkness, no one talked. The car was warm and cozy, and when Peter reached to turn on the radio and tune in a station that played music, it seemed the right thing to Garrison, an accompaniment to the reverie that he sought.

By Portland, he was willing to feel that all his worries were behind him. The three of them were in Maine now, in a zone of irreversible enchantment. Whatever the world was, it had stopped back there at the state line. Ahead lay Lewiston and Augusta and Waterville and Bangor, the big towns. And from there on, it would be woods and mountains all the way, through Aurora and

Beddington to Baring, and at Baring north again, to
Woodland and Princeton, and then hooking back west at
the turnoff into Grand Lake Stream.

He stopped for gas at the north end of Portland, and
while the boys used the bathroom, he thought to call
Joan again, to tell her how it was going to be okay. But it
didn't seem possible to do it anymore—not now that
they were here. In Maine. Wouldn't it undo the magic to
talk about it?

The boys came back to the car laughing like lunatics,
Peter to the rear of Andy, his big hands steering Andy by
the shoulders.

"Who's for eats?" Garrison said, once they were
back in their places again. "This is lobster country,
don't forget."

"Yucch," Andy said.

"What're you yucching about? You ever had a lobster?"

"I don't have to have one to know they're yucchy."

"I've never had one either," Peter said.

"You willing to give it a try? Or is your mind as
closed as the old chap's here?"

"Yucchy," Andy shrilled gleefully, and with his fingers he made wriggling gestures of menace in front of
Peter's face. "Here comes the *yucch!*" he growled, and
when Peter grabbed Andy's hands and kissed them, everything in Garrison dissolved.

"God, I'm so happy," he said, and then he hurried
on. "Now the theater folk on old Broadway, those that
claim to know a thing or three about lobster, they have a
lot to say for a place up here called Boone's. What say
we get directions and try it?"

"Fine by me," Peter said.

"Not by me," Andy said. "Unless you can get a
hamburger there."

"Pardner," Peter said, reaching his arm around Andy
and hugging him close, "I don't reckon thar be a chuck-

wagon in all these Yoonited States cain't rustle up a little chopped meat and fry it in a ball if they've a mind to. So what do you say, pard? The old trail boss has spoke his piece, and it's either Boone's or starve."

"Boone's!" Andy shrieked, delighted.

Garrison nodded joyously. He wanted to pick the both of them up and carry them there on his shoulders.

The meal was a great success, an old-fashioned shore dinner, Andy taking a taste of Peter's steamed clams and lobster and even conceding that he'd tasted worse things in his life, but not many. They finished with ice cream and each with a wedge of strawberry chiffon pie that seemed to rise a foot off the plate. Garrison ordered coffee for himself and for Peter, and when Andy asked if he could have some too, Peter intervened and Garrison said yes, he'd make an exception.

All through the meal, the thing that gnawed incessantly inside him lay quiet. It seemed hours since he'd had his last seizure, and even when they'd stepped out into the night and stood in the parking lot, looking up at the sky, he still felt safe from serpents, restored to himself, strong, immortal.

"Cold," Andy said.

"Me too," Peter said.

They ran for the car and piled in, Garrison hurrying to start the engine and turn on the heater.

"I must be nuts," he said as they pulled out of the parking lot and began wending their way back to the highway. "You fellas aren't dressed for what's ahead, and neither am I. What I'd say we need is outfits, by God! Agreed?"

The boys cheered.

"You bet!" Garrison said. "The works—all that woodsman stuff. Right?"

"Right!" the boys chorused in reply.

"Then, by God, I know just the thing! L. L. Bean, by God!"

Freeport. Freeport, Maine. He knew the town from all the mail orders he'd placed over the years, all those sporty things Joan was always finding in the catalogs, clipping the pages for him just in time for Christmas. And he'd heard stories about the place from lots of people who did their summers in Maine, how it was open around the clock and always mobbed. It'd be a great treat for the boys.

Besides, it was only about fifty miles up the coast, and that was the way they were going. Then he could get right back on the Interstate and make it to Augusta for the night, before the boys got too tired.

He turned the heater down now that the car was warming up, and as they headed out of Portland, they were singing again, Peter's choice.

Ninety-five bottles of beer on the wall,
Ninety-five bottles of beer,
If one of those bottles should happen to fall,
Ninety-four bottles of beer on the wall.

The place was big, all right, and the parking lot, which was big too, was jammed. Even at this hour, people were streaming in and out—kids mostly, teenagers and people in their twenties, youngsters with backpacks, boys and girls who looked as if they'd just come in from the trail. Garrison cruised through the parking lot, but there wasn't a space in sight.

"I don't believe it," Peter said.

"Hey, old thing!" Garrison slapped Andy's knee. "You awake? Take a look?"

The boy was groggy from the road and all that food. He did his best to look alert. But when Peter lifted him to his lap, Andy's head sagged.

"Maybe we should skip it," Garrison said. "Just go

on to Augusta and get our stuff somewhere in the morning.''

''Hey, pardner, look alive!''

Peter jogged the boy up and down.

''No, let him sleep,'' Garrison said.

''And miss Bean's? Miss world-famous L. L. Bean for a little shut-eye? Come on, Andy, upsie-daisy!''

The boy opened his eyes.

''I'm awake, Papa. Promise.''

''You think you can hold it for maybe an hour?''

The boy nodded vigorously, and Peter slapped him on the back.

''That's the spirit! That's my old trail-blazer!''

Garrison pulled around to the entrance. It was no use looking for a space anymore. He let the boys out and told them he'd catch up with them in the boot department, and then he drove back onto the street and started looking for a parking place nearby.

He found a spot and locked the car. But he remembered something as he drew the key out, something he couldn't imagine he'd forgotten about, but was glad that he had.

The gun, the Buntline. This would be a good time to get rid of it.

He fitted the key back in the lock and opened the door. He reached in and felt beneath the seat. Then he leaned in and pushed his hand from side to side and all the way back.

It was gone!

They weren't in the section where the boots and shoes were sold. They weren't anywhere around there. Garrison moved up and down the rows of chairs where people were trying on footwear. He kept looking at the same people, checking their faces again, as if he were seeing them imperfectly and if he looked one more time, they'd turn into Andy and Peter.

The place was a madhouse, crowds of people waiting to get the attention of salesmen. He kept circling around, forcing his way between salesmen and customers, grabbing at people and trying to make them hear.

He was winded—and the words came out in a rush.

"A boy. Blond. Two boys, a little one and a big one. Did you see them? They were supposed to be around here, and one of them's big and the other one's little. Seven years old. He's wearing a navy blazer and short pants. The big one's got on a white windbreaker. Tall. Almost as tall as me."

But they all looked at him as if he were crazy or drunk—and he could see their eyes travel knowingly to his hands, the bandages, and then back up to the cuts on his face, the untrimmed beard, the deep excavations around cheeks and eyes that cancer was beginning to dig.

"Why don't you try the PA system," somebody suggested. But Garrison never heard.

The place was gigantic. He covered the second floor and then went back down to the first. He tried the second floor again, retracing his steps, his brain unreeling a morning years ago, the rooms of a small apartment, the bellowing silence that had answered his calls.

Come out, come out, wherever your are!

He reached out to a passing salesman and held him tight by the arm.

"The store! Are there back exits? Is there another way out?"

"Sure there is!" the man yelled and jerked his arm away.

"I'm sorry," Garrison stammered. "Is this all of it? The whole store?"

The man looked as if he were about to call for help. "What?"

"These two floors," Garrison said. "That's it?"

"*Three* floors, mister. There's a basement floor too. Hey, what the hell is the matter with you?"

Garrison ran. But he never made it all the way down. Between the second and first floors, he saw them coming up the stairs, Andy cradled in Peter's arms.

"Conked right out on me," Peter said, smiling.

Garrison's voice was hoarse. "He's all right?"

"Right as rain," Peter said, still smiling. "Wanted to see the canoes down in the basement, but just couldn't keep his eyes open. Just on my way up to get you."

"Yeah, well," Garrison said, pain raging in him now. "Okay—I guess that's okay, then," and he put out his hand to touch Andy on the forehead as if the boy's temperature needed checking.

"I'll carry him and you can do the shopping."

"No," Garrison said. "Let me take him. We'll get what we need tomorrow."

They turned around on the stairs and went back out to the car. Peter held the seat forward, and Garrison lifted Andy into the back. He took off his sportcoat and put it over his son, and then he did the same with one of his sweaters.

"We'll get the heat going and he'll be fine," Peter said. "Poor tyke, it's too much excitement for him, don't you think?"

All the way to Augusta, Garrison kept silent. But Peter jabbered away. He wanted to talk about everything now, the years with Willa, the awful life he'd had.

"What we lived in, for instance. But Mother had to have her privacy, and that's how she got it—by building a crazy thing like that. She's brilliant, though. Maybe she's the most brilliant woman in the world. But it doesn't make any difference. I hate her. Just the way *you* hate her. Look what she did to us. All the years she robbed us of. It was terrible being a boy in that place. It was terrible being so alone. For a long time I blamed you for it. You see how mixed up I was? Isn't it crazy? I mean, instead of putting the blame where it really be-

longed. I'm not ever going back. If it's okay with Joan,
I'll live with you. What's Joan like? I'll bet she's beautiful. Because Andy's so beautiful. He's the cutest little
fellow. Listen to him. He's *snoring*. It must be great
being a father. I'd like to have sons, I think. Just the way
you did, Dad.''

Garrison heard the boy yawn.

''But I'd stay clear of a wife like Mother, though.
She's brilliant, sure, but she's all wrong for a wife. I'll
bet Joan's the opposite. What I don't get is how the two
of you ever got married if you never got a divorce from
Mother. Or did you? I mean, I don't know all the facts.
What is it, the time just runs out? I should know things
like that. Steiner. That was clever, don't you think? I
thought of it right away. But she was a nice woman, that
Mrs. Chambers. I think she loved you as much as I do. It
was when you told about Grand Lake Stream. You don't
want me to take the wheel now, do you? I mean, if
you're too tired, I could take over for a while. There's
nothing to worry about. Dad? Look, I know why you're
so quiet all of a sudden. You're *worried*. Tell the truth.
Oh, I can tell. Hey, but listen, don't be scared. I *have* it.
I took care of it for you. You didn't want me to know
about it because you didn't want to frighten me, but I
found it when I drove us from that filling station to Mrs.
Chambers's place. Well, sure. I mean, I always adjust
the seat. The Land Rover, the Jeepster, I always give
them a little push. It's a habit. So when it wouldn't move
. . . You were fast asleep. Bushed. Totally conked out.
Just the way the old trail-blazer is right now. I don't
mean to upset you, Dad, but that was *dumb*. That's the
first place they look. I mean, if we'd gotten stopped or
something, they'd go right for under the seat. Is *that*
what you did it with? That guy you killed? Anyway, skip
it now? Just don't worry about it. I took care of it.
You're not angry anymore, are you, Dad?''

Garrison couldn't see him in the small illumination

from the dash. But when a car passed, Peter's face was briefly lighted up.

"Dad?"

He tried to keep his voice very calm.

"Just tell me where it is."

"It's better if you don't know. I mean, if you knew, then you'd give it away. It'd show in your face. This way, you're *safe*. Just forget about it. I'll take care of it. The way I thought of Steiner just in case."

"You have it somewhere? You hid it?"

"Of course," Peter said, his voice cheery in the dark. "I'm looking after you. Don't worry, I'm going to handle things. You know, one thing I owe Willa for is being smart. I mean, maybe you don't know how smart I really am. But I'm not carrying it or anything like that. That's the *last* thing I'd do. It's okay. Put it out of your mind."

"You really should tell me," Garrison said. "It's not right for me not to know. The thing's dangerous. It'd be better if I knew where it is."

"Not on your *life,*" Peter said, and put out his hand to touch Garrison's shoulder. "Listen, Dad, I don't want to take any chances. If you knew, you'd just be nervous about it—and then all we'd need is for a cop to stop us. For anything. Just for speeding, say. Or a busted taillight. No sir, it'd be right there on your face. A man like you? Uh-uh, it'd be the first thing out of your mouth—'Officer, I don't have a gun hidden anywhere.'"

Again Garrison heard him laugh.

"Just take it easy," Peter said. "I told you—I'm looking after things. For everybody. For the three of us."

"I want that gun back," Garrison said.

"I know you do," Peter said. "But don't worry."

It was quiet in the car for a time. And then Garrison heard Peter's breathing, in perfect timing with the small sounds coming from the back.

"You should thank me," Peter said, and he yawned

twice and then stretched out his legs as if preparing for sleep.

He stayed on the road, passed Augusta by, and went all the way to Bangor that night. He had no choice but to go on, and no reason to turn back. The next day they'd be there, and everything would be wonderful again. Grand Lake Stream. It was a magical sound in his head.

The gun. He had to get it back. But how? Was it possible he was overreacting? He was so suspicious of Peter. But why? Was it fair? Wasn't the boy just looking out for him? The past was the past! That was how Peter wanted it, and that was how it should be. Bygones, behind them, and nothing ahead but Grand Lake Stream. He was ashamed of himself for not letting the old feelings go. It wasn't fair to Peter. It wasn't fair to the great times ahead. But the gun. He had to have it back.

He tried humming to himself. He tried to confine his attention to the road. He tried working out the details of the white building on the hill, the austere placement of the dark green shutters. How many on each side? Four? Six?

But all he could see was the long black barrel of the Buntline. He wanted to reach over and feel Peter's pockets. And then he was ashamed of himself all over again.

It was three in the morning when he made it into Bangor. He registered first, at an out-of-the-way motel, and then went back out to the car to wake Peter and carry Andy in.

"You give them a phony name?" Peter asked as he unlocked the door and held it open for Garrison to get through.

"Let me get him into bed first," Garrison whispered. "You take the other one and I'll sleep with Andy."

Peter locked the door and went to the bathroom. He left the light on when he came back out.

Garrison kissed the sleeping boy and eased him under the covers. When he looked up, he saw Peter with a finger to his lips and motioning for him to move into the light, where they could talk without waking Andy.

"How come? You should have given them a phony."

"It doesn't matter. Not really. Besides, I'm running out of cash and I'll have to pay with a credit card. Now go to bed."

Garrison kissed him, and then he held him and hugged him hard, despite himself feeling for the gun in Peter's pockets.

But of course it wasn't there. It couldn't be. Not with that strange long barrel.

"I'm not tired," Peter said. "Maybe I'll go out and walk around."

"I'd rather you stayed here," Garrison whispered.

"It's okay," Peter said, whispering too now. "You get some shut-eye, Dad. I've still got the room key."

He held it up to show it in the light—and for a crazy instant it made Garrison jump, as if a deadly weapon had flashed into view. Peter tossed the key up and caught it, and then he put his lips to Garrison's cheek.

"Sleep tight," he whispered.

Garrison watched him go, tiptoeing across the room and slipping silently out the door. It filled him with dread, the way Peter seemed to be managing things, taking charge. But didn't the boy just want to help? He was immensely intelligent and mature. He'd had to be, living a life so alone, a life without a father.

It was ridiculous, this uneasiness. It was just his fatigue and pain distorting things, making everything more than it was. He made up his mind that in the morning he wouldn't have it, he wouldn't allow it at all.

He lay down beside Andy, turned onto his side, and carefully reached his arm around the small still form.

It was wrong to let anything ruin this. There were only so many days to go. In the morning they'd get themselves outfitted, warm clothes and everything else. And after that, the drive through the mountains, to Baring and Princeton, and then to Grand Lake Stream.

He felt the pain coming, but he refused to let it make him gasp. He inched the blanket higher to where it covered his son's shoulders. And then, when he was sure he'd done everything he possibly could, Garrison closed his eyes and surrendered himself to sleep.

22.

It was as if all the light in the world were shining in that room. The heavy curtains were parted, and Garrison could see a picture-book day streaming in through the venetian blinds.

He rolled over and saw the boys dressed and sitting on the other bed, Peter showing Andy how to make a whistling sound by cupping your hands together and blowing through a space between your thumbs.

But Andy couldn't do it.

"I think my hands aren't big enough," he said, though he wouldn't give up trying.

Garrison watched. It made him feel as if he'd turned to a warm liquid, seeing his sons together this way.

He got up and kissed them and sent them off to breakfast in the coffee shop while he took his first shower in days. He felt reborn. But when he looked in the mirror to finger back his hair, he could see how far from life he already was.

It didn't matter. Nothing mattered, so long as he had these perfect days.

He had coffee and toast while the boys finished up, and then they went next door to the office and paid for breakfast and the room, the boys stopping to pick up pine cones and toss them as the three of them strolled dreamily back to the car.

It was on the seat. He saw it when he opened the door. It rested where the driver sat, and under it was a note.

Garrison brushed the Buntline to the floor. He

snatched up the piece of paper and held it squashed in his hand as he reached over and pushed open the opposite door, Peter tilting the seat forward for Andy to get in back. But when Andy started in, Garrison caught him by the shoulder.

"Up here, old thing. I want all my singers in front."

"Just thought he might want to stretch out," Peter said. He put his hand next to Andy's head and stroked his hair to one side as Andy squeezed in next to Garrison.

Garrison turned the key. When the engine caught, he raced it and kicked the Buntline under the seat. He reached into his pocket for a cigarette, and when he brought his hand out, he left the note behind, and then he pulled around to the front of the motel and back onto the street.

He saw the sign for Route 9. He checked the mirror and starting easing the Pinto to the right. He looked again just before he was set to make his turn.

It was then that he saw the cruiser in the mirror, the rack of blue lights across the roof, two lit and three flashing on and off.

He felt Peter tap his shoulder. "Do not anticipate," Peter said as Garrison pulled over and stopped.

Garrison watched the trooper approach, the sauntering walk, a man with all the time in the world. He saw the aviator glasses and the cavalry boots and the thin, straight line of the mouth.

He rolled down the window and got ready.

"Good morning, sir."

"Officer," Garrison said, and nodded.

"Nice day."

"Yes," Garrison said.

"I'll take a look at your license and registration, please."

Garrison got out his wallet. He found his license and handed it through the window. "Pete, check in there," he said, and nodded at the glove compartment. "It's a rented car, officer," Garrison said.

"Is that a fact?" the trooper said. He bent down a little and looked through the window, first at Garrison and then at each of the boys. "You got Iowa plates on this vehicle, but your operator's certificate says New York. How's that?"

"Been traveling," Garrison said. "Simple as that."

He took the registration from Peter and handed it out through the window.

"Is it?" the trooper said.

"Pardon?" Garrison said.

"Is it as simple as that?" the trooper said.

"That's right," Garrison said.

The trooper studied the registration and the license, and then he looked in through the window again.

"Is there something wrong, officer?" Garrison said.

"Where you headed?"

"Grand Lake Stream."

"Doing a little hunting, are you?"

"Just sightseeing," Garrison said. "Maybe some fishing."

"This time of year?"

"Well, I don't know," Garrison said. "This the off-season or something?"

The trooper frowned. He handed back the license and registration.

"These your boys?"

Garrison nodded. "My sons, yes."

"You fellas having a good time?"

"You bet," Peter said.

"Yeah," the trooper said, getting up to his full height. He stepped away from the car and swept his eyes from back to front, and then he leaned in through the window again.

"You mind opening it up?"

"The trunk?"

"That's right."

Garrison took the keys out of the ignition and waited until the trooper got out of the way, and then he pushed open the door.

He unlocked the trunk and held the lid up while the trooper threw back the mats and poked his hand around in the wells behind the rear wheels.

"No luggage?"

"Getting our gear and things on the way," Garrison said. "It's just one of those impromptu trips you sometimes go on."

The trooper stood away from the trunk and eyed Garrison. "Can't say I know about those." He smiled. "Thought you said you'd been doing some traveling. Out to Iowa, right? You been doing all that without clothes?"

Garrison smiled. "It takes all kinds," he said.

"Is that right?" the trooper said. "You can close that now," he said. "Close it and get back in your car. But I don't want to see you riding three in front again. You got room enough there in the back, so use it."

The trooper started back to the front of the car, and then he turned as if remembering something.

"What happened to your hands?"

"Cookout," Garrison called without hesitation. "Fire sort of got away from me."

"Well, watch it," the trooper said.

Again he turned away briefly and then turned back again.

"You can drive all right with those?"

"No problem," Garrison said.

The trooper didn't answer. He kept on going this time, and when he was back behind the wheel of the cruiser, he motioned for Garrison to come ahead and pass him. But Garrison stayed where he was until Andy had climbed in back.

Then he made the turn onto Route 9.

It was getting colder now as they made their way

through the mountain country to the east. They'd have to get warm clothes soon. But he knew there would be nowhere to buy what they needed until they reached a big enough town. Princeton, say. He could read the note then, do it while the boys were busy picking things out. Or he could stop for gas in Beddington, say he needed to use the bathroom.

But Garrison knew he couldn't wait that long. He pulled onto the shoulder, turned off the engine, and took out the keys.

"Just be a second," he said.

"What's up?" Peter asked.

"I think I dropped my cigarettes in the trunk."

He got out and opened the trunk. He pushed the lid all the way up.

The message was printed in Peter's precise hand, and it startled Garrison to see it again, that meticulous formation of letters he remembered from the notebooks. All false, Peter had said. But was this false, too?

Dearest Father—I realize how difficult this is for us. I am tense and you are tense. Let us do our best to hide this from Andy. Let us do our best to love and trust one another. I am sorry I upset you about the gun. Here it is. It must be disposed of, but you know better than I how that should be done. I love you and want to protect you. Your son, Peter.

He let the paper fall to the ground and slowly lowered the lid of the trunk. He stood there for a time while he lighted a cigarette and looked out over the magnificent country around him. To the east lay Lead Mountain. In a few hours they'd be there, in Grand Lake Stream.

He understood that life could be like this, no pattern, nothing you could be dead certain of. He pushed down on the lid to make sure the latch had caught, and then he got back into the car and smiled gratefully at his sons.

There wasn't much to Princeton. The highway widened and went through town, and that was where everything was, one long strip of stores and service stations, set off here and there by a church or a school or a meeting hall. Trucks piled high with logs and sometimes with lumber stood off on either side of the road, so that it was difficult to see the storefronts and pick out the right place.

Garrison went the length of the town, turned the car around, cut into the curb, and took the first free space he saw.

"All out!" he bellowed with enthusiasm. "Last stop before Grand Lake Stream!"

Andy dove over the seat, but Peter pushed him back.

"Not until we get you fixed up," Peter said. He pulled out of his windbreaker and tossed it in back.

"No," Garrison said, "that won't be necessary."

"It's getting cold out there," Peter said. "Besides, I've got this heavy swe⋯

Andy was deligh⋯ ⋯ ⋯ the arrangement. He tumbled over the seat ⋯ ⋯ ⋯ let Peter zip him up, and then he pushed his way out of the car, giggling with pleasure. For a time Andy stood on the sidewalk, hiking up the hem of the windbreaker until he got it so that he could skip away a little distance and try it out for size. And then he came tripping back while Peter got out and Garrison locked up.

"Gentlemen," Garrison said.

He put out his hands and the boys came to him.

"This is good," Garrison said, and, with their hands in his, he started up the nearly deserted street, knowing he was as happy as a man ever could be.

It was early afternoon. The day that had dawned so bright in Bangor was bleak in Princeton. Yet Garrison didn't feel the cold. Even when he saw snowflakes, he still felt warm. And then he felt hot, massively hot, his organs roasting on a spit. The pain. It was like a girder shoved into his groin. The breath went out of him, and with it his strength. He tried to catch himself, to keep

from falling. But for some reason his hand couldn't find
a place on Peter, and Garrison went down, slumping to
the sidewalk like a bucket of glue pouring out.

He could feel Andy's hands on his back, the boy trying to grab at him and haul him back up. He wanted to
say, "Don't, don't, I'm all right." But he knew that if
he tried to speak, a scream would come out instead.

He tried counting. He thought if he could keep on
counting, everything would come back and be just the
way it was.

He opened his eyes at the count of eight. He couldn't
see just yet. But he knew his eyes must be open.

He rolled over and laughed.

"Hey, Henry Henry! Fooled you again, by golly!"

Garrison grabbed his son and held the boy to him so
that the boy could not see his face.

"You think you're the only clown on the block? Is
that what? Didn't you see that snowflake hit me?" Again
Garrison forced himself to laugh. "Eye!" he whispered,
and when Andy moved his face into position, Garrison
kissed his eye. "Wrong eye!" Garrison declared, then
got to his feet as though nothing had happened. "I ask
for an eye, and you give me the wrong one. I ask for a
couple of noses, and what do I get?"

The boy was staring at him as if he hadn't made up his
mind yet.

"Hey, old thing! You lost your sense of humor? All
right, so I thought you saw that snowflake wallop me
one. Give a fella a break."

The boy seemed willing to accept this. His face took
on a scolding expression.

"A thing like that's embarrassing, Daddy. Promise
you won't do it again."

"Only when I feel like it," Garrison said. He was still
dazed and half blind, but he made himself smile goofily
and keep on smiling until he was sure Andy was convinced.

It was then that he realized Peter was missing.

"Hey, scout, where's Pete?"

Garrison looked behind him. He saw some men grouped near a storefront, but when they saw him looking their way, they turned their faces as if to show that his presence disgusted them.

"Over here!"

It was Peter, yelling. The boy stood at the curb across the street. He was waving with one hand and pointing with the other. "I've found just the place!"

Garrison waved back and took Andy's hand. He was crossing the street when he remembered everything, the three of them walking abreast, his knees buckling, the coarse wool of Peter's sweater, the way it felt when the heavy yarn was yanked away from his fingers.

Garrison stopped in the middle of the street.

He saw Peter grinning. He saw the arms folded, the thick gray sweater, the scuffed boots he used for climbing rocks.

Somewhere down the quiet street, a truck was starting up.

Garrison held his son's hand. He stood where he was, his head swimming, snow falling in his face.

"What's the matter?" Peter called, and still he was grinning. Even from this distance Garrison could see the exuberance of that grin—and the stunted tooth it revealed like a wink.

No, there was nowhere else to go. Not now, there wasn't. And maybe there never had been.

"We're coming!" Garrison finally called back.

He gripped his son's hand and continued across the street.

It wasn't until he had the trunk open and was fitting in the bundles of clothes—mackinaws, bulky sweaters, wool shirts, heavy fisherman's trousers, double-thick socks with blood-red bands going around the top, knee-high all-weather boots for the boys, warm caps, and plenty of thermal underwear—that Garrison realized he had better call ahead. It'd be dark by the time they got there, almost suppertime, and he'd better fix it so that they had a place waiting for them, food ready and a fire going in their room. The lodge, they'd have fireplaces in the rooms, wouldn't they? And lots of wholesome food, seconds for the boys if they wanted them?

Garrison laughed at himself.

"Good Lord," he said aloud, "I don't even know the name of the place."

How was it he hadn't thought of this before?

He slammed down the lid of the trunk and let the boys back in the car.

"Wait a sec!" he called to the salesman who was watching from across the street.

The young man crossed over, looking as if he expected Garrison to say he wanted to buy some more things.

"Yes, sir?" the young man said, and stood with his hands in his pockets, his back to the drift of the snow.

"We're headed for Grand Lake Stream," Garrison said.

"Yes, sir."

"You know the area?"

"Yes, sir," the young man said.

"Well, what it is, is that I haven't been there since I was a kid. But I remember there's this fishing and hunting lodge up there, a big white building on a little hill. You know the name of the place?"

"No, sir," the young man said. "Can't say that sounds like anything I ever saw."

"Yeah, well," Garrison said. He reached over and wiped his arm across the windshield. "I don't know which lake it's on, Grand Lake or Big Lake, but it's a big boxy building with green shutters. That doesn't sound familiar? A long path going up to the front porch?"

"No, sir," the salesman said. "You sure you're talking about Grand Lake Stream?"

"Oh, yes," Garrison said, "I couldn't be making a

mistake about a thing like that. There's a small general store right where two roads cross?''

"Yes, sir.''

"Lakes on either side?''

"Yes, sir.''

"And off to one side, on one of the lakes, right near the shoreline, a big white building? I don't know, maybe they've painted it a different color?''

"No, sir,'' the young man said. "I know it up there real well. My cousin and me go on over for smallmouth bass all the time, and I got an aunt who works at the fish hatchery on the stream. No, sir, no big building like that, that I know of, sir. No lodge that looks anything like that. Years ago maybe, but not now. Unless it's off back in the woods somewheres where I never saw it. Could be that's it, you know.''

"Sure,'' Garrison said. "That must be it. I guess I must've gotten it a little mixed up, is all. I'll find it. I'll ask at the general store.''

"Yes, sir,'' the young man said. "You could do that, I suppose.''

"You think they'll be open?''

"Yes, sir, I think so. If you don't take too long.''

"Thanks,'' Garrison said. "And thanks for helping with all that stuff.''

"Yes, sir,'' the young man said, and started back across the street. Garrison saw him take a little jump when he got halfway across and then use the snow to skid himself the rest of the way to the curb.

The snow was thinning when they started out again, but the wind was picking up. Small gritty flakes flew in frantic gusting bursts across the windshield, ticking against the cold glass like pebbles thrown by the handful. The road was icing fast, and from time to time Garrison could feel the Pinto give way to long, slow glides, the rear wheels suddenly losing traction and spinning lazily downhill.

"I sure didn't plan on anything like this," Garrison called to the boys as he worked to keep the car under control.

"All the better," he heard Peter say.

The boys were sitting in the back now. Andy had his hands cupped to his lips, and when Garrison checked in the rearview mirror he saw Peter rearranging Andy's thumbs.

"That's what makes it fun," Peter said. "And that's what we're here for, isn't it?"

"You bet," Andy mumbled into his cupped palms.

Garrison glanced in the mirror again. He saw Peter looking back at him, grinning.

23.

He could feel it rising in him, the weary elation and near-hysteria that comes on when you are drawing close to the end of a long journey. He could sense it in the boys too, bouncing in their seats, restless to be done with all this waiting, to be inside somewhere, comfortable and safe.

The Pinto made its slow, relentless way along the road into Grand Lake Stream, the air cold and the night coming on, the snow stopped now, the tires whipping a steady percussion to go with the overwrought feelings that mounted inside the car.

Garrison sang with the boys. But it was neither the melody nor the words that was at work in his mind, wheeling it and wheeling it through all the days of his life.

He turned the heater up, and pulled out the knob to put on the headlights. The long, straight road through the trees lit up in blinding white. It was as if the small car were moving in a dream through an unending tunnel of frost. He could hear the tires beating on the crusted snow, the boys' voices lifted against the wild snowy silence.

Eighty-one bottles of beer on the wall . . .

He blinked his eyes, and then he rubbed them hard to clear them of what couldn't be true. Everything was bright, so very bright. It seemed that a nimbus of furious light was shining in the distance, a small sun rising at the other end of the road. Again he blinked his eyes, and when he opened them, he saw towering color, the wide world alive with beginning again, leaves and pine needles like billows of dark green spume. He knew that it couldn't be real, that it was nothing more than a dream of summer, a dying man's wish for the life he'd never live to see. He was seeing things, and he knew it—but he let himself see them, the fragrant cavalcade of stately trees that lined the road to Grand Lake Stream. It was all coming back now, the fluted music of a lifetime ago, a boy sitting high beside the father he loved so much. *Sing along now, B.W.! This here is it, boy! So sing along for all you're worth!*

> *Oh, the bear went over the mountain,*
> *The bear went over the mountain . . .*

He let the car roll to the side of the road. He pulled the emergency brake and left the motor running, then he reached under the seat and said, "Nature calls."

Outside the car, the air was icy and the fallen snow blew in riotous swirls against his face. He crossed the road and started walking in the opposite direction, and when he'd gone what he guessed to be far enough, he turned to face the trees. He wanted it to land as far from him as his heart could make it go.

He reached back his arm and brought it forward hard. He threw it into the dark trees with all the strength he had. Then he turned and went back up the road, calling, "Hey, Pete! Andy boy! I ever tell you how come the bear went over the mountain?"

The Pinto was empty. There was no one in the car.

He put his head down behind the seats to make sure.

"Fellas?" he called softly, as if they might be somewhere very close by, teasing him, hiding just outside the car.

His heart cracking open, Garrison pushed himself away from the car, wheeling in the road, shouting in all directions.

"Boys! Boys! It's dark out there, and cold!"

He listened for their voices, for the sounds of their feet in the snow.

"Peter! Andrew! I'm serious now! Boys?"

He strained to hear. He sent out his hearing into the far sockets of the night.

"Fellas! Old thing! Hey, Petey boy, we've got to get a move on now!"

He turned and turned, listening to the tall trees creaking in the cold. And then he heard something else, like laughter perhaps, or the distant remnant of their song.

He moved in the direction of the sound, stepping down into the woods adjacent to the car, his shoes catching in the frozen underbrush.

It was louder now, a little louder, like laughter or singing.

"Boys! I'm not kidding! Andy! Pete!"

He heard them clearly now—laughing like loons—or screaming.

His hand touched the searing surface of a tree, the ice burning though the bandage of gauze. From behind him the headlights fed a gloomy halo of phosphorescence into the woods, a kind of gassy presence, as if a giant jellyfish floated luminously among the trees, a gelatin clouding the frosty air. He rubbed his eyes and tried to see better, and when he brought his arms down, he felt so very tired. Drowsy even, as if his body had breathed a narcotic vapor and was gradually relaxing into sleep.

He kept moving downhill, lifting his knees high to free himself from the frozen tangle that snatched at his shoes, his motion clumsy, like a man struggling against insurmountable fatigue.

And then he heard it very clearly. Shrieking laughter? A child crying out?

"God, God, God!" he screamed, heaving himself forward now, shouldering hysterically through the ghostly light.

"Andy!" he screamed, his eyes blinded by the white-hot fragments of the nightmare assembling in his brain, all the pieces falling unthinkably together, real and terrible, the gross reality of evil itself.

"My God, what have I done!"

He could see them now, standing against the greasy black shimmer of the lake beyond, the white windbreaker like a sheeted figure draped against the curtain of the night.

Garrison hurtled down through the trees, then vaulted from a lip of frozen turf and landed hard on the first wide rock, his heart yawning open with the frenzy of his screams.

"Please, God! God Jesus! Peter! Don't!"

He could see them moving there, just above him, two faintly revealed shapes, and in his ears he could hear a hushed droning, like the slumberous hum of a small motor running very, very slow.

Anasazi.

Garrison flung himself onto the next rock up, his arms outstretched, his hands out in front of his face.

"Get away from him! Andy, get away!"

There were only rocks in front of him now, things that were forever in a man's way. He threw himself against them, he forced himself up, he pushed out at everything and clawed his way to a place where he could set himself and jump.

"No!" Garrison howled.

It was the last of his prayers.

And with the last of his strength, he leaped to the last high rock, then lunged to save what he could.

24.

THERE ARE THINGS we'll never know. Who can tell us what Ben Garrison intended as he plunged down from the lakeside road, thrashed his way in terror up through that black snarl of trees and brush, dove through the darkness, and then stood there, gaping out at his sons from his footing on that first snow-covered rock? Perhaps there was nothing in his mind except the horror of what he thought he saw, believed he heard. Did Andy cry out in fear or in joy? Did Peter move to push his brother? Or to snatch him back from the concrete pilings sunk into the lake below?

The rockpile's there to this day, there on the north end of Big Lake. The owner never finished the house. I can see why it would work out that way, why he'd never want to live on the site. But it would have been an interesting house, the thing the owner had in mind, half of it clinging to the steep shoreline, the other half fanned out over the water. The pilings were already in place.

Naturally, the lodges had been hauled down years before, to make way for new housing for summer residents. I know it would be an astounding irony if the construction site where it happened had been a part of the grounds where once had stood the lodge Ben sought. But there's no telling. For the simple reason that he'd never known the name of the thing. Isn't it remarkable, what a child will remember and all his life dream about, never really knowing what he actually saw? But it was just the opposite with Peter. For him, a name was all there was.

Anasazi.

In the end, it proved to be nothing, just the name the Navajo gave to the ancient tribe that had once inhabited the same region of the Four Corners area that the Navajo migrated to in the sixteenth century. They found some ruins, and they made up a name for the dwellers who had long ago occupied them, called those ancient people the Anasazi.

It's interesting, though. Because, in the Navajo language, the word means "enemy ancestors."

I wonder if Peter knew the meaning of that word. And if he did know, then how? Did Willa tell him?

Of course, the word is plural, isn't it? Ancestors. Enemy ancestors. Perhaps in Peter's mind, Anasazi stood for Willa too.

But this is just wild guessing. To the boy, it could have been nothing more than a word, one with a curious sound that fascinated him for no more reason than that.

Yet there's no mystery about the thing Peter took with him when he left the cave, that bag made out of thin black cloth, a shoelace as a drawstring to close it like a pouch.

It was in his hand when the game warden found him in the morning, its contents not anything you'd ever guess. Another shoelace. That's all. The kind businessmen use. Waxed, woven very tight, and dipped in paraffin to keep it strong.

God knows what the thing meant to Peter. It means nothing to anyone else.

It's all guesswork—and I suppose that's partly why Ben's story obsesses me so. Was it all just the random fall of the dice? Or was it meaningful, something more?

These Anasazi, they lived in caves, and for a time they practiced something that almost seems to fit. They strapped their infants to boards to flatten the back of the baby's head. These boards were meant as cradles, cradles that gave the cranium a certain shape, a distortion it would have for life, something you and I would see as abnormal, but to the Anasazi it was how a person should be.

Who can figure out people? Who can ever guess what they're liable to think?

I've searched through Willa's books.

There's nothing in any one of them about this ancient tribe the Navajo named the Anasazi.

Sometimes you wonder. Sometimes you think it's the absence of a thing that's more important than anything else.

Like Ben.

He wasn't there for all those years when a boy was growing up. But he was there at the end, there with his sons when they stood on those rocks. To push Peter off? Or to grab Andy back from going over?

Later on, when he was dying and talking to me, sometimes coherent, but mostly not, even then Ben wasn't sure of the answer himself. But was he thinking anything at all when he vaulted to that last high rock, his eyes half blind, his body shrieking with the agony of the cancer that had gotten loose from his pancreas and was crawling all over his guts?

Ben Garrison saw his sons moving in the night. He heard their voices. Were they struggling with each other or were they playing? Did Andy cry out in terror? Or was what Ben really heard a cry of delight?

I know this.

Ben Garrison was a good father.

When he landed on that last rock, there was nothing in his heart but a good father's love.

The game warden found all three of them in the morning.

He saw the Pinto standing empty, and he went to take
a look. He had to make his way through the same trees
and brush that Ben had fought his way through when
he'd raced to get to that rockpile before it was too late.

The game warden didn't like those rocks. He didn't
care at all for the thing they meant—more city people
moving in around the lake the following summer, knocking down trees, tearing up what nature had taken so long
to put in place. He didn't like the bulldozer that was
parked down near the shore, and he didn't like the ugly
little mountain of rocks it had shoved up so somebody
could have a beach where God hadn't intended. Most of
all, he didn't like the insult these people were giving to
his lake, putting down big blocks of concrete right in
where the kids used to come to catch minnows for bait.

From where he was now, he could see a man up there
not dressed for this weather, although the sun was strong
now and the snow had melted off. Was he asleep? It
looked that way. Asleep or dead drunk, which was getting to be more and more the case when these outsiders
came fooling around where they didn't belong.

The boy looked okay. Dazed a little, but spry enough,
wearing a warm white windbreaker and sitting on his
haunches in that cross-legged style boys always seemed
to favor so much. Probably was something wrong with
the man, seeing as how the boy sat there leaning over
him, a pretty big boy to be sitting in a little-boy way like
that.

When the game warden got closer, he could hear him
too, and the sound of him was just as little-boy as the
way he sat, a kind of whining or whimpering. Anyway,
some damn silly pleading that the kid just wouldn't quit.

The game warden found the third one down below. It
was just by accident that he did—because there really
wasn't any reason to look. But from here you could get a
grand view of everything, the lake never more beautiful

than when the sun's still hanging in the pines across the water.

He saw the dark blue blazer laid open in the front, the arms out wide like a child trying to fly. From where he stood, the face looked peaceful. It looked like nothing more than that a small boy had picked his spot and fallen fast asleep.

But the back of the head had hit concrete, and only an idiot couldn't tell you it must have been as flat as a board.

No, not even Ben Garrison could say what happened on that last rock—except that he'd reached out to stop time, to turn off the light in a nightmare, and touched life, his dead son, instead.

He made me swear to look after his people, and I decided marriage was the best way to do it. Is Joan still young enough to have another child? We think so and we're planning it, come what may.

As for Emily, the woman is nothing at all like Willa. And besides, our daughters are too old to make over. Don't you have to catch a child right at the start to twist its heart and make it hate?

It's absurd to worry. I'm not suggesting history can't repeat itself. But never the same way twice.

And Peter? What about *him?*

Nothing. There's nothing further to say. I understand the boy is graduating from high school a year ahead of time, and that in all other respects he's getting along just fine.

As a matter of fact, I had a letter from Willa a few weeks before I began writing all this down. Not a letter, really. Just a handful of sentences to explain the check she had enclosed, her share of the meal I'd bought her when she came to New York for the film. She said she wanted to square accounts, and she apologized for taking two years to do it. An oversight, she said, because she hated being in anyone's debt.

After her signature, she added a postscript. Here it is, just as she wrote it.

Peter never speaks of the accident anymore, but he often talks fondly of what a wonderful boy Andrew was. He's asked me for Joan Garrison's address. I think he wants to write her and say as much to her. I believe this would be good for him—and good for Mrs. Garrison. Can you supply it? Her address? Or should I have Peter write to her in care of you?

BERKLEY HORROR SHOWCASE

Read Them Alone...If You Dare!